Foxes on the Hill

Foxes on the Hill

by
Serena Sue Hilsinger

Gambit
INCORPORATED
Boston
1969

To Hal

A Postcard from the Volcano

Children picking up our bones
Will never know that these were once
As quick as foxes on the hill;

And that in autumn, when the grapes
Made sharp air sharper by their smell
These had a being, breathing frost;

And least will guess that with our bones
We left much more, left what still is
The look of things, left what we felt

At what we saw. The spring clouds blow
Above the shuttered mansion-house,
Beyond our gate and the windy sky

Cries out a literate despair.
We knew for long the mansion's look
And what we said of it became

A part of what it is . . . Children,
Still weaving budded aureoles,
Will speak our speech and never know,

Will say of the mansion that it seems
As if he that lived there left behind
A spirit storming in blank walls,

A dirty house in a gutted world,
A tatter of shadows peaked to white,
Smeared with the gold of the opulent sun.

—Wallace Stevens

Author's Note

The characters and situations are fiction.
The landscape is real.

Contents

Part One

April: Afternoon at the Crematory

"No, you're quite right," Claud Sarum said. "It is not exactly a church."

The old woman in front of him listed with the weight of her shopping bag and waited for the rest of what he had to say.

Claud said nothing. Instead he sent himself a bulletin. The speed and confusion of the events of the last week had been so extreme that bulletins were necessary, not by the hour, but by the minute. The bulletins Claud sent himself came from the man who was on the scene, were addressed to the man who was not, and they stated, simply, when, where, who, and why. Without them Claud was sure he would lose his hold on the world completely.

It was the last Saturday of April. He was in the Hudson View Crematory and Chapel. The old woman, whom he hardly knew, was his mother-in-law, Mrs. Sortine. Rachel, her daughter and his wife, was about to be cremated.

Having got the facts straight, Claud unbuttoned the jacket of his properly dark suit, forty-two long, bought from a rack on the previous afternoon. He could not deny that it needed to be altered. He had fattened from a forty-two to a forty-four in a matter of months. He was not really vain, but he liked to think of himself as young; nevertheless, year by year, and inch by inch, inexorably, his stomach advanced upon him, giving the lie to his delusion. Claud sucked in his stomach and straightened his shoulders, reminding himself that he was only thirty-nine and still the younger son.

The older son, his half brother, Richard Bennett, stood two or three yards away. He and his wife had flown over from England for the occasion. From the breadth of his well-fitted jacket to the point of his glistening shoes, Richard was an exclamation mark of distaste. Claud damned him to the furthest corner, without roads and wires, on the surface of the earth.

The gods chose either to ignore or deny his imprecation; Richard was still there.

Claud surreptitiously tugged at his left pant leg. The suit would have to be altered at once. Fortunately, he knew a fellow (the poor chap lectured evenings to matrons on the art of the Incas) whose cousin was a tailor. He would get the address tomorrow. The cut of the crotch chafed him sorely. His wife, Rachel, was "gone," as they euphemistically expressed it. (She had blown her head off in a hotel room, which was not "to go" in any common sense of the verb.) As a result, the laundry had not been sent out on the usual day. He was denied even the small comfort of boxer shorts, for only briefs had been left in the drawer.

The problem was not only the suit and the briefs, it was also the heat. It was an unseasonably warm April. The door of the chapel was ajar and New York steamed in. It seemed to Claud that one had a right to expect relief from the heat in such a place, a certain sanctified chill, which the chapel of the Hudson View Crematory did not provide.

Thirty years ago, on the hottest day he could remember, his

father had taken him to visit Salisbury Cathedral, and it had been cold inside. "Here are the roots of our name and family," his father had said, and they had looked at Magna Charta and at an ancient clock, and they had been cold on the hottest day of the world. The clock had ticked for six hundred years, but it had no face. The idea of it amused him still.

Claud almost smiled. However, this was not even a church, much less a cathedral, as he had just tried to explain to the small, stooped body of his mother-in-law. Mrs. Sortine was still there before him, still looking up at him, awaiting some further explanation of the nature of the place. Claud prayed that someone would interrupt before the old lady swung her shopping bag at him and demanded redress for her wrongs: namely, the violation by burning of the sanctity of her daughter's death and the damnation of her daughter to the Seventh Circle of Hell for the crime of self-murder. Claud saw Rachel clearly. She was in a dark wood. She lifted her arms and was immediately transformed into an ancient tree whose gnarled branches yearned toward an absent sun.

He accused himself of being bookish. Hell was a subject with awesome possibilities, but his imagination did not reach beyond the pages of Dante. Looking apprehensively at his mother-in-law, Claud finally spoke.

"We felt we should carry out Rachel's wishes."

It was almost impossible to believe that his breath, lips, and tongue had conspired in saying it, but there the sentence was, malingering with the humid air which seeped in from the hot streets.

It was a lie and he was sure the old lady knew it. Of course Rachel had not been consulted. Rachel's wishes were guess (although Claud was fairly sure that she had been renegade enough not to hold out for a cathedral funeral). Because they belonged to no parish, attended no services, and had no plot, cremation was a matter of expediency. After all, one could not simply order six feet of ground in New York City, bury one's wife, and erect a stone. Lela Reld, an old friend of Rachel's, was responsible for the present arrangements. It was to Lela that he had turned in his confusion, and she had got up a funeral for Rachel. It was Lela's party.

As Claud scanned the back of the chapel looking for her, Lela came in. He wished she'd close the door instead of standing there, uncertain, blinking—the sudden dark of the chapel so obviously baffling her after the light of the street. Lela had his son, Colton Mark, by the hand. The woman who usually cared for the boy had quit—inconsiderate old bitch —and Lela had decided it would be simplest to allow the boy to come to the funeral. The change in his son's routine was one more example of domestic anarchy, but, fortunately, the lapse from a decent order was almost over.

Claud looked at his half brother once again, this time with gratitude, for there, steadfastly, at the side of poor Richard (plucked untimely from his English hearth and tidy English garden by this most unforeseen and awkward of circumstances) was dear sister-in-law Anne, tall and handsomely haggard, stalwart to the last. She had said they would stay until he could get hold of events. He could, perhaps, put up with dear brother Richard and his severe impeccability if Anne were there to ease him into a new pattern of life. At least he might have clean shorts once a week and the knowledge that his son was cared for. Anne would cope, despite her paintings and her alarming inclination toward madness.

He had asked her this morning, directly she arrived from London and offered to stay and care for them, how often she was mad these days. She had replied forthrightly: "I am sometimes mad, but only on Wednesdays, with company coming and not a crust in the house to serve." What was one to make of a woman like that? (It was certainly better than having no woman at all in the house, Claud reminded himself.)

Either bored or annoyed with the lack of conversation, his mother-in-law, Mrs. Sortine, had wandered away to find herself a seat. Claud watched as Lela presented Mark to his grandmother. Mrs. Sortine creaked down to receive the child. It was obvious that both regarded the embrace as an unpleasant necessity. Mrs. Sortine's face hung over the boy's shoulder and questioned Lela intently, while her stolid, embroidered shopping bag sagged to the ground. Her left hand never deserted the handles. Claud recognized the symptom. Long a victim of New York buses, Mrs. Sortine had learned the art of survival.

The ceremony of affection over, Mrs. Sortine bent herself into a chair, rested her bag on the floor by her side, and spread its handles, drawing out a missal and a rosary. While the old lady teased the beads, Lela and Mark stood poised next to her with an air of enforced reverence.

Lela had the hair of a mouse and the eyes of a cat, and her figure was good, Claud appraised. They had suddenly become allied through the death of his wife, and he felt the need of an honest but not unflattering belief in the physical fact of her. She looked as if she needed a decent night's sleep. He waved to her and beckoned to his son.

Making his way down the center aisle to meet the boy, Claud surveyed the strangers and acquaintances finding their way to seats: folding chairs arranged in weaving rows. Clearly, the man who had set up the chairs must have been either moronic or drunk; clearly, the overhead of the Hudson View Crematory and Chapel was low.

Burning was a desirable rite, Claud reminded himself, chosen by Dido and Joan. Rather awkwardly, he held out his hand to his son.

Lela Reld watched until Mark Sarum was safely in his father's hands; then, with despairing relief, she sank into a chair and estimated the assembly: a fair showing for such short notice.

It was good to be sitting down with an hour of vacancy before her. An hour was the least it could respectably take. She had been up before dawn and driving to the city with the first ray of the sun. She was tired. Lela leaned back and reviewed her day.

First there had been two hours in the car with her friend and neighbor Beth Stead, who had shopping to do and agreed to come to the service for Rachel in payment for a ride to New York. The traffic had been terrific and the conversation dreadful. Luke, Beth's infant son, was teething, and Beth had talked about nothing else. For five years Beth had been either pregnant or nursing, and to her, teething was a subject as varied and infinite as the cosmos itself.

Lela accused herself of lack of sympathy (after all, Luke was her godson, surely she owed him some kind of loyalty) and of unfairness (after all, Beth was the solid earth upon which the world was built—surely there was much to be said for solidity), and resumed accounting for the day. Despite the traffic, she had perfunctorily expelled Beth at a bus stop and arrived in time to pluck Claud's English relatives from their nine o'clock plane.

Bless Britannia! Anne and Richard Bennett had not only decided to come to the "funeral" but also to stay on awhile with Claud and the boy. Claud Sarum and Mark Sarum had been riding her bareback, each to a shoulder, and if someone hadn't come it might have gone on for months. Meeting Anne Bennett at the airport, she found herself patting the woman on the shoulder, stranger though she was, as if testing the strength of a mount.

She had delivered the English to Claud's apartment, taken herself off to Stern's for a black dress and hat, returned to the apartment, changed clothes, and collected Mark. Claud had already taken the others on ahead.

Now she was finally sitting down. The ceremony had still not begun. She wished they would get on with it. She wished she had a book, desperately wanting—and almost believing she had earned the right to—relief from the fact of the next hour.

Funerals were surely the most difficult of occasions. Now, at the tender age of twenty-eight, she had got mixed up in one (not only mixed up in it but solely responsible for the logistics of it).

Claud had called Tuesday night. It was all very sudden. She had just put the potatoes on to boil. Claud asked politely after everyone they had in common. She was amazed at the length of the list as, phone to her ear, she gazed through the dark hall to the stove in the lighted kitchen. There was the red enamel pot and within it brewed disaster.

"Yes, everything's fine," Claud had replied automatically to her automatic question. On that instant white foam blossomed above the rim of the red pot, as though the thrust of an after-burner were about to propel it up to and through the barrier of the ceiling.

"Fine!" she echoed, slowly moving the phone from her ear to the cradle, crediting Claud with a third martini.

"No!" Claud shouted, just as she was about to break the connection. "No. It isn't fine at all!"

Rachel had shot herself dead, he announced, and he hadn't an idea in the world what to do next. Rachel's mother would be no help at all, would insist upon masses, incense, and iridescent Madonnas. Surely Lela understood that. Moreover, it was suicide; a Catholic service was out of the question. His half brother, Richard, could not arrive before Friday at the earliest. The problems were immense. There was the body, for example. Something had to be done with it. And then there was poor little Mark . . . Could Lela please come down?

The potatoes had exploded according to promise, extinguishing the pilot flame. With escaping gas and the acrid smell of scorch drifting to her through the hall, Lela had finally agreed; she would come down.

Her husband Daniel said no. She was a fool to get involved; it would only upset her. But, she explained, it was a matter of duty, almost a matter of conscience. She owed something to Rachel (here she had been purposefully vague). Still, Daniel maintained that she was a fool. Claud was an adult and presumably a man. He ought to handle the thing himself. He was older than they by nearly a decade. Lela would only succeed in making herself sick.

Nevertheless, she had gone down the next day and taken on the mother of the body, Mrs. Sortine, who had not yet been told.

Lela and Rachel had been at college together, and Lela knew what there was to be known about Rachel's relationship with her mother. Having got herself a scholarship, Rachel had left home one September morning. She had, from then on, sent a letter and a check a month, and visited on Christmas morning. She had introduced Claud and Mark on the occasions of marriage and birth. In short, Rachel had all but denied her mother.

With that information at hand, Lela had taken a cab to the Bronx (which had cost her a fortune) and confronted Mrs. Sortine across a bowl of wax fruit. She had explained, in a voice which she hoped was appropriately modulated, that Rachel was dead, and suggested, perhaps too subtly, that Rachel had taken her own life. Rachel had not been feeling quite well lately, she invented, hoping that Claud would be completely acquitted. Mrs. Sortine had proved distressingly tractable. "Yes," she said politely and somberly, "yes," and offered a cup of coffee. Did she really understand? "Yes, yes, Rachel, my child, is dead," Mrs. Sortine answered, carefully, deliberately, but without feeling.

Lela had wanted more. She had wanted some sign that this old woman in a room in the Bronx had expelled from her womb, with what is reputed to be the human extremity of pain, a first and only child named Rachel, and that the woman had now taken fully and definitely into her mind that the child was dead. She went over it once again, looking Mrs. Sortine full in the face. The old woman said, "Yes, yes" and drank her coffee. Lela contributed details and embellished them: the muzzle of the rifle in Rachel's mouth, pieces of hair stuck to the wall of the hotel room. "Yes, yes."

Remembering so clearly her conversation with Mrs. Sortine, here when the service was about to begin, Lela wanted to scream aloud, there before everyone. She had always been willing to concede her essential depravity, but the depths of it were really appalling . . . to torture the poor old woman simply to satisfy her own myopic vision of the rightness of things.

Mrs. Sortine had been the first day of Lela's initiation into the ceremonies of sudden death. On the second day, having decided upon cremation as the only sensible means of disposal, she and Claud had consulted the yellow pages of the phone directory and found:

HUDSON VIEW CREMATORY AND CHAPEL
Riverside Drive
Serving Manhattan
Modern Gas-Fired Chamber
Free Use of Chapel with Pipe Organ
Tel. 111-2138
(Reverse tel. charges on Cremation orders)

Both a large coffin, to transport the body to its burning, and a small urn, to contain the consequent bone and ashes, were necessary, the Crematory director had explained. A matter of law, he had said; but whether it was truly law or merely precedent or perhaps only the ghoulish invention of a man who made dying and grief his business, they hadn't had the time to discover. She and Claud had allowed themselves to be browbeaten by the director's dissertation on taste in such matters. They selected a medium-priced coffin and urn. If they absolutely refused to inter, the director had added, he himself could recommend a tasteful but medium-priced columbarium. Otherwise, Claud would have to accommodate the urn of his wife's ashes himself, for scattering was forbidden. Bone fragments, sometimes four or five inches long, settling on another man's picnic, the director explained with graphic emphasis. "But surely," Claud had protested, "in this day and age, they can pulverize bone."

On her third day in New York she had got on the Sarum phone and engineered a well-attended funeral, as if it really mattered, as if Rachel were being married (rather than cremated) to an Eskimo or Hottentot and it was necessary to pack the hall so that the absence of disapproving relatives would not be noticed, as if she had said to herself—which she had not—"the least I can do is give her a proper funeral." It was bizarre and she was exhausted.

Now it was the fourth day. Chairs scraped to attention and the silence of expectancy invaded the chapel. A man walked to a lectern and invoked the Lord. When the prayer was completed, he lifted his head to address the mourners. His mouth opened and Lela half expected: "Dearly beloved . . ."

While the solemn voice gathered them there with more appropriate words, Lela gazed around the chapel once again and was vouchsafed a good clean look at the face of Gail Lessing, who was sitting near the door. Gail was one person she had not called and urged to attend the service for Rachel. The three of them had been at college together at an age when intensity and jealousy wove the texture of life. At the moment, Lela chose not to linger upon the landscape of Gail's face. She could swear the woman was gloating.

Behind Gail, the rear door of the chapel opened discreetly and Beth Stead made her way quickly down the aisle, rustling infinite shopping bags. It seemed to Lela that getting there on time was the least, the decent least, Beth could have done.

"Here I am as I faithfully promised. Late but here," whispered Beth, finally settling into the empty chair next to Lela. "For God's sake be quiet," Lela hissed back and then gave her attention to the voice from the front of the chapel.

Lela had chosen the details of the service. A short introduction and excerpts from the Psalms: so she had convinced the director of Hudson View, who seemed to feel that something more elaborate was in order. The short introduction was just coming to conclusion. The quiet conversation of the voice from the lectern gave way to a more sonorous intonation. The civilities were over; excerpts from the Psalms would now begin.

Our soul is escaped as a bird out of the snare of the fowlers;
The snare is broken, and we are escaped.
Our help is in the name of the Lord, who made heaven and earth.

Suddenly, Lela bent forward in her chair. She had paid lip service to lunch by eating a piece of old Swiss on a slice of dry bread, and it was about to come up. Daniel had been right; the complications of sudden death had made her sick. The name of the Lord wasn't helping a bit. It was Daniel she wanted (for, according to all the lawbooks and vows, one could legitimately expect aid and succor from a husband in a time of need), but the last time she had looked around he had not yet arrived.

She was afraid to lift her head, afraid to turn her head; it was more comfortable leaning over a bit. Not too much to be noticed, though. Just a little, as if she were moved by Rachel's death. If that mouthing bastard at the front of the chapel would just get through it quickly, and if Daniel would just come, then, then, everything would be fine. Beth beside her, wallowing in Saks' labels, was dead asleep and no help at all.

*If I take the wings of the morning, and dwell in the uttermost
parts of the sea;
Even there shall thy hand lead me, and thy right hand shall hold
me.*

It was Daniel's right hand Lela wanted. She lifted her
head ever so slightly and, as the voice proclaimed a moment
of silent prayer, Daniel Reld appeared. In spite of the nature
of the occasion and her nausea, Lela watched with some
amusement the difficulties he was having getting himself
into a seat, for Daniel was over seventy-six inches long, most
of it leg, and a good two hundred and fifty awkwardly distributed pounds in bulk. Finally, with as little noise as possible,
he achieved a victory over the narrow aisle of chairs, sat down,
and stretched his legs out underneath the seat in front of
him.

The expression on Daniel's face was a howl, and Lela was
sure she knew exactly what he was thinking: he was wondering what he was doing one hundred miles from anything that
made any sense.

He hated the city and they had almost not married because of it. Paintings, music, plays, she had protested. "You
go whenever you like," he said. And so they made love on the
ground within the shadow of a farm machine which looked
like a dinosaur. There had been some awkwardness about
buttons and considerable pain for Lela. Nevertheless, they
had been married quietly two weeks later and noisily a month
after that for family and friends.

The silent prayer was over and the voice from the front of
the chapel began again:

*O Lord, how manifold are thy works!
In wisdom hast thou made them all:
the earth is full of thy riches.*

So is this great and wide sea,
wherein are things creeping innumerable,
both small and great beasts.

There go the ships: there is that leviathan,
whom thou hast made to play therein.

Although she had chosen the passage, it did occur to Lela to wonder what exactly ships and a whale had to do with Rachel and her useless death. Nevertheless, things did seem to be proceeding nicely. She herself was feeling rather better, reassured by Daniel's presence. Claud, Mark, and the Bennetts had taken, appropriately, the front row of chairs. Lela looked critically at the back of Claud's head. Although it did not look stricken, at least it was decorously bowed. The bereaved were behaving themselves. Anne Bennett had an arm around Mark's shoulders. That was a good sign. Anne Bennet would cope. Mark was the problem, of course; he was only eight years old. To be dead, Lela had explained to him, was to cease to breathe, to cease to live, not ever to come back. He must not look for his mother because she was not coming back. Lela was not at all sure she had hit the right, the eight-year-old note. Anne Bennett would have to take it from there.

For nearly a half hour Lela rested, at one with the lullaby of the King James cadence. Then suddenly the nausea was back. Lela prayed for the end of the voice from the front of the chapel.

And I shall dwell in the house of the Lord
forever.

There was the silence of a conclusion and then the company arose as if on one pair of legs. Lela pushed quickly through the crowd, now praying for the strength to reach the ladies' room.

The lavatory of the Hudson View Crematory was luxuriously appointed. The tile was immaculate, the air deodorized, and machines dispensed vials of perfume, clean towels, and foil packets of Alka-Seltzer. Leaning over a toilet bowl in one of the booths, Lela catalogued the appurtenances of the place while her nausea ebbed and the cold sweat which covered her body dried. Finally she flushed the toilet and left the booth. Avoiding the mirror above the sink, she splashed cold water on her face.

The outer door swung open and Beth Stead rushed in.

"Are you all right?"

"No!" Lela replied, pulling a paper towel from the wall dispenser and wiping her face. "Do you know if Daniel is out there?"

"Yes, yes. He just asked me to come in after you. He's right outside with Sarum and his family. What's wrong?"

Again the outer door swung open, and Anne Bennett marched in.

The room began to spin again; Lela put her head down over the basin as Anne Bennett came to her and felt her forehead.

"My dear child, you're ill!"

Resisting the desire to congratulate Mrs. Bennett on her powers of detection, Lela simply said, "Please ask my husband to come."

The next thing Lela heard was Daniel's voice, saying the expected: "I told you you'd make yourself sick."

"Mrs. Reld has been taken ill. Her husband is with her. We had better go on ahead," Anne Bennett explained to her husband Richard and to Claud. Putting a comforting arm around Mark, she steered them all toward their waiting car.

When they were settled and ready to depart, the head of the director of Hudson View appeared over the edge of the half-opened back seat window.

"I hope everything was to your satisfaction," he whispered ceremoniously. The family nodded affirmation. "Shall we deliver or would you prefer to come for it yourself?"

"What did you say?" Claud asked in a baffled voice.

The director closed his eyes in momentary deference.

"The urn," he explained.

"We will call you tomorrow. Drive on!"

Anne Bennett's command was immediately obeyed and the director barely retrieved his head as the car window became a moving guillotine.

Slumped against his sister-in-law and laughing like the end of the world, Claud exclaimed, "The old lady, my God, we've gone and forgot the old lady!"

After the ceremony, finding herself neglected by everyone, Mrs. Sortine had decided upon a trip to the center of town and hailed a cab for a treat.

"Forty-fourth and the Avenue of the Americas," she painstakingly instructed the cab driver. She was always careful not to call it Sixth; she thought that an obligation as sacred as the pledge to the flag, a formality intimately related to the process of acquiring citizenship. Although she had been a citizen for years, sometimes she still woke up in the sweat of the night for fear she had forgotten the words of allegiance, expecting a midnight call from a man from immigration who would require a recitation on the spot. No such visitor had come in all these thirty years, but still Mrs. Sortine woke in the night.

Shopping bag by her side, Mrs. Sortine relaxed in the comfort of the cab. There was nothing more to worry about. The worst had happened.

Part Two

August: Weekend at the Summer House

I

In the kitchen of the summer house, Beth Stead anxiously awaited the cleaning lady. At 7:36 the old woman limped up to the door, and Beth knew immediately that something was wrong.

"I don't know what it is, I tell you, Mrs. Stead, I don't know what it is. I'm a jinx, Mrs. Stead, a jinx. I never saw the beat of it."

Mrs. Vanidore crossed the kitchen, dropped two paper bags on the floor, and took out her working shoes. Beth Stead stirred her coffee and poured another cup.

"Come have a cup of coffee. Trouble again?" she asked sympathetically, quelling her annoyance, for if there was one thing which she could not cope with and ought not be required to cope with, on this day, of all days, it was the eternal specter of malevolent fate which sniffed at Mrs. Vanidore's heels like an underfed dog.

"Trouble! Hah! Yesterday—one day—twenty-four hours— I crack a rib and the Army rejects the kid. All in one lousy day. Trouble you say!" Mrs. Vanidore bent over painfully and changed her shoes.

"Don't mind if I do," she said, accepting the proffered coffee.

"Milk, Mrs. Vanidore?" Beth asked weakly, for annoyance had given way to apprehension. There were five guests arriving, and nine rooms full of sand and salt to clean, and only she and Lela to do it if Mrs. Vanidore was stricken.

"No, thanks. No milk. Never touch it. I ask you! Mrs.
Stead, I don't know what it's all about. My husband Jack
passes blood. Did I tell you that? I see it with my own eyes,
right there on the sheet. Go to a doctor, I says to him. Go to
a doctor before they carry you out in a three-by-six box. Give
up the booze and go to a doctor. But he don't listen. The
big lunk just stands there pulling out his teeth."

"What?" Beth asked, absorbed beyond her will in the
eternal what-happened-next.

Mrs. Vanidore obliged.

"Yeah! Pulling out his own teeth like roses off a bush. He
says it don't hurt a bit. No wonder, they're floating in booze.
Two grown men around and me working like a nigger every
blessed day of my life. Does one of them lift a finger? Not
even to change a light bulb. There I am on the cellar steps
with my arms full of sheets, and the light don't work. Down
I go, flat on my face. I couldn't draw a breath all night. Just
cracked, the doctor says, just cracked. Got to wear one of
them girdles. I told the doctor last night, I told him, the
rib's the least of my problems. I can't eat anymore and I don'
see good. There's something wrong with my system. Vita
min pills, he says. Vitamin pills . . . I ask you. Then the kid
comes home from his physical, dragging his tail. The Army
don't want him. High blood pressure, no less. His parents
bleeding and broken, and he's got high blood pressure. I say
to him, I says, what do you want, a medal or something?"

Mrs. Vanidore groaned in conclusion.

"You can't clean house with a cracked rib. You'd better
take the day off," Beth volunteered reluctantly.

"No, no. I know you got people coming. I'll do the down
stairs like I promised you."

II

STILL HALF ASLEEP and suspended between the motions necessary to insert a pillow into a pillow case, Lela Reld stood at the open French windows and stared at the gray mast of the sloop anchored in the sea beyond.

"I realize you think you're unsuited to the degradation of housework, but must you simply stand there staring?"

Lela turned toward the voice.

Beth Stead, blond, prematurely stout, full breasted and proud, stood, hands on hips, in the doorway of the bedroom. The morning was to be devoted to laundry and lunch; the afternoon, to the arrival of guests. Thus Beth, mother of four sons and wife of a poet, had decreed, and so it would be. A long, well-got-up luncheon, beginning at best with vichyssoise, was a definite possibility, if Lela could be pried into a modicum of activity with a lever of measured sarcasm.

There was often a formality about Beth's speech and thought, and even when pregnant, she played the harp with dignity. The harp and the dignity and a small, carefully invested fortune were ancestral, descending from her great-great-aunt. For Beth, the deity—her husband Matthew—and their four sons were the kingdom of earth and the fullness of life. They were her riches and her boundaries. They were enough. She was a thoroughly happy woman, she liked to tell herself, and she almost believed it.

Matthew was an often absent and somewhat irresponsible

deity. He was absent now but expected momentarily. For almost three months he had successfully contained his wanderlust, when suddenly the demands of domestic felicity had seemed impossible to bear. He had escaped to the Hebrides for three weeks, and the escape had been well timed. The children were paying their annual visit to grandparents and Beth was more or less sated with the satisfaction of his presence; she was pregnant. The Relds, with whom the Steads were sharing the house for the summer, were still there, so she was not alone.

A week before, Matthew had addressed an airmail postcard from Skye to the large summer house standing on rocks beyond which stretched the sea:

Hello,

This by flashlight in a field. I came here yesterday. Spectral medusae crowd the seas. Last night a pack of wild dogs passed by me as I slept. This morning a shepherd said, "They have devoured men." Tonight I am not at my ease. I hike toward the Black Cuillin. Shall be back in London on Wednesday and with you on Friday.

Matthew

("I don't believe a word of it," Lela had commented. "Fancies of a younger poet.")

It was Friday, the day Matthew was to arrive and the day of the arrival of guests. It was one of the last days of summer.

Beth joined Lela by the open French doors. The room, like all the rooms on the second floor, was large, sparsely furnished, and opened onto the balcony which girded the north, east, and south sides of the house and overlooked the sea.

"The project at hand is beds, my dear," Beth announced. "The sheets please, with zeal. Mrs. Vanidore has back trouble and rib trouble. In fact, if she is to be believed, her entire system is deranged. Consequently, her usually invaluable assistance may prove to be less than valuable today."

Together, in silence, they finished making the bed and left the room. Beth's floor-length lavender dressing gown sailed down the hall. Lela followed it, slapping the rigid soles of her sandals against the bare wood floor, and then turned off into her bedroom where Daniel was still asleep.

Daniel was dreaming of a solar eclipse, a phenomenon which had occurred early in the summer. Lela and Daniel had awaited the spectacle on a rock by the sea with the expectation of being moved by the cosmos into the lofty dimension of pity and terror. They had not been disappointed. Nature performed superbly: sudden, unearthly dark and cold; the hysteria of gulls; the ocean motionless; the moon, a perfect black circle, and, around it, the sun, a blue-green-white light.

Now, at the end of summer, on a Friday in the early morning, as the hot sun assaulted the room, Daniel dreamed the eclipse, until the familiar slap-slap of his wife's sandals upon the floor violated the solar silence and a fly settled on his ear. The solar eclipse became a wild boar.

Lela ignored the mound of Daniel in the bed and walked to a table on which lay two piles of paper. One pile was a story for Mark Sarum called "Euzilpha and Carduff," printed in large block letters, for the Sarums and Bennetts were coming to spend the weekend, and Lela wanted to have a gift for the boy. The other pile contained several pages of Lela's long angular script comprising one sentence.

A Short Essay About this House

Here in 1775 died Walter Winslow of wounds sustained in a battle between the good people of this town and the British warship Hawk—here he died in his modest and ordinary home, survived by his widow, Rebecca, who thereafter climbed down the rocks and walked the beach each day until she could walk no more and then lingered for twenty years in bed, listening, as the snow and the wind weakened the walls, until she died, aged 104, a blessing and a relief to her nieces who inherited the ravaged house and the handsome oak double bed of the twenty years of dying (unfortunately, the rest of the furnishings—meager but necessary—were left to a second cousin who had visited Rebecca twice and sympathized with the pains in her legs); nevertheless, the nieces moved into the house and spent the winters in the oak bed playing games of double solitaire, ignoring the fact that their quilt was sometimes white with snow which had drifted through the cracked house, and occasionally attended by a man-of-all-work named George who had been brought up by his disappointed mother as though he were a girl; although he had grown gnarled and wizened, the erstwhile transvestite in him revealed itself in the kerchief he always wore around his head, the kerchief he wore to the wintry funerals of the nieces, the kerchief which repelled and disgusted (despite George's efforts to ingratiate himself) the next Winslow heiress, the niece of the nieces of the widow of Walter Winslow: Eliza, tall and rawboned, who picked blueberries and told fortunes and thus survived; Eliza, who in her later years took in "Black Rob," a toothless Negro, an itinerant hog butcher, who lived in the cellar of the house, and finally in the house itself as Eliza grew old and peculiar and lonely, and who took tender care of her until she died; and then, when the walls of the house fell in, "Black Rob," the master of all he surveyed (the ocean, and the rocks, and the fallen boards) dwelled once more in the cellar, until he could no longer patch the cellar walls, and ice lined the floors, and his toes froze, and the Constable, at the behest of a concerned citizenry, had him carried to the poorhouse

*where, of course, unused to such luxury, "Black Rob"
died within the week, mourned by no one, least of all by
the ruined house which lay scattered upon the rocks until
1868, when the wealthy spinster Lyda found it, or more
accurately the site of it and one or two floorboards; and,
having climbed the rocks and razed the ghostly boards,
she determined to build a house after the manner of Mid-
Victorian Italianate (for Lyda had been dutifully abroad
and dutifully impressed by what she saw), and thus she
instructed her architect; aghast but well paid, he went
about his work with scornful diligence, erecting the
piazza and balcony unnecessary and impractical in any
but a southern climate, remaining, nevertheless, what he
had always been—that most unique of creatures—a
reasonable, an eminently sane man, and Lyda was pleased
with him and his house and was content for a few years
to sketch the ocean, and then, after a chance visit to the
widow and twelve children of a man who had been killed
in a grog shop, she led a temperance union, and then for
several years suffered—mildly but incessantly—from an
obscure nervous ailment (in 1880, disturbed by the noise
of a whistling buoy, she wrote to the Secretary of the
Navy, and the buoy was forthwith removed, despite the
loud and perhaps justified remonstrances of endangered
lobstermen); however, the following summer she took to
her withered embrace a clergyman sixteen years her
junior, and the local newspaper reported, dryly, that Lyda
was much improved in health and that the buoy had been
returned; they lived happily and died almost simultaneously despite the difference in their ages and the house
became the burden of a series of undistinguished descendants of the clergyman, until finally, in 1935, it became the proud possession of Henry Porter, who had
been shipwrecked off Cape Hatteras in 1929 and delivered
by his rescuers to the local Salvation Army where he sang
a hymn and was given fifty cents; Henry Porter, who ably
conducted various enterprises involving non-existent com-*

modities and thus rose rapidly; Henry Porter, who married late and finally adopted that necessity for a businessman, a son; Henry Porter, who bought the house on the rocks overlooking the bay and the sea and painted it yellow, the house into which we now intrude ourselves.

Lela straightened the pile of papers. Sooner or later she would get on with it again. For the most part it was lies, the product of random reading in the local library: old newspapers and privately published memoirs, as well as the accumulated gossip about six or seven houses in the area, for the librarian (herself the great-great-granddaughter of a sea captain and still in tenuously mortgaged possession of a house with a widow's walk) had proved to be an artful and willing purveyor of the local oral tradition.

There was some truth in it, nevertheless. Henry Porter still lived, although he neither enjoyed nor approved of the process. (In 1944 Henry's adopted son, the only thing Henry had ever loved, had joined the paratroopers. Like Icarus he was soon undone.) It was from Old Henry (so he had been called since the day his stepson died) that Daniel and Lela had leased the house and bought the boat, a sixty-year-old Friendship sloop, christened *Philemon* by Matthew in a bacchic moment with a bottle of Budweiser beer.

One November morning Lela and Daniel had driven to the sea, climbed the rocks, and found Old Henry inexplicably seated on the veranda of his large, boarded-up, yellow summer house. Negotiations for the house and boat had proceeded rapidly, for the Relds were eager and Old Henry was indifferent.

Daniel's body remained inert. His breath went in, went out, the doors to the balcony were open, the muffled explosion of the sea came regularly.

Resisting with will—for there was so much to be done—
the rhythmic ambience of sleep and summer, Lela took a pen
and on the top sheet of script marked with some satisfaction
(for at least it was fact) the day, the month, and the year.
Then, looking up at her image in the mirror above the table,
she thought of her friend, Jean Macleod, who was expected
at noon.

"It is bone structure; it is all in the bone structure," Lela
informed her reflection in a whisper, as she stretched the skin
of her face taut and found nothing more extraordinary than
the common nose and inevitable chin of faces which are not
unusually deformed.

III

ONE HUNDRED AND SIXTY miles from the summer house, in a small room with little ventilation, Room 4 of a Connecticut guest house, Mrs. Jean Macleod drank the last of an insipid mixture of warm tap water and instant coffee. A long-time inhabitant of the refuges for transients both here and abroad, she had found this measure an effective, if somewhat unpalatable, means of stimulating the organs of wakefulness. Gagging slightly, she folded a blue nightgown into the open suitcase on the bed, closed the case, and snapped it shut.

Mrs. Macleod was to be the weekend guest of Lela and Daniel. It was to that end—a not too uncomfortable bed within the sound of the sea—that she reluctantly exerted herself so early in the morning.

Although aging and plump, Jean Macleod had beauty. She knew it and she carried it well. She was rendered uncomfortable and slightly unbalanced by the weight of the suitcase in her right hand and the awkwardness of her beaver coat draped over her left arm. Having experienced, with the intimacy of discomfort, all the continents of the earth, Mrs. Macleod had learned that climate was not a thing one could trust. She always carried, never packed, her winter coat. Nevertheless, she negotiated the steep steps of the guest house with certain dignity, like a mature swan—squat but graceful—which finds no turn in the river strange or overly difficult.

As Mrs. Macleod got into the automobile she had rented and placed the suitcase on the seat beside her, she remembered the manuscript which had lain—as it always did—on the table beside her bed. She opened the case and was reassured to find it couched safely beneath the blue nightgown and above her strictest corset (saved for those special occasions—thankfully they were less and less frequent as she got older—when decorum was best served by discomfort).

She patted the manuscript tenderly, with connubial condescension, for its author was her late husband, a boanergestic preacher who, enchanted beyond the limitations of ordinary obsessions by his passion for medieval scholarship, had attempted an accurate but entertaining account of everyday life in the fourteenth century. The Reverend Macleod, long since dead, had never completed the book. From Alexandria to Oslo to Madrid to London to New York, and back again, for ten years of journeys, the unfinished manuscript of *One Week on a Medieval Barony*, its yellow foolscap fading, traveled with Mrs. Macleod and lay beside her bed. She read it often, but never beyond page eleven, at which point she would inexorably sink to sleep.

Mrs. Macleod still mourned her husband in a general way, as one does the loss of involuntary beliefs and old truths. Sometimes late at night, if she were kept awake by a change of diet or lack of proper ventilation, or if she were awakened, as she had been recently, by bad dreams, she would march rather foolishly around her hotel room, muttering, "Damn death, damn death!"

As the car turned away from the Connecticut guest house, Mrs. Macleod asked of herself sharply, "What time is it?" Her watch proclaimed 8:22; the church chime clanged 8:15. Her watch was at least eight minutes slow, she knew, and there-

fore the church chimes must be wrong. She was overly conscious of time. A week before she had flown home from
Oslo, her flight overtaking the sun somewhere above the
North Atlantic. She realized that questions of time were still
really questions of place. She did not quite know where she
was yet.

Mrs. Macleod rounded a sudden curve in the road and
swerved the car just in time to avoid hitting an ancient farm
cart with an old man and two children aboard. As her car
drew past the cart, a young boy stood and waved to her.

Mrs. Macleod did not wave back, for she suddenly remembered lines from a poem:

> *Children picking up our bones*
> *Will never know that these were once*
> *As quick as foxes on the hill* . . .

And then she worried and wondered if the child had noticed,
had thought her indifferent perhaps, or cruel. The morning
mist rose across the random stone walls.

IV

On the second floor of the summer house, Lela smiled as she approved the simplicity of the bedroom she had furnished and arranged for herself and Daniel, singling out for her particular approbation—which took the form of a deep curtsy and a presentational sweep of the arm—the two-part oak captain's chest with brass handles. She had bought it from a local junkman and she knew every inch of it with the peculiar intimacy involved in the resurrection of solid objects, the intimacy of sandpaper, tack cloth, and linseed oil.

Having accomplished a narrow escape from the charge of the wild boar, Daniel opened his eyes, observed his wife suspended in a curtsy to the chest, and cleared his throat significantly. Lela smiled vaguely at him, barely tolerating the invasion of her privacy, and left the room. Behind her she heard Daniel's unsuccessful attempt to cover his laughter with a pillow.

Arming herself with sheets and a pillowcase from the linen closet in the hall, she strode into another bedroom. There upon the bed, flat, immobile, and smiling, was Walter Bridge, an old and close friend of both the Relds and the Steads. He had arrived quite unexpectedly on the previous day. He and Daniel had been up most of the night drinking, and Walter was still fully dressed. Depositing the sheets on the dresser, Lela went over to the bed and stared down at him.

It occurred to Lela that, with the possible exception of her husband, Walter was the person she most cared for in the world, although she hardly ever saw him. Walter always arrived unexpectedly and never stayed long enough to convince her completely of his reality. Walter was the first juggler of the world (so she silently crowned him as she looked down at his sleeping smile). He could keep an infinite number of balls in the air at once. He could whip up any foolishness to its fullest froth, and when he did so, all disbelief was suspended and the atmosphere was heady with delight.

Walter had some passionate pact with life, some important connection. Compared with him, they were all anemic. He had something they lacked. He gave something they needed. It had been an aimless, discontented summer, but now with Walter among them, Lela felt that for the moment things were complete.

One of Walter's most important occupations was the creation of his own legend, a magnum opus at which he worked assiduously and relentlessly. He claimed to owe his name to his grandfather, who had been found, as an infant, in the shadow of Brooklyn Bridge, and thus named after it. He claimed to owe his fortune to his father, the son of Brooklyn Bridge. The details of his father's rise to fortune changed occasionally in the telling (as did the face of Walter's character), depending upon Walter's audience.

Mr. Bridge (son of Brooklyn Bridge, and father of a reticent but nonetheless engaging Walter Bridge) had been chauffeur to a wealthy eccentric who chose him as the recipient of hundreds of thousands, to spite his expectant heirs. This was the version Walter told to women over forty, if they were married and lacked perspicacity.

Mr. Bridge (son of Brooklyn Bridge, and father of a beautifully virile animal named Walter) had been chauffeur and, to put it crudely, as Walter did in a tone of amused restraint, man-of-all-work to one of New York's most successful madams, a position he fulfilled with such adroitness that he became a partner in the enterprise and something of an expert in some of the more exotic intricacies of the business which madam preferred to leave to a man. This was the version Walter told to women under forty if they were unmarried and lacked perspicacity.

For all men who lacked perspicacity, an abundant breed Walter abhorred, he created a synthesis of bad movies, about a prominent but unnamed gangster and his trusted Negro wheelman, who saved his money and avoided arrest.

Walter's friends were less concerned with his fictional past than with his factual present. He was capable of remarkable lucidity, and yet his imagination was not earth bounded. In short, he was gifted, quite the most gifted among them. They all expected him to do something, but the exact nature of his hypothetical achievement remained a mystery. They waited for Walter to perform that which they could not even conceive.

Walter had been to college with Matthew and Daniel and had concluded his formal education at a fraternity dinner given to celebrate his election to Phi Beta Kappa. Over dessert he had produced, to everyone's surprise, a one-way plane ticket to Hong Kong. Walter had returned from China a year later with astounding stories about the yellow race, preeminently about the women of the yellow race, which Daniel did not wish to believe and Matthew did not wish to disbelieve. Neither Lela nor Beth had been allowed enough of his repertoire to form a desire one way or the other, for if there was anything that Walter Bridge (whose humor denied nothing and defied everything) respected, it was the wives of his friends, the women who—on those few occasions when it was necessary—took care of him.

They were all vaguely concerned about him. Since his return from China, he had not seemed to settle down to anything. It was difficult to be sure, however, for his exact activities and whereabouts were usually unknown.

"You oughtn't to drink so much," said Lela to his sleeping smile, as she unlaced his shoes. "What's the point? You don't make any sense, you know, you don't make any sense at all." She put his shoes on the floor and drew the shades to keep the light from his face.

"You're good. Did anyone ever tell you that?" Walter asked as he awoke.

"No one but you, and only when you're drunk or sick."

"You're a liar. I'll bet old Dan tells you all the time."

"Don't be vulgar and besides it's none of your damn business anyway."

"I was not being vulgar," he called after her.

Lela slammed the door, and was again aware of stifled laughter as she walked down the stairs.

In the kitchen of the summer house, Beth sat on a stool and leaned her elbows upon the makeshift counter Daniel had erected the day before. She stared with distaste at an empty fifth of rye and a bottle of bitters which someone had forgotten to cap.

"Walter and Daniel," she muttered, "Walter and Daniel have been drinking Manhattans. All night, of course. And what are we to do with Walter?"

He had simply arrived, on this of all weekends; there wasn't a bed in the house. He would have to sleep on the balcony or on the veranda. He would prefer it, of course, concluding that if he were not treated with ceremony, he need not respond with ceremony. "It will be all right," she tried to tell herself. "After all, one can't put one's young bachelor friend into the same room with the old widow friend of someone else." Nor could one ask the widow lady—a thoroughly good sort, Beth reminded herself, there was no use blaming Mrs. Macleod—to sleep on a mat out of doors. But of course it would not be all right. The English couple were coming and had, no doubt, heard about the burning of schools, the shooting of Negroes, men in sheets, flaming crosses. They would wonder why the only Negro among them should sleep on the floor. It would be difficult and all so silly; they had all slept on the floor at one time or another. Walter had arrived with a small tape recorder in one hand and a hand-sewn leather duffel bag in the other, fully expecting to sleep on a floor. Of course, all of that could not be explained to the English; particularly not to the man, an Oxonian with the idiosyncratic pronunciation of his species. Although Richard Bennett said everything three times successively, his simplest sentence was usually beyond Beth's comprehension. A subject as complicated as Walter could not be explained to a man who could not be understood.

It would be difficult. Matthew would arrive, see it all, and storm. Matthew would try to make it right. He would ludicrously and awkwardly mount his highest horse and announce, after three brandy highballs and from that virtuous but precarious height, the whole straightforward truth. Walter was a well-educated, independently wealthy Negro who liked to sleep on floors. Although it was true, Matthew would make it sound like fiction of the most absurd order. Meanwhile, Walter would be off someplace—recording the cries of gulls, that was what he had said he had come to do; yes, Walter would be off recording the gulls, never eating with anyone else, oblivious and indifferent to the effect he and his damn gulls were having on the English vision of the American Race Crisis. Eating separately and sleeping on the floor. No doubt the Oxonian would write—directly he returned to England—a staunch letter to the *Guardian,* in which everything was repeated thrice, declaring that he knew, from personal experience, that all Americans, even the most liberal, the best educated, the most northern, were brutes and bigots who mistreated Negroes. It would be difficult.

Beth knew there was no use blaming Walter or Mrs. Macleod or Matthew or the Oxonian; it was, of course, all Lela's fault. Her deliberate perversity was responsible for this impossible assortment of guests on the day of Matthew's return. She was also responsible for not having put a coat of varnish on the counter (she had promised to do it), and that too would have to be done before Beth could devote herself to vichyssoise, crabmeat salad, and a gelatin mold (lime for the color), what Beth hoped would be an acceptable simulation of a well-got-up, handsomely presented luncheon to be served at two. Lela was also responsible for—Beth looked at the cupboard doors above the counter—"The Whale Spits Out Jonah Upon the Dry Land"—a print of a stained-glass window which Lela had cut in half and affixed to the two doors of the cupboard to cover peeling paint and a large crack in the wood. She had also removed the cupboard knobs in order not to distort, mutilate, or interfere with the regurgitation of the whale. When the cupboard doors were closed, one half of a praying Jonah stuck out of Leviathan's mouth. It was now necessary to pry the cupboard doors open with a knife in order to reach the sugar.

"She has no sense of the fitness of things," muttered Beth. "Jonah in the kitchen."

She looked once again at Lela's handiwork and allowed herself to smile, knowing that if there were one thing that could survive the weekend and the next forty years of private and public catastrophe, it was their balanced love, their mute, disgruntled affection for one another.

Yes, it would be all right, Beth convinced herself, as she took a can of varnish and a brush from the cupboard below the sink. After all, it was Walter, not the English, who mattered. She couldn't remember the last time they had seen him. He never seemed to have an address. (It was, for example, as she had remarked annually, impossible to get hold of him for christenings. To which Matthew had replied—annually— "Since you persist in this shibboleth, I am relieved, for his sake, that you can't find him.")

Beth realized that she had been missing Walter without knowing it. She was glad he had come, and it would please Matthew so. Absentmindedly, she began stroking the wooden surface with a brush of varnish. It was the day of Matthew's return. The thought was a constriction in her throat. She moved her body back and forth with the stroke of the brush and invented a strange melody for the rhythm and the thought.

Passing the kitchen door, Lela heard Beth's song and did not interrupt. The unvarnished counter, like the arrival of guests, was problematic and best left to the course of things. She walked down the hall and paused in the doorway of the living room. Mrs. Vanidore, suddenly aware of her presence, groaned painfully as she bent down to dust the leg of a chair.

Meanwhile Walter had pulled himself off the bed and unpacked his duffel bag, which contained *The Old Farmer's Almanac*, underwear, and a flute. These and the portable tape recorder he arranged neatly in a dresser drawer.

V

Fifty miles from the summer house, in a Boston hotel room, Richard Bennett, dressed in a light gray suit, starched white shirt, and black tie, sat down upon the edge of his wife's bed, bent over, and felt the dampness of the pillow against his hand and his wife's feverish skin against his face. He took her in his arms and ran his hand along her back, aware first of the annoying, long ragged tear in her nightgown and then of the intriguing pressure of her breasts against his chest.

"Now do stop crying, Anne. This isn't reasonable. Last night it was a trivial disagreement of moods, nothing more. All that is the least part of our lives and my love. Where do you get the odd idea that it matters so much to me?"

"It does matter, Richard." Anne Bennett moved within the circle of her husband's arm and brushed her hair from her face. To be getting old, she thought, was to have hair like straw and to forever feel like a hag.

"I suppose you've not slept at all," he whispered. "It was silly of you not to have called me. I sometimes think you enjoy working yourself into these states." He kissed her forehead. It was half an endearment, half a surreptitious attempt to determine if she had a fever.

She moved so that she could see his face as she answered him. "Of course I don't enjoy these 'states.' How can you be so absurd? But there is utterly no point in our both losing sleep. Left alone, you always sleep like the dead. Come now, admit it, you know you do."

"I only know that when I wake and find you like this it frightens me."

"It is only the usual thing—nerves, insomnia, call it what you will. As I have told you time and again, there is absolutely nothing you can do."

"It frightens me," he repeated petulantly.

"Well, it's ridiculous of you. I am simply . . . highly strung, is, I think, the usual phrase. Do stop magnifying insomnia into suicide. I am not such a fool as Rachel. Most likely I shall outlive you by a century at least."

She wondered why they had to go on talking. She had not slept; why must he insist on talk, talk, talk.

Fresh from a long, deep sleep, and a little ashamed of the fact, Richard continued to talk: "When you're like this you make me feel so selfish, so small. You become so cold."

In a moment I shall scream, Anne thought, I shall scream loud enough to knock the walls of my skull in.

She did not scream. Instead she replied in a voice clear with the consequent frustration of not having screamed: "Now we're back to it. At the core of everything. The trivial disagreement (as you so absurdly refer to it) of last night, and all the endless 'last nights' backward in time for twenty years. My frigidity."

"Oh for God's sake!" In spite of his sound sleep, Richard was also irritated. "Stop being melodramatic! You're not frigid."

"All right then, my occasional frigidity."

"Frigidity is not occasional. Either it is or it isn't, and in your case it most certainly isn't. It is always a mistake to argue about words before breakfast."

"But Richard, I haven't let you . . . one never knows quite how to say it without sounding indecent . . . couch me in almost two months. It has been that long, hasn't it?"

"I wouldn't know. I haven't been keeping a calendar of our sex life."

"It's only normal that you should reproach me." She put a hand to his cheek and laughed at him. "Do be normal; please reproach me. I would feel ever so much better about it if you did."

"Now let's not have one of your dissertations on the normal, not before breakfast."

She leaned back and laughed again. "Quite right, my dear. I can't carry on with this; I'm much too tired."

Richard continued to cradle her in his arms until there was a knock at the door. Feeling that things ought to be brought to a proper conclusion, that some sort of modulation was definitely in order before he moved away from her, he leaped upon a quotation which he delivered as tenderly as possible, realizing, even as he spoke, that it sounded absurd.

"I praised her body *and her mind.*"

"Oh Richard," she hooted, "come off it. You hardly sound real. Hand me my robe will you, and do answer the door."

Richard removed himself reverentially from his wife and opened the door to the bellboy, who was abnormally tall, ugly, and slightly spastic. The tray he held to his shoulder wobbled dangerously. Richard took it from him quickly and tipped him.

Anne had a glimpse of the bellboy, and, as soon as the door was shut upon him, she burst out:

"My God, what a queer looking creature. What does this country do to its children?"

"I only had a brief look at him, but I would guess that the problem is congenital, not national," Richard answered, brushing underwear off a table to make way for the tray. He had married an untidy woman. The fact always surprised him.

"Intelligent, I think, certainly sensitive, too much so perhaps—extraordinarily ugly . . . can't manage his body yet, I suspect . . . I dare say I can use him," said Anne. Reaching for a small sketch pad and pencil, she began to outline with deliberately crude strokes her momentary impression of the bellboy.

By the time Richard had finished pouring two cups of coffee and had measured cream and sugar, the sketch was completed.

"Finished and with only eighteen lines, which is just about his age. Being so horribly young, he deserves no more."

Richard handed her a cup and glanced at the caricature.

"Good God!"

"Dreadful, isn't he. I have it in mind to do a vast mural sort of thing and I shall stick him—a small but prominent him with yellow skin—in the upper left corner. I shall make him a sort of mask. In fact, I shall have three masks, comedy and tragedy, all very conventional and stylized, and this fellow in the middle."

"All three in the upper left?" asked Richard dryly.

His wife was a painter; her work was often praised and occasionally purchased. Several critics agreed that although it seemed a little behind contemporary taste, time would prove it of some importance. Richard was proud of her success and her commitment, but he did not pretend to understand her work

"Then," Anne continued, ignoring his question, "fifty years from now, when I'm dead, quite dead, and the worms have picked my bones, he'll come across my mural someplace or other and recognize himself as a young man. He'll be dreadfully upset . . . you see, he's just that sort . . . no defenses . . . wears his skin inside out . . ."

"If that's the case, why do it?"

"Because his face is useful and besides it suits my mood," she answered.

"I hate it when you talk that way, writing your own epitaph and the rest."

"Nonsense, it's very good for me to treat myself with clinical detachment; you yourself have said so. I should think you'd find posterity a reassuring thought. Perhaps you'll be discovered for what you are, a charming, handsome, well-dressed angel, who gracefully combines the best of both Testaments: the patience of an afflicted Job with the gentleness of Jesus . . . so there!" Anne kissed him on the cheek and got out of bed.

"Are you really predisposed to stare while I haul this wreck I call myself around in an effort to make it presentable?" she asked, rummaging in a suitcase.

"Yes, otherwise you never will get ready."

Anne spoke from the bathroom over the sound of running water:

"I suppose we must go."

"We've promised, you know. Actually, I'm very much looking forward to talking to Daniel about his work. I've been thinking of doing an informal piece about the aesthetics of science."

Anne came out of the bathroom and occupied a long, expectant silence by pulling a dress over her head.

"Actually, that sounds like a rather splendid idea," she said finally. "Doesn't it ever occur to you that if it weren't for me and your money, you would no doubt do something very important one day?"

"I suppose the little money I have might be blamed, but it's certainly nothing to do with you. I much prefer dabbling. We've been all through that. Here, let me give you a hand." Richard addressed himself to zipper and buttons.

Richard had inherited a scant income and a comfortable house. He occasionally lectured, he occasionally wrote essays, and he frequently encouraged the young, both with his money and his time.

"What do you make of Daniel?" he asked.

"Of course, I never understand a word of what he says, but the words he uses about science of all things are extraordinary: elegance, beauty, symmetry . . . He seems very much the man in the tower. God, I wish we weren't going. The prospect of all that young American idea of health: everyone bathing nude in the sea, tumbling about, and fornicating on the ground . . ."

"That is *your* idea of health; not the Relds'. American brute health is a British illusion, as we both very well know."

In his mind, Richard could see very distinctly the thin blue paper of an air letter and the handwriting of his half brother, Claud, describing his new bride, Rachel:

> She has everything I need—energy, vivacity, and ambition. I'm such an indolent bore—she will re-make me beautifully. Rachel isn't pretty in the usual meaning, but handsome, yes, and so lively, so clear and bright and such fun, and you and Anne are bound to admire.

At the time Richard had dismissed the letter as the usual bridegroom babble, embraced the idea of his new sister-in-law as a typical healthy American girl, registered habitual annoyance with his brother's prose style, and replied to the letter in his usual tone of elderly indulgence.

Richard was fifteen years older than Claud, who had been the result of a late pregnancy in a second marriage. Richard's attitude toward Claud had been at first embarrassed, then disdainful, and finally fatherly. It was with paternal relief that he viewed Claud's marriage, believing that there would be stability and children.

Richard was intelligent, certainly a modern man, without most of the prejudices and quirks which sometimes accompany independent wealth (even meager independent wealth); nevertheless, in some subterranean passage of his consciousness there were vague but profound memories of maternal grandparents, stately substances who raised the thought in him that either he or Claud ought to continue the blood (no matter how diluted by their separate sires). He and Anne had no children and therefore, by marrying, Claud has assumed the obligation.

After the birth of the child who appropriately bore the maternal name, Colton, and several years of married purgatory, the details of which Claud had not confided, came Rachel's suicide. The event was enough to dismiss forever from Richard's mind belief in the promptings of ancestral ghosts, for the child who remained might very well have done better not to be born. Now it was also impossible for him to believe in his original preconception of Americans as a simple, healthy, cheerfully vulgar, but essentially harmless race. They were nearly always vulgar, very often sick, but never harmless. Although he looked forward to visiting with them, Richard was still not entirely convinced that Lela and Daniel were the exceptions which proved the rule.

Richard stared at a spot of sunlight on the floor, unaware of Anne, who was now dressed and had nothing left about her of anger or tears. She interrupted his thought:

"Of course we'll go. I like Lela tremendously and shall ask her to pose for me. The boy will like the sea. It will be a pleasure to watch him. Children are delightful when they face natural immensities. Come on, you've promised us to Claud for breakfast." She took his arm as he rose from the chair. She was always moved when he brooded like that, staring at the floor, not knowing where he was.

He sensed her concern, looked at her, showing his appreciation that she had got herself up so nicely, and thought: I feel it now, what I've felt every day since we met, the thing you refuse to believe in.

However, he had learned a long, if not wholly comprehensive, list of the things he could, with impunity, articulate, and so he made no declaration but asked a simple question:

"You won't mind terribly?"

"No, not at all. I really do want to see Lela. There are questions I must ask her. You must promise me one thing, though."

"And what is that?" he asked.

"Not to repeat everything thrice."

"Whatever are you talking about?"

"I'm talking about the fact that whenever you are with Americans you repeat everything you say three times, as though the whole race were either deaf or moronic. I'm sure they must find it a bit unnerving."

"I do nothing of the sort," argued Richard as they left the room.

In the lobby of the hotel they joined Claud and Colton Mark. The maternal name was not the sort a boy of eight could be expected to bear with equanimity. Although his uncle insisted upon Colton, everyone else called him Mark.

Anne led the way through a room of breakfasting travelers to a quiet table at the rear, followed by the well-dressed Richard and Claud, who was disgusted. (Why couldn't they just sit down by the door, why the parade, he wondered.) Mark brought up the rear. He was small for his age, but well formed, and still rather in awe of hotels.

VI

THE CAR STOOD POISED at a stoplight. Mrs. Macleod's right hand moved up, across, and down. How one does these things automatically, she thought, without knowing anything at all about gears: what they are, what they look like, what they do.

The light changed. Her foot pressed the accelerator.

"Children picking up our bones will never know, that we were once as quick as foxes on the hill," she chanted aloud, and then she performed an act of penance.

"It does not do to shun the young," she said to herself, for she still questioned the click in her mind which had led her not to respond to the young boy who had waved from the farm cart. Pulling off the road, she beckoned to a barefoot adolescent. His shoes were tied together and hanging around his neck, and he had a sign in his hand (he was holding it upside down) announcing his destination, a town through which Mrs. Macleod would pass.

"You're not running away from home, are you?" she asked, opening the car door.

"No, that's where I'm going," he replied.

Tentatively putting one foot into the car, he asked, "Are you sure?" He had hitchhiked often enough to know that elderly women with a look of chastity did not, as a rule, accept as passengers well-grown fifteen-year-olds with a look of puberty.

"Quite sure, quite sure," she replied, thinking that the boy seemed well-mannered. Childless herself, Mrs. Macleod's reactions to the young were usually determined by their manners.

"I will take you where you want to go, and in exchange you must tell me all about yourself."

The Bennetts and the Sarums had finished breakfast and stood in the hotel lobby awaiting the car Claud had rented for the weekend. Anne rested her hand lightly on Mark's shoulder. She was aware that this was a privileged gesture. As a rule, Colton Mark did not allow demonstrations from women; Anne and Lela were perhaps the only exceptions, and Anne was proud of the fact. She was still chafing Richard about the peculiarities of his conversation with Americans.

"But you do, Richard dear, really you do, without even realizing it. Hello, hello, hello. Beautiful day, beautiful day, beautiful day. Without a doubt, without a doubt, without a doubt. Everything three times, isn't that so, Claud?" she appealed to him, resisting the impulse to push his shoulders back, for in the last few days he had adopted a melancholic stoop.

"Precisely," replied Mark, relieving his father of the burden of conversation.

"Keep a civil tongue, Master Colton, keep a civil tongue." Richard feigned severity, adopting, as he often did to amuse the boy, the tone of a headmaster.

The morning sun reflected off the surface of the airplane punished the eyes. Having arrived from London and disem-

barked at New York before dawn, Matthew Stead now observed the plane he was about to board. It would deposit him
at the distance of about an hour from his wife and the house
overlooking the sea. He shaded his eyes with his hands.

Matthew was a portrait of craggy golden youth lapsing
(however defiantly) into the indistinction and overfeeding
of maturity. Ruefully, he often referred to the condition as
early middle-aging, a terminal illness. Nevertheless, there
still hung about him the impression of crude nobility. To his
embarrassment, Lela often called him the Earl of Murray. In
his own way he was a braw gallant and played well at the
more contemporary, indoor equivalents of the ring, the ball,
and the glove. If he died young, he would be mourned by a
number of queenly women (among them his wife, who had
survived his four children and his poetry, which was invariably about other women).

At the last possible moment Matthew ran toward the
plane—hair, tie, and jacket flying—and announced to the
amused stewardess, who obviously found him attractive:
"Well, I'm coming after all."

At the summer house Lela again passed the kitchen door.
Beth's strange melody had ceased and there was the strong
odor of spar varnish. It was time to consult about lunch, she
decided.

"Vichyssoise? Oh God, must we?" Lela asked in reply to
Beth's recitation of the proposed menu. "And a mold? Gelatin makes me nervous, particularly green gelatin. We once
turned off the refrigerator and went away for three weeks.
But there was a head of lettuce left in it . . . and . . ." Lela
remembered how it looked and her stomach keeled over.

"The vichyssoise will smell of varnish. Couldn't the counter have waited until after the weekend?" she asked weakly.

"If we are going to do it, to entertain, I mean—and let me remind you that you are responsible for this extraordinary potpourri of personalities . . ."

"This what?" Lela interrupted, incredulously.

"Please let me finish. If we are going to do it, we ought to do it well. You cannot invite people of that sort . . ."

"What sort?" Lela again interrupted.

"The Bennetts' sort, that's what sort; you cannot throw peanut butter and jelly sandwiches at them."

"Oh, don't be silly; they're perfectly nice, perfectly simple people."

"Simple!" exclaimed Beth. "You can hardly call Anne Bennett simple."

"She is the last person in the world to care what we serve for lunch, as you would understand if you knew her better."

"Well, I don't care to know her better, thank you!"

Lela began to understand. Beth was really saying that she did not want Matthew to know Anne better. Matthew's taste had recently veered rather sharply to older women. Lela wondered for the thousandth time that summer how she had got herself into so complicated a world. It was, after all, the season for rest and simplicity.

"You have nothing to fear from Anne Bennett, I promise you, and that is the golden truth," Lela stated. You have just made a mistake, she told herself silently, as she placed her hands on Beth's shoulders.

Beth turned away, but it was clear that she was not angry. Lela offered a prayer of gratitude. Matthew's infidelity was not a subject she wished to pursue with Beth, for that would invariably lead to convolutions and distortions of their pleasantly simple intimacy. She had been a fool to bring it up, but it was a common pattern—if she placed the smallest fraction of her foot in the sea, the undertow was irresistible. Lela did penance.

"I'll make the vichyssoise," she promised. Beth left the room without turning toward her.

Lela pried apart "The Whale Spits Out Jonah Upon the Dry Land" and took a book from the shelf of condiments.

"Mrs. Armbreaker's recipes for joy?" asked Daniel, making a sudden entrance and kissing the top of her head.

"Vichyssoise. I thought you were still in bed. Coffee on the stove."

"Beth looks on the verge of a hurricane. What a smell!"

"My fault. Both the hurricane and the smell. Vichyssoise is the result. Here, read, while I try to gather the necessities."

Daniel took a sip of coffee, cleared his throat importantly, and began in an exaggerated basso:

" 'Yes, the last s is pronounced. Most Americans shun it in a "genteel" way as though it were virtuous to ignore it. Be sure to serve the soup reduced to a velvety smoothness. If you like, do as the Joneses do in regard to the last s, that unfortunately may pass unnoticed, but ostracism should come in the wake of the tiniest ignoble lump left to mar the dish.'

"God!" commented Daniel. "Armbreaker thinks she's a poet."

"She bears the taint of a so-called academic wit. Does she ever say how one makes the soup?" asked Lela.

"Potatoes, chicken consommé, cream, chives, and leeks."

"Sounds like an ugly species of insect."

"Leeks, not leeches, darling," he explained.

"I don't even know what they are."

"You can use onions instead."

"I suppose I'll have to. Give me a quick cross reference to chicken consommé."

"Why don't you just use a cube of bouillon?"

"Beth would never approve."

"All right, if you insist." Daniel flipped pages. "You need nasturtium leaves."

"You're joking!"

"No, ma'am, it says very clearly—nasturtium leaves."

"Picked by the light of a full moon, no doubt. I think I'll have a drink to see me through the vichyssoise. Notice I pronounce the final s. That is, I'll have a drink, if you and Walter have left anything."

"Must you? It's so early," Daniel protested.

"Bit hung over, dear?" Lela proceeded to uncap the remnants of the whisky and vermouth and to fill a coffee cup with ice.

"I can't watch." Daniel left the kitchen, calling over his shoulder: "I've hidden a bottle of Jack Daniel's underneath the sink. It might go down more easily than that crap."

Lela collected potatoes, onion, the bottle of Jack Daniel's, and the cookbook, spread the objects in a straight line on the kitchen table, closed the doors of the cupboard, paused to contemplate "The Whale Spits Out Jonah Upon the Dry Land," and then sprinkled sour mash over ice cubes in a coffee mug. Pronouncing with exaggeration the final s, she toasted: "To Vichyssoise."

VII

Spinning words in his mind, Matthew looked out the plane window at the landscape below.

"Above the perimeter of that particular world . . . (Of latitude and longitude, I know nothing; Daniel would know, for at any given moment of space and time he knows emphatically and with exactitude where he is.) Above the perimeter of that particular world . . . (At the undertaking of this thirty minutes of thought in this year and this age, it behooves us, indeed it is necessary, to recognize, with humility, as though in the presence of Supreme Beings and Prime Causes, the possibility if not probability of worlds other than ours.) Above the perimeter of that particular world, that map beneath me (here today, gone tomorrow), I will close my eyes—so—and rest . . .

"*A Short Episode in the General Scheme of Things*: I came to London, London, London town, fair town—not really so fair, but there was a lady there, taller than real, cold as marble and I, needing a night's accommodation, a gay prince of a blade (hardly a blade, if truth be told: too heavy around the waist and a bit gone at the jowls, but let it here and at once be added, prince and blade enough to make an assault), I told myself marble is finite and a tall lady easier than truth. There in a Lyon's Corner House I stirred a spoon in English

offee, which is unpleasant to look at and unworthy of taste,
while the tall marble lady faced me, watching the rhythm of
my hand, her long hands displayed like half-furled antique
ins upon the marble tabletop. How to begin, I asked my-
elf, how to begin? With a gesture of directness, of course.

"One stalwart stride brings me to her table. 'Come with
me,' say I to her. I assume 'yes' though she neither looks nor
speaks. Out goes my hand and sure enough she takes it. The
ovely lady is going to stoop, I say to myself, or my name isn't
olly! 'Scot?' she asks. 'American,' I answer. 'I suppose you
want me to take you home.' On the instant and before I
eply we're off . . . sure as my name *is* folly . . . to some
ort of studio place overlooking the river. Not being particu-
arly well versed in the care and feeding of cool, middle-aged
London ladies who are on the make, I am not quite at my
ase. She does not speak at all, but then why should she?
take off jacket and tie and lounge upon the floor, leaving the
est to her. A half cigarette later, she appears, naked and mov-
ng beneath her slip, but I can tell from the look of her, she's
lothed in irony; it hangs about her from the neck to the an-
les like a heavy cloak. And this is what we go to the ball in, I
hink to myself with a laugh. Nevertheless, I take her face in
my hands and ask forthrightly: 'Are you quite sure?' A gal-
ant, princely blade am I to the last, knowing full well that it
s simply a matter of the slightest touch, the movement of
one hand from cheek to lip to chin, down the neck and along
he shoulder blade, then along the boundary of the arm—a
matter of one slow movement accomplished with finesse.

"And so it was. One small incident in the general scheme
of things. And now . . . And now . . ."

The plane dipped to its destination. Matthew fastened his
eat belt upon command.

And now there would be the sea. And now there would be the sea and the rocks. And now there would be the sea and the rocks and the summer house. He wanted that house. He would talk to Daniel as soon as he arrived. They must buy the house. They could manage it between them, without dipping into Beth's capital.

"And now there will be Beth," Matthew said to himself and his plane touched ground.

The boy's voice was hoarse as he thanked Mrs. Macleod. He had talked about himself for a very long time. Although she had heard very little of what he had said, it was with something akin to regret that she watched him jump awkwardly over a low hedge and head up a path toward a cottage. There was green all around—a heavy green despite the lateness of the season—the intrusive dank perfection of some sweet flower, and the humid hum of insects. Trees hung over the road; she breathed deeply in panic, and shifted from neutral to first.

"And we were once as quick as foxes on the hill."

With relief, Anne Bennett noticed that the automobile was indeed as good as the rental agency had promised. Fortunately, it drove itself, for Claud, who was at the wheel was hardly giving the project the necessary attention.

The poem was on her mind. The poem from which Richard had so absurdly quoted. She could not capture the whole of it. It was no good saying a few words of it to herself, she had to see them on a page, or a picture that they made.

Finally she began to see it. The book was covered in green leather. She saw herself sitting in her large ancient arm chair; its upholstery was worn: the faded leaves of barely visi

ble peonies had loose threads, the points of which brushed
annoyingly against the thin skin of her left wrist. She held the
book with her right hand. The words on the page became
visible. She saw the title: "A Memory of Youth." And there
were the first three lines:

> The moments passed as at a play;
> I had the wisdom love brings forth;
> I had my share of mother-wit . . .

The next lines were blank. She could not make out anything
until the lines that Richard had quoted:

> Believing every word I said,
> I praised her body and her mind . . .

Again an appalling blank. The words which followed were not
there. Again she put her mind to it. There was the chair, the
fire, the irritation on her wrist, the hot reflection on her cheek,
and solitude, for no one else was in the room. The words began to appear:

> Yet we, for all that praise, could find
> Nothing but darkness overhead.
> We sat as silent as a stone,
> We knew, though she'd not said a word,
> That even the best of love must die,
> And had been savagely undone . . .

"Darkness overhead, darkness overhead, savagely undone, savagely undone." Anne read and reread the lines, feeling the
threads upon her wrist and the heat of the fire on her cheek,
until young Mark, riding in the front seat next to his father,
broke the code of silence, proclaiming inexplicably:

"The sea is coming; the sea is coming."

"*Catastrophe* is in the air!" Mrs. Macleod's mind italicized with purposeful melodrama. "Not in the air; in the light," she added, for the early morning sun was gone. The gray over sea, rock, and house seemed tangible, but of an irregular texture like worn velvet.

"Hardly catastrophe." Her voice accompanied her mind with a flat groan. "Something trivial, something shabby. A closet drama, in which rectitude does not triumph, brought to a crisis by the high humidity."

Her car rocked up the winding rutted road toward the house. The house, upon whose elaborate and definite forms the eye could rest, provided relief from the dull ambiguous landscape of near rain.

Mrs. Macleod's arrival was heralded by the curious gulls, or so it seemed to Lela, who watched the birds' circling commotion overhead from the kitchen window as the car pulled up the driveway. She stirred the soup once, turned off the stove, and ran to the front door, reminding herself that the soup needed to be chilled.

Mrs. Macleod waited to be embraced.

"Dear girl, have you been drinking already?" she asked.

"You don't know what I've been through," Lela replied.

VIII

THE SUN'S SURRENDER to fog was complete. The vivid jade of the stained-glass window had dulled to teal. On the eleventh step, underneath the second stained-glass window, the welcome had slipped, the greeting had fallen. Neither Lela nor Mrs. Macleod understood why.

In one of the second-floor guest rooms, Mrs. Macleod sat upon the bed next to her open suitcase with her eyes closed. She saw it again. A window overlooking winter. The earth and the air were gray, and there was only the occasional clarity of snow on a black tree for relief. Lately it had occupied her more and more; sleeping and waking, she saw it.

Lela stood at the open French door of the room, staring ruefully out over the ocean. The mast of the *Philemon* was eclipsed; the leaden groan of a foghorn had just begun. It was going to be a failure, she knew, for there they were—not even looking at each other, unable to speak, an empty ocean between them—left with only the platitude of their good intentions. It would all be a failure.

Lela saw the weekend unroll like a carpet upon which danced she and Daniel, Beth, Matthew, and Walter. Children bearing the distortions of their own adult heads. She heard them chanting nursery rhymes. She turned quickly and faced Mrs. Macleod.

Mrs. Macleod, rapt before the window of winter, had more important things to think about.

Without warning, Claud turned the car sharply down a dirt road.

"Directions," he muttered apologetically to his passengers as they were thrown to one side.

On a deacon's bench in front of a red frame building eight painted pots in a row spelled out: ANTIQUES.

As he got out of the car he saw Anne lean toward Richard and knew that she was remarking about his sullenness, exaggerating his want of humor and conversation.

"Damn them," he thought, "damn them all to hell. With their incessant 'come to the sea and bring the boy; come to the sea and make yourself whole.' "

The voice in his mind executed a singsong rise and fall, accompanying the aphorisms that no one had actually spoken but everyone had thought.

He jerked open the door of the shop. The crowded interior danced with the motion.

Claud penetrated the shop like an explorer in a promised land, touching and smiling. It was a magical shop. The Lord's Prayer embroidered: five dollars with frame. For madame's dressing table: a length of forest green, upon which, in textured relief, lambs and lions couched together in peace. No doubt in the past it had been covered by jars of grease, lotion, cream—the necessities of milady's toilet; no doubt the lambs and lions had also been eclipsed by a silver-backed brush with dirty bristles, an object of revulsion to some gentleman. Upon an antique escritoire: a silver pen. "For words of love to men of soul," muttered Claud, caressing the pen.

The proprietor, Hezekiah Stowe, stepped forward and,

with improbable precision, at a distance of six feet, spat into a
Satsuma rose jar, as Claud reached for it.

"It preserves the scent," Hezekiah explained.

Claud ran his hand over the surface of the jar. In a golden
field, gold encrusted butterflies kissed red and white chry-
santhemums. The jar was ornate and trod dangerously near
the boundary which divided good taste from bad; nevertheless, Claud found it handsome.

"I'll take it, spittle and all," he announced, setting the jar
down on the green velvet cloth. For a moment he thought he
saw the hands of his wife Rachel, tracing, with their slight
tremor, the outlines of the lamb and the lion.

Having received monosyllabic directions from Hezekiah
Stowe, Claud returned to the car and held up the rose jar for
Anne's inspection.

"An object for Lela," he announced, as though entitling a
work of art or a dramatic presentation. "After all, one may
not arrive empty-handed."

"Good God, must you be so testy?" asked his brother
Richard. "The weekend has just begun."

Anne ignored her husband's outburst. "Satsuma. Very
nice," she approved. "Lela will like it. I remember seeing one
like it before and thinking it lovely. Just now I'm not sure
where."

Claud handed the jar to his son, commanding tersely,
"Open it, Mark. It smells."

As Claud started the car there came to Anne, suddenly and
very distinctly, the odor of rhododendrons, their blossoms
fully opened and on the verge of decay.

"Where was it?" Anne asked herself. "Some shop in London? Or was it in the country?"

Slowly and carefully she reconstructed the time and place.

The Satsuma rose jar was in a window with an elephant tusk and a collection of very old clay pipes (dredged up from the Thames, according to a placard). Care had been taken that the jar should repose with grace: purple velvet in careful folds surrounded it.

She had got it clear now; time recaptured, as they said. They were spending the month in London and she had not been polite to one of Richard's young men. There were six a day of them, or so it seemed, talking books at the top of their lungs and forever queued up in front of the loo. Having failed once again, having not come up to scratch (wasn't that the current phrase?), she had taken the underground to Kew Gardens and come across the shop with the rose jar in the window.

Charing Cross, Earl's Court, Hammersmith, and a crowded tube. "Guiness is Good for You." The plaid socks on the gentleman opposite had appalled her. "Pardon, please, is this the Ealing or the Richmond Train?" "Richmond." "Oh dear, that isn't right!"

The underground emerged overground. There was an impact of light but the sun had gone in. At Turnham Green it rained: tennis and cricket came to a halt. Chaps in white trousers ran off swinging their rackets and bats, calling to one another, laughing. Gardens and garbage and toy houses swimming backward in the cold gray light. Kew Gardens. Way Out. And as she came out into the street there had been the shop and the jar.

Bad weather at Kew or a Cold Day for Sperm. Now why did she do that? An unexplained click in the head and the insertion of an irrelevant obscenity. Because the day had begun with the trouble with Richard perhaps, and because she could remember so clearly the damp warmth of the greenhouses, how they had seemed like hermetically sealed breeding grounds.

Outside there had been a cold wind for spring and desultory rain. Inside, the tops of giant palms curved with the curve of the roof. Thin delicate vines, seemingly as frail as insubstantial twine, but in reality possessed of some inner sinew, some toughness, bore their heavy fruit: breast-shaped pendant gourds. The air was like scented oil; there were lilies in a pond and pregnant fish. Feeling faint, she had gone out into the bad weather.

Sitting overlooking the fountain and the artificial lake, sitting among the statues of the royal beasts (between the black bull of Clarence and the griffin of Edward III), feeling the cold fountain spray blown by the wind, watching the darkening sky, the male duck's pursuit of the female, the young gardener tending roses with his long-handled shears, schoolchildren with sketch pads, all the trees leaning as the wind blew—she had come to no conclusions, nor had she been more than usually sorrowful—no, merely empty and rather glad to be alone.

There had been rhododendrons that day, a rose jar in a shop, her failure, and rain.

Soothed by the rain beating its regular pace against the car windows, Anne slept.

Having arrived at Logan Airport and cabbed into town, Matthew boarded the bus which would take him home. The bus moved on toward the sea. Isolated drops of rain became a brief downpour and then a steady muffled stream. Matthew was soon asleep.

There was a black screen and on the black screen "London" in white letters. "Roll 'em," shouted a voice across the screen of Matthew's mind. "Take one!"

Slowly there came into focus one of the Admiralty Horse Guards, standing at attention in an archway, dressed in a tall plumed hat, white pants and long black boots with his sword hanging at the correct angle.

"Technicolor," commented Matthew. He was seated at a distance from the screen.

Two boys pushing bicycles approached.

" 'ey, Alf, look at this bloke!" cried one.

" 'ow does 'e keep 'is bloody 'at on?" asked the other, pointing to the strap secured between the guard's chin and lower lip.

"Ask 'im!" suggested the first boy, squaring himself in imitation of the guard's stance.

" 'ow do you keep it on?" bawled the second boy.

" 'e won't talk," commented the first knowingly.

" 'e'll talk all right," answered the second. He unzipped and took aim at one of the tall shiny black boots.

"Fade out," shouted the off-stage voice. For a moment the screen was black and then there appeared across it "Pause" in large white letters.

"And now a crowd scene," commented Matthew, as another picture began to take shape on the screen. He saw himself step up to the screen and take a hand microphone.

"Ladies and gentlemen," he announced, "on the right side of the screen you see before you one of the Horse Guards gone berserk. He is pursuing two boys on bicycles around Trafalgar Square. Notice the drawn sword which he brandishes. Notice his boots, his scarlet tunic, his amazing hat. He has lost his impassivity. That is his problem.

"And there, ladies and gentlemen," continued Matthew, the hawking orator, "there right slam bang in the middle of your screen, oblivious to bicycles and madness, there are the blokes, chaps, lads, boys, or whatever you choose to call them, depending upon your age, class, and temperament. There they are, four abreast, arms linked like the Musketeers, hair down to their shoulders, their eyes afire, laughing with the laugh of the hyena. There they are, studding up and down in front of Nelson in their pointed Italian leather boots. Of course, Lord Nelson, guarded by lions, impervious to everything, most particularly pigeon shit, is too high up to care. Observe them well, ladies and gentlemen, they are the hope of the world, the seed of the future; as you can see, they have the rightful vanity of conquerors." Matthew bowed himself back to his seat.

"Fade out!" shouted the off-stage voice.

"Pause" appeared once again.

Moments later there was a wall with a sign: "Bayswater Road," and a row of modern flats. Finally the screen was filled with a close-up of the ancient facade of a church and the inscription which it bore. The letters were worn, difficult to make out:

Let the pictured walls within speak of the past . . .
Is it nothing to you, all ye that pass by?
Come and rest awhile.

The door of the church swung open. Sunlight streamed down and angled off fragments of glass. One wall was down. The debris of two decades littered what had been the floor.

Brakes screamed. The bus wrenched out of motion. Thrown forward in his seat, Matthew awoke.

"Yes, it *has* been a warm summer, but I am often reminded of winter," replied Mrs. Macleod to Lela's remark about the weather. "It is the landscape of age, you know."

"It is a cold house without the sun, rather chill and damp. I'm afraid it's going to be a very crowded weekend and not a very pleasant one, if we have bad weather. We were having five; one came unexpectedly. Matthew comes back today; Beth, Daniel and myself—that makes ten in all," said Lela.

At that moment, Beth passed the door of the guest room. Lela called to her and, taking her hand, drew her into the room.

"You remember Jean Macleod."

"Yes, of course, we're very glad you could come." Beth extended her hand to Mrs. Macleod.

"I'm afraid most of the responsibility for the care and feeding of guests falls upon these firm shoulders," Lela explained, pushing Beth to a sitting position on the bed.

"It must be difficult. Such a large house; so many people," Mrs. Macleod mumbled, gazing past Beth and out the French door.

"Beth's children are with their grandparents and Matthew returns from England today," said Lela, stirring conversation and feeling the effort hopeless. They had no nasturtium leaves or whatever ingredient it was that was needed.

"How nice," Mrs. Macleod commented flatly. "Hmmm," she hummed, brushing fore and middle fingers across her brow and through her hair.

"Scotland. Actually, he's just been to Scotland, except for a stopover in London," Beth corrected.

"Dreadful country. From Carlisle to Inverness there isn't a foothold. One is either hanging from a cliff or at the bottom of a bog." Mrs. Macleod stared out to sea as she spoke.

"He was on Skye." Beth was passionately precise.
"The end of the earth, to be sure," said Mrs. Macleod.
In silence the three women stared at the small patch of sea framed by the open door until Beth broke the spell.
"I must drive the cleaning lady home," she said, "and find soup plates on the way back."

IX

Two or three miles from the summer house lay the nearest town, stretching its open mouth into the sea. The town divided itself between fishing and tourists and suffered certain civic neuroses which were inevitable results of this dissociation of its personality. Its statuary was immaculate and an ordinance forbade spitting. However, the behavior of the gulls along the piers was less than fastidious, and there hung about the place the stench of fish, stale beer, and collective hypocrisy. The lean fishermen cursed the tourists with the fat behinds but scrambled for the coins they tossed.

It rained straight and hard on the sea. Led by the screeching of hungry gulls, the fishing boats wrenched and rasped along the horizon. Their dogged, slow progress was a countermotion to the leisure of the lean pleasure craft closer to land, left sail-less and deserted at their moorings.

"Here now, why don't I wrap you in part of my mackintosh; it's such a very large one. We can easily share it."

Anne and Mark stood on a pier in the rain, watching the boats, while Claud and Richard asked final directions. Mark had no coat and his light trousers and shirt were streaked with rain.

"If you look there," she said, pointing to the horizon, "right there at the boat with the blue stripe on the hull, you won't even know it's happening." His reluctance to be close, even momentarily, was a constant challenge.

She crouched to his level and began unbuttoning her coat. "It's such a simple thing, you know," she said, smiling.

Mark watched her smile as though it were an event, an isolated act. It happened slowly, and, although he could see it took effort, he knew it was genuine. He knew that if he touched her mouth it would have a slight vibration. He would not allow himself tenderness, not in the giving or in the taking. He had made up his mind about that a long time ago. Instead, he smiled back at her, very pleasantly, very reasonably, so that she would not be hurt, and moved away.

Anne rose, buttoned her coat again, and cursed herself because she had forced the moment, had asked of him what she herself could not give, because some spot of vanity within her had demanded satisfaction. She had wished his trust not for its own sake, but because he would give it to no one else.

The car horn sounded. She followed Mark back to the car, where Richard and Claud were waiting.

"He's drenched," Claud accused, surveying his son with distaste.

"I'm sorry," said Anne.

"Take my jacket." Claud pulled it off with exasperation.

Mark shook his head negatively. His short legs did not reach to the floor of the car, but he was agile and evaded his father's efforts to put the jacket around him.

Claud struggled with the boy briefly and then threw himself against the steering wheel, laughing with dry, hoarse sobs. His passengers waited in rigid silence. Finally he lifted his head, turned the key, and released the hand brake.

Anne leaned back and closed her eyes with relief. It had been a mistake, this effort, this excursion, this journey to the sea. Four months had passed without event. The tension between Claud and Richard had not erupted into crisis, Mark had been somewhat unresponsive but never difficult, and Claud had not—since the day of Rachel's cremation—embarrassed them with his appalling laughter. She too had managed nicely, had run the household smoothly and enjoyed New York. The problems of insomnia and frigidity were facts of her life; they had not been more severe in America than in England. Now, suddenly, all was wrong. Richard was angry, Mark, upset, and Claud, disintegrating before their eyes. She felt fatigue and fear of life, that the next step might bring disaster.

Much better to sleep and not to think.

From the bathroom came the scent of lavender bath oil and the sound of Walter reciting:

> *"Under the keel nine fathom deep,*
> *From the land of mist and snow,*
> *The spirit slid: and it was he*
> *That made the ship to go.*
> *The sails at noon left off their tune,*
> *And the ship stood still also."*

"That's Walter Bridge, God help us," Daniel explained to Jean Macleod as he guided her down the hall. He was showing her the house at Lela's request.

In the kitchen below, Lela put the vichyssoise in the refrigerator to chill and, turning to the window, watched angular Giacometti people through the old, distorted glass. Man walking and woman walking. They became, as they passed closer to the glass, more distinct, until finally she had them: Neil and Gail Lessing and a suitcase.

"Now we're in for it," Lela muttered, "now we're really in for it." She wished the Lessings away and waited for the front bell to ring.

On the steps of the veranda the Lessings did not ring the bell; they argued.

"We look like things the cat dragged in, disgusting rodent things, and you smell like a locker room. If just once you could let us do something in a sensible way," Gail hissed.

"The assault on the Relds was your idea, dear heart," Neil snarled. "Cheek kissing and nostalgia for the old days at school . . . well, here we are . . . Decant the syrup and tune up the voice which cloys, and we'll have one hell of a time O!" He rang the bell.

"A two-mile walk in the rain—you're out of your mind, you really are," Gail accused.

Neil watched the working hinges of her jaw and, when she stopped talking, he stared at the slit of her clenched lips, writing on the wall of his mind: "You foul bitch." The words hung unpronounced in the mist between them.

Gail observed, clinically, the concavity of his chest and the collapsed billow of the damp white shirt which covered it.

"You stupid, ugly fool!" Her silent shriek was as audible as the waves slapping the rocks.

"I've got a week's vacation; I want some exercise. Why don't I just leave you here and go on about my business?" Neil stepped off the veranda and started down the drive.

The shadow of Lela behind the screen door spoke.

"Gail? Is it you?" she asked in what she hoped were tones of breathless, pleased surprise.

"Yes, us, of all people. We were a few miles away and thought we ought to stop by for a hello. It's been so long."

The pronouns were an appeal to her husband and traveled the mist between them. Turning back to the veranda, he committed himself once again to the surface peace and waved to the shadow.

"Hello, Lela, you're looking good."

"Fine, Neil, fine," the shadow replied absently. "Come in, you both, you'll be drenched."

She led them through the hall and into the kitchen describing the house and the summer as they went.

"Take off your things. I'll heat some coffee. Where are you staying? What are you doing so far north?"

Vacation, they explained, sun and sea, and they all laughed in a general way about the weather.

"We stayed the last two nights in the town. Neil went fishing, but now we're on our own . . ." Gail ventured.

"Well, Gail . . ." Lela decided upon the aggressively honest, flat-chested, short-haired, straight-from-the-shoulder tone which had characterized their relations at school. "I can't put you up here; we're expecting hordes—it just can't be managed; *but* . . ." she placed her hand on Neil's shoulder, for he was about to protest, "but we can easily—and want to—dine you, wine you, and find you a bed somewhere among the not-too-distant neighbors." She waved vaguely in the direction of the road leading to the town.

"They're forever using our rocks, our sea, our booze, and, occasionally, our patience. They'll be happy to oblige. It's really a crime that you've chosen just precisely this weekend, when we've got two continents converging upon us."

She poured them coffee and considered the possible effects of Lessings on the projected order of things, concluding that it was already so dreadfully complicated, further complication might simplify. Strangers, strangers, she invoked to herself, let them come in armies, let them conquer, for surely this is mad.

"Come," she said to them, "bring your cups and come into the living room. Neil, you must talk to Daniel, really you must, and tell him what you've been doing."

"I'd like that," Neil replied. The prospect of a talk with Daniel was good. It would be difficult, of course, for Daniel was an academic and a theoretician, while Neil was an experimental physicist in industry; Neil knew that in the universe of split hairs called Academe, the difference was not merely professional and intellectual, it was also social. Doubtless, Daniel was a snob about his work. Still it would be good to talk to him.

Lela called up the stairs, "Daniel, Daniel!"

The Lessings seated themselves, balanced their cups, remarked on the floors—worn but parquet—and agreed that old houses were surely the best, for one felt settled.

Lela's call reached Daniel in their bedroom where, after demonstrating to Mrs. Macleod the glorious captain's chest and the virtues of the view, he had been called upon to deliver a definition of Celestial Mechanics, for Mrs. Macleod hadn't an idea in the world what such a strange phrase could mean. For herself it meant a whimsical picture in her mind: God with a beard on a cloud pulling switches. Daniel had tried to explain that it was a lesser science, a cataloguing of data, and he blessed his wife for the interruption. He deposited Mrs. Macleod in her bedroom and they were both grateful for the dispensation.

Daniel paused in the doorway to the living room.

"Hello, Lessings!" he called, managing the situation with the necessary mingling of humor, surprise, and seeming pleasure, for these were Lela's friends, a pair belonging to a tide of similar intrusions which violated periodically the usually placid waters of their life together.

"Yes, aren't they a lovely surprise," said Lela, grinning at her husband.

Mrs. Macleod lay upon her bed and drew slowly on one of the few cigarettes she allowed herself in a day. She enjoyed it and regretted the sound of a car coming down the drive. The others were arriving; it was necessary to move, to exert oneself, to walk down the stairs.

Walter and Mrs. Macleod collided at the top of the stairs as Beth plunged down past them, calling back, "Have you two met?" She disappeared around the curve of the stairwell, apologizing. "You see, it may be Matthew."

Walter and Mrs. Macleod shook hands laughing and followed Beth downstairs.

Hearing a car in the drive, Daniel went to the front door, glad to be released from talking with Lessing. He had never liked talking with Lessing.

"Oh do move, Dan," Beth urged as she tried to see past him. "It may be Matthew."

"No. Just Claud and his family," he said.

Beth retreated from the hall into the living room and was confronted with the fact of the Lessings. She had met them once before at a party given by the Relds and had announced to Lela that they were clearly two of the most impossible people on the face of God's earth. Gail was a pushy vulgarian, and Neil, too embarrassing a spectacle of nerves to be shown in public. Beth finally acknowledged the Lessings.

"Well, hello."

"Oh Beth," cried Gail, "I had no idea you'd be here! I've been hoping we'd run into each other again sometime."

The full force of Gail's effusion was lost, for Beth immediately interrupted in her most pointedly formal voice.

"Lela, your guests are arriving. I think we should welcome them."

Beth beckoned regally as she spoke and Lela followed obediently. In the hall she noted with relief that Mrs. Macleod and Walter seemed to be getting along very well together. They were poised at the foot of the stairs looking at the design of one of the stained-glass windows.

"A bird," suggested Mrs. Macleod, "a very clumsy phoenix, perhaps."

"Very heavy wings," Walter agreed.

"This should be amusing," Mrs. Macleod said, turning toward the group at the front door. "You had better give me your arm, Mr. Bridge."

"Claud!" shouted Daniel from the door into the mist. "Come along up!"

Anne Bennett, with Mark Sarum by the hand, came up to the veranda first, whispering, "Listen to the sea, Mark, listen to the sea." Mark looked back to make sure his father and uncle followed. Lela came to him, knelt down, put an arm around him, and clasped Anne's hand.

"Oh Mark, stop being so silly," Lela scolded, for he stood stiff against her.

Anne felt it necessary to apologize for his resistance. "He's being impossible today; I don't know what we're to do with him. I leave him to you. I really do."

Richard stepped onto the veranda, gave Lela a friendly pat on the shoulder, and extended his hand to Beth.

"It's very nice to see you again, Mrs. Stead. Very nice. Very nice indeed. Funerals and their aftermaths are, unfortunately, occasions uncongenial to the pleasure of new friends."

Beth wondered what one could possibly say to a sentence like that. With or without the excuse of a funeral, the man's language was beyond belief. She was saved from the complexity of a response by the image of Matthew turning the curve of the drive, his bag in his hand and his jacket thrown over his shoulder.

"There he is!" Beth pushed past the guests and down the steps of the veranda.

Matthew dropped his bag, drew Beth close to him, and waved his jacket like a flag of conquest at the others. For he was back, he was home, and he had been missed. This woman, this stranger (even now, with his arms around her, he wasn't sure he could name his sons in order)—she had missed him.

"Matthew, Matthew, Matthew," chanted Beth, "Missed you, missed you, missed you." With her arms about his waist, she moved her body to that melody.

"Like crocuses in December and oysters in June," he mocked gently in a whisper.

From the doorway Walter and Mrs. Macleod looked out at the new arrivals.

"How *are* we all to fit in?" she asked.

"I, for one, mean to sleep on the floor," Walter announced.

"Oh, I'm afraid I couldn't get down that far, dear me no."

"I'm sure you'd manage it beautifully," he replied gallantly.

A little beyond the threshold, Lela still knelt with an arm about Mark, holding Anne's hand.

"Jean, come here. This is Anne Bennett, and I've just been telling her about you."

Mrs. Macleod took Anne Bennett's free hand, and, for a moment, the four of them were poised in the chain of their connecting touch.

Matthew and Beth came arm and arm onto the veranda. "Look everyone, the weather is lifting," Matthew announced, waving his jacket again with his free hand as though proclaiming a victory. The mists opened. A ray of sun broke against the mast of the *Philemon*. The bells of noon struck from the town.

"How very nice," said Anne to Mrs. Macleod as the first bell chimed.

The Lessings came out onto the veranda upon the second chime.

Gail's voice clashed with the third chime: "We've not had a chance to be introduced in all this excitement of arrivals."

"These are the Lessings," announced Daniel, vaguely aware that the introduction was perhaps not properly executed. At the fourth chime the gulls began to scream an answer.

"God, Walter, how did you get here?" Matthew embraced him.

"On a black panther with golden wings, how else? I'm dry, man. Best we go inside."

"I haven't been on a sailboat in years." Richard watched the *Philemon* tug at her mooring.

"We'll take you tomorrow," Lela promised.

"Oh, but I can't swim, not a stroke," Anne protested.

"Eleven," Mrs. Macleod mouthed silently, looking down at Mark.

"Twelve," he pronounced emphatically.

The sound of the last chime disappeared on a widening eddy of air. The gulls silenced themselves. The weather had lifted. The sun was out.

X

Anne came into the dining room as Lela placed white soup bowls upon the rich wood of an old table. The rose jar stood open in the center, its fragrance escaping.

"You were quite right; the view from the balcony is superb."

"I've been telling you so all summer in my letters, but you wouldn't be persuaded."

"I've been meaning to thank you for keeping in touch; it was very kind of you to be concerned."

"It wasn't kindness. I enjoyed writing. Claud is a difficult person; it can't have been easy for you these last months."

Instinctively, Anne gathered a sea shell from a side table, a plum and an orange from a bowl and arranged them around the gold field of the rose jar. "It's been surprisingly easy. We've hesitated to come for fear of disturbing the ease, and we have been right to worry, for these past two days Claud has indeed been impossible."

"I ought not to have insisted that you come. I thought the sea and the sun . . ."

"Yes, of course, you couldn't have known; anyway, it is necessary for us to find out if Claud can really take hold, for we want to go home. I suspect we shall find out this weekend."

"At home you have a house and friends . . ."

"And a landscape." Anne gazed out the window at the sea, as she spoke. "You would find it disappointing. Small lakes and minor mountains. But it is where I walk, what I see, and I've found that I can't work without it."

"But your pictures are almost always of people."

"Yes, but the shapes of the people are in the forms of the place where I look every day. Yes," Anne mused, looking far out at the line between the sea and the sky, "one wants to go home. There are the suicides and there are the survivors —everywhere—there is little that one can do. We want to go home."

Lela finished laying the table and joined her at the window. "You're quite right. There is little anyone can do. You ought not to let them keep you."

"The boy rankles though. Having no children of our own, we feel we ought to, would like to, do something for Mark."

"I feel that too. Mark's the one in all of this, the real unlucky dove."

"What were we talking about?" Anne's fingers traced a design on the pane. "Your letters. They were very gay and talked of everything, everything in the world but the girl. Why do you never tell me about Rachel? Why does no one ever speak of her? It is as though she never existed. Neither Claud nor Mark nor you has said her name once in all these months."

Lela paced to the other side of the room, observed the table, moved one bowl slightly to the left, and replied coldly:

"She hated her mother for no apparent reason, married Claud for no apparent reason (except, perhaps, for the want of a landscape), and killed herself for no apparent reason. In short, she was not a reasonable woman."

"She, she, she . . . Why don't you say her name?" Anne demanded, facing Lela across the table.

"Rachel! Rachel! Rachel!" Lela shouted at her.

"Vichyssoise," interrupted Anne, for Gail and Neil Lessing had suddenly come into the room, "how marvelous!"

"You've met the Lessings, Anne?" asked Lela, managing the transition neatly. "Gail, do smell," she added, indicating the rose jar.

The others soon followed, packing themselves around the table, perching on a haphazard selection of unstable chairs gathered from all parts of the house.

The dozen white soup bowls were Beth's triumph; Lela alone could begin to appreciate it. Their neighborhood was sparsely inhabited, and to have found, not only a neighbor at home, not only a neighbor of generous inclinations, but also a neighbor in possession of twelve matching soup bowls was a striking combination of luck and enterprise.

Nevertheless, the moment belonged to Lela's soup, an even more striking feat of luck and enterprise. Beth recognized the fact and acknowledged it handsomely.

"Admirable," she announced from the head of the table where she and Matthew presided with robust dignity like figures from a pantheon, "truly admirable."

"Against the tide," muttered Mark, in one of his rare lapses into speech, as he pushed his spoon from the inner to the outer rim of the bowl.

Although both remarks were unique events, Lela did not hear them, for she had identified their neighbors, the Woodwards, as the only possible donors of twelve matching soup bowls and the thought of the Woodwards was disquieting. The Woodwards, she knew, would willingly put up the Lessings, but she wondered about the results. The Woodwards were peculiar and the Lessings were humorless; decidedly, the consummation of their qualities was not to be wished.

Beth had distributed salad and mold, and Lela noted there would just be enough to go around once.

"How do they make it? Is it perfume?" Gail's voice reached Lela.

"That's a question only Anne can answer."

"What is the question?" asked Anne, who had been speaking in whispers to Richard.

"About the potpourri," Lela explained, "its contents and method. English ladies ought to know."

"Potpourri." Anne reached for the rose jar and moved it theatrically under her nose.

Magnificent, thought Matthew, she is truly magnificent.

Anne incanted the spices as though they were the ingredients, supernatural but effective, for the transfigurations of worlds.

> "Rose leaves, lavender, myrtle, and bay,
> Rosemary, balm, and musk,
> Thyme and violet, geranium too—
> And nutmeg, cinnamon, mace.
> Pepper, lemon peel pounded thin—
> Cool and dry and press."

"Do you do some up each autumn?" asked Walter from across the table.

"Good heavens, what do you take me for—the daughter of the rector? The wife of the squire?"

"Hardly. A prophetess who got left behind, or a Druid with class, perhaps," he countered.

"Eat your mold, Walter," commanded Lela, rising to clear the table.

"Sweet child, dear lily of the valley, I can't," he protested, "please take it away." Lela piled his plates on a tray and moved to the other side of the table.

"The soup was beautiful, dear," whispered Anne, putting an arm about her waist, as Lela leaned forward to collect the platter of half-eaten mold, "and I'm sorry I upset you."

"Thanks for the lovely jar, Claud, I can't think what thing I like more," Lela said.

Claud rose slightly in his chair and bowed his head to her as she moved on to the next place. Lela detected more irony than gallantry in his gesture.

"Basil," murmured Mrs. Macleod, who had been the daughter of a farmer and the wife of a minister, "we always put in basil."

In the fall, she remembered, late in the fall. Wood smoke burning leaves, the tree trunks and branches in their dreadful clarity. . . . "No, no, Jean," her mother called, "leave the jar covered; leave it covered until Thanksgiving . . ."

"Lela won't give us coffee, so there's no use expecting it," Daniel announced, rising to help her clear the table. "Water or wine, wine or water, keeping it pure, we are."

The guests departed—out of doors, or upstairs for naps. The Lessings remained.

"This was very nice of you, but now we must move along," said Neil to Lela.

"Well, it's not been half nice enough. Won't you let me arrange to bed you down with the neighbors? Do stay long enough to try our sea. We're very proud of it."

She knew as she spoke that to persist in this was perversity, she was complicating muddle; but she had spoken and it was

:oo late. Neil tried to reject the invitation but Gail's enthu-
.iasm was adamant.

Lela drove the Lessings to the Woodwards.

The Woodward house also faced the sea. It was an unusual
ouse, a shock to any sensibility accustomed to the ordinary
rchitecture of ordinary America. Approached from the road,
he house revealed only the 45-degree angle of its roof. The
ouse was jammed into a cavity in the rocks and the front of
t was completely glass.

Stone steps wound down the face of the rocks to the yawn-
ng glass portals of the Woodward cave. They climbed them
:autiously.

"How did they manage it?" Neil wondered with an en-
;ineer's interest.

"I think it's beautiful." Gail looked down the sheer drop of
ock to the sea beneath and shuddered slightly. The breeze
rom the sea was cold in spite of the sun.

"Seth is some sort of contractor, enormously wealthy, semi-
ctired, I think . . ."

Seth Woodward emerged from the house, highball in
and. "For Chrissakes, Lela, you make me sound antique
nd overweight." He was neither, and proud of the fact.

"These are Gail and Neil Lessing, old friends of mine. I
vondered if we might spill them over into your guest room
or a night? We're full up. Is Sonja here?"

"Sonja's off shopping, but we'll both be delighted, you can
e sure." Seth shook Neil's hand and maneuvered his athletic
mmensity, made more than necessarily manifest by his tight
olfing shorts, into a position from which Gail's ample form
ould be easily appreciated.

"We've been telling your hosts all summer . . . any-
ime we can give them a hand . . . We use their beach, you

see. Now, come along in!" He pointed his glass toward the interior.

They followed his gesture; Gail, eagerly, with a delighted smile and a wave of the hand to Lela, Neil, more cautiously, clasping the small suitcase which he had carried from town.

"Now, be sure to come over as soon as you're settled in, the four of you," Lela called after them.

"I'll see to them; don't you worry about a thing. This is just what we need—Sonja and I—we've been bored to tan trums this whole week."

Lela found his pronouncement less than reassuring. The sliding glass jaws of the house closed. Climbing back to the road, she tried herself for desertion and irresponsibility and found herself guilty. She felt the proverbial burden of the man who saves another's life. Many years ago she had taken on Gail as a close friend. For a short time, she had pleasured herself in her own forgiveness of Gail's vulgarity, in her own charity. In order to satisfy her own perverse emotional needs she had preyed upon Gail's envious devotion to her. That was a very long time ago, she reassured herself; but still the awareness of it made the blood rush to her face.

As she started the car, Sonja drove up alongside.

Coarse black hair tied in a tail. Tanned to mahogany. Clad in primary colors. Long-limbed, lean-flanked—Sonja impressed herself upon Lela's vision in fragments. With an effort Lela brought the pieces together and spoke to her.

"I've left you two of our overflow. Seth said you wouldn' mind."

"How delightful. What are they?"

"Married couple. Neil and Gail Lessing. Can't thank yo enough."

"Our pleasure. Did our bowls survive? Beth was in such

rush, I didn't get a chance to tell her to be careful of them. Impossible to replace, you see."

"They're fine!" Lela shouted, driving off down the road.

A mile down the road she turned off onto the shoulder, braked suddenly, slamming herself against the steering wheel. Sudden panic in the middle of the afternoon—it was absurd, to come as it did, with the sun making the world gay; there shadows of gulls' wings danced on the rocks; the sea was fairly leaping out of itself on a brisk breeze. Yet still she felt it, a panic like trying to scream while asleep and dreaming.

Finally she started the car and moved once more toward the summer house. Rounding a curve, she saw the house in front of her on its peninsular mound of rock, and halfway down she recognized the figure of Jean Macleod, who had negotiated the steep rocks to watch the surf. Jean was apparently unaware of Mark who stood several yards above her also watching.

The salt spray transformed itself into snow and Jean was young again, alone in her father's house, supported and surrounded by her father's land. She sat at a rough wooden table. Upon the table there were gourds, a sprig of wintergreen in a tumbler, and a cluster of chestnuts.

"It is late for horse chestnuts," murmured Jean.

There was a window before her. She watched the tedious winter trickle down the sill, and, beyond, the bald hill with its line of stone walls crawling to the summit. Suddenly, a hawk began his round rite; he hovered, dove, grazed the ground, and angled into disappointed flight. One uneasy crow called an omen-black call.

The chime from the town clanged twice and, abruptly, Mrs. Macleod shook herself out of vision. As a girl, she had been a fool. She was still a fool, an old fool lately frightened by dreams. Shifting her gaze, she saw Mark standing above her and motioned him to her.

Mark scrambled down the rocks, stumbled, clutched her.

"Shall I tell you a strange secret?" she asked.

He nodded emphatically.

"Every seventh wave is always a big one."

"One," they whispered in harmony.

"Two. Three. Four. Five. Six."

The seventh wave struck like lightning and thrust needles of spray high into the air. They tasted salt on their lips.

Mark pressed himself against Mrs. Macleod. The white spray thrust up, devoured the air. He too remembered the winter.

The snow fell softly, hit the ground. His fingers on the windowpane got cold, made marks. The fire looked hot, but he was too far away to feel it. He sat in the big chair which made his feet stick straight out in front of him. Then his mother came to him and asked if he wanted to take a walk in the snow. That was the first time and so he went very quickly to the closet to get his snowsuit. It was too high; it was on a hook and the hook was too high and it took a long time to get it down, and when he had it down he rushed to put it on and that made it take longer. He was afraid she would go without him. She watched but didn't help until he was ready for the hat, the funny hat with the long tassel; she clamped it on his head and smiled and took his hand. They went out of the house and looked into the cold and soft snow So much of it . . . all over the houses, all over the ground all over the trees. And she said . . . and that was the first time . . . snow could cover many miles of houses and of ground and of trees. They walked . . . big holes in the snow rom their boots . . . they walked and she threw a ball of snow into the soft white air. They were the only things in all of everything that weren't white. Where, where, where, he asked, where does the whiteness come from? There's a great machine in the sky, he told her, and it makes all the snow and pours it out over everything. Don't be silly, she said, snow comes from clouds, just like rain. He made a song about it anyway.

> *Snowball, snowfall,*
> *It comes down just like a wall.*
> *Humpty Dumpty sat on a wall,*
> *He sat and watched the snowfall*
> *Fall.*

His mother laughed and laughed.

XI

At the cave of Woodward the party was just begin ning. In the living room, Seth addressed the bar with skill an mixed the first round of drinks. Sonja manipulated th phonograph and smoked. She looked—Seth thought—lik a long and dainty monster dreaming of executions.

"I hope this is going to be as interesting as it looks," sh said.

"That, I think, depends on us," he replied, smiling, fc he liked her best that way, long and a little wicked.

"Unpacking, are they?"

"And changing. I suggested something more comfor able. I have my heart set on her wearing stretch pants."

The phonograph unrolled gutter French from a hai voiced chanteuse.

In the guest room Neil and Gail unpacked and change(with furtive glances at the art nouveau which hung upon th wall over the enormous bed. The wife of the most recent assassinated politician—four feet high and framed in ebon —followed them with her optical illusion eyes as the moved. Hollywood's latest suicide pointed her opuler breasts ceilingward.

They joined the Woodwards. Speechless, Neil indicate the bedroom with a sweep of the hand.

"But they are nothing, Neil my boy, nothing compared with these!" Seth presented his most treasured artifacts which were stacked against and dominated one wall:

CAMPBELL'S SCOTCH BROTH
24 CANS
IF IT'S CAMPBELL'S IT'S
GOT TO BE GOOD
3¢ OFF
LIMITED TIME
ONLY

"I don't have to tell you that they cost a pretty penny."

Gail approached the display with wonder. "I've heard of it, but I didn't know that people had it in their houses."

"Most people don't; most people are antediluvian." Sonja coiled and uncoiled herself on a zebra rug.

"Darling, let me do the honors."

"Of course, my love." She salaamed.

Seth handed around drinks. "Now listen, my children, and you shall hear . . ."

Neil and Gail settled on a green sectional sofa, curved like an avocado, and chose to be enthralled.

"Why must everything be dead? Dead art, dead décor, dead music. The past, always the past. I want my world, the one I live in. Movies, ads, cars, three thousand kinds of soap, and dear old mother's homecooked best in a can. If God is, at all, he's got to be in a soup can. Intellectual fog in pain is not for me. This is it . . ." he gestured histrionically toward the soup cartons. "This is real and I embrace it; I celebrate it! Now don't get me wrong; I like your friends. This is the year of the college professor, and as plagues go they're better than most. Negroes would be better yet; they're the future. Jews would be worse. Jews are ghosts, the past; they're too finely tuned, for this is the age of the thick-skinned."

Seth continued without pause. "Daniel and Matt are the finest of fellows and Lela's alluring in a breastless way, but they're all too vague for me. I want to make the girl on the billboard; that's really the way to feel sometimes. I want to mount that flat surface and push it out all over her."

He stopped for a moment and eyed Gail's obvious discomposure with amusement.

"Yes, little lady, I want to be the most alive in this world at this moment." He walked to the couch, bent over, and kissed her on the mouth.

Gail's awkward confusion—she had met Seth's kiss with stiffly puckered lips, like a child imitating the movies—struck Neil as immensely funny. He threw his head back and laughed at her, and then joined Seth at the bar while he stirred another pitcherful of drinks.

"Frankly, I thought this new art was something quite different," Neil argued. "I thought it meant satire and contempt, not embrace and celebration."

"I see the two as one experience. Mind you, I've been talking about my personal reaction, not about the intention behind this stuff, or about what the critics say," Seth explained. "In the beginning I laughed and sneered at what these fellows were doing," he gestured again at the soup cartons, "but suddenly the old values gave way and I wanted to be one with the things around me. I wanted to be real and full in my own moment without making judgments, without —memory or desire (isn't that the phrase?). Everything else —everything other than billboards and orgasm (I realize they are the sort of symbolic simplifications you may find

useful for argument)—seemed suddenly superficial and absurd, because everything else was other than real; even the
necessary getting and spending was other than real." Neil
poured the women drinks and Seth gathered his thoughts
with a long swallow. He slurred on.

"We, all of us, are born and die with and in space and
time. Everything within or beyond or beneath is subjective
and various and neither true nor not true. The billboard is
my space; soup cans are my landscape; my time—the se-
quence which supersedes the clock—is the tick of my body.
So, you see, I am left, and not unhappily, I must confess, with
soup cans and orgasm."

"Don't forget liquor, my love; it makes you almost as
eloquent as orgasm does," Sonja intruded.

"True, true. I'm talking too much. Now, tell us, what do
you think of our grotto?"

"Fascinating!" Gail replied so promptly that Sonja tit-
tered.

Neil was more thoughtful.

"Well, the house is interesting, of course, but the things
you've been saying . . . I'm not sure that your justifications
for this art and for your own disinterest in everything but
the present are either logical or ethical . . ."

Seth interrupted with laughter, "I hope to hell they're
neither!"

"Then you would agree that this is all egocentricity and
showmanship?"

"And six parts gin to one part vermouth," contributed
Sonja.

Seth ignored her. "Yes, Neil, for myself alone. A way of
life. Egocentricity as you say."

Sonja retwined her legs into another position and wondered if her thighs seemed heavy in slacks. The boy interested her; he seemed less pathetic, less hollow-chested after a drink and a change of clothes. The way he slumped into the couch, nervous, thoughtful, pulling at a lock of hair, attracted her. His shrew of a frump didn't deserve him.

"You see, we are not nice people; we're not at all nice, and our not being nice is not a mistake, it's deliberate," she announced wryly.

"Subtlety, dearest, subtlety," cautioned Seth archly. "Show, don't tell."

"Oh God, you'd better have another drink. I'd rather have you drunk than coy. He's absolutely unbearable at the halfway point."

"Allow me this time." Neil stirred and poured flamboyantly.

"My wife has pushed me down the rabbit hole and I intend to see it through to the other end."

"Stout lad, that's just the spirit."

"Do rabbit holes always come out someplace? Aren't they ever one way?" Sonja asked naïvely.

Neil remained silent, but his mind addressed her:

And in your eyes, that hard hunger, what's it for, madame? What can we do for you? No mere knightly gift: a partridge in a pear tree, for example, will do, I'm sure. Oh no, yours is a subtler taste, and taste I will, I suspect, before this rabbit hole has run itself out. What will you have? Fornication of a complicated sort, I wager; crudity, of course, but crudity aware of itself, nasty perverted crudity, crudity which is vulgar rather than coarse . . . silly physical contortions, all sorts of very up-to-date variations to hide the fundamental fact that you don't like it very much but wish you did. Well, madame, I'll be happy to oblige, and you, I think, will be very well pleased—as pleased as you're capable of being.

Neil turned and served his wife.

"Sweetheart, drink up, the party's just beginning."

Lela watched Jean and Mark from the living room window. The boy sheltered against the woman who seemed neither to accept nor reject him. They were both absorbed in the sea.

Daniel came up behind her and pulled her against him.

"You come and go and I haven't seen you for days. Or so it seems right now."

"I've been thinking of you," she murmured.

"When?"

"When you came down the stairs and there were the Lessings."

"And I thought about you," Daniel said. "I thought, silly Lela, pretty Lela, come, come, come."

"Yes, but you were up most of the night; you're tired, poor dear."

"Oh no I'm not. I'm just fine."

"I've just deposited the Lessings."

"What an awful change of subject!"

"I've put them with the Woodwards and I fear that I've done wrong. I think there's something strange about Seth."

"I know there's something strange about Sonja!"

"What do you mean?" Lela pushed him from her. "What haven't you told me?"

"Nothing. It's just instinct. Hey now, quiet yourself, darling."

"Then you really don't *know*, you're just guessing."

"That's right. Still, I'm convinced there's something wrong with that woman."

"Oh damn. You ought to lock me up in a cage and not let me interfere with people."

"Stop being ridiculous. You didn't interfere with the Lessings; they interfered with you. I won't have you beating yourself about those fools."

"Oh why can't one just live simply and alone!" she moaned.

"Why indeed." He smiled ironically. "But since we can never seem to manage it, you'll be happy to know I am about to do my small part for this happy, happy weekend. I'm going to take Claud for a walk. Greater love hath no man." He kissed her on the nose. "I'm on my way to round up Walter and the dog as shields. Have you seen the animal?"

"Oh dear, no, I'd completely forgotten him. Give him a call. He's probably not far."

They walked into the hall and Daniel turned to her at the door.

"Lela?"

"Yes."

Striding down the drive, he whistled shrilly between his teeth. A lean, gray, awkward hound charged toward him and rubbed against his legs.

"Well now, we've gone and forgotten you, poor boy, good fellow. People, people, too many people, and no time for you at all. Walk, boy? Walk?"

Jean Macleod wondered why she had come. It would be a weekend of people, a weekend of the clash of unsheathed egos, a weekend of he said, she said, I am, I want. She was too old for all that and too tired for it. She simply wished to be left alone.

Mark moved slightly away from her as if he divined her thought.

"No, there's no need for you to do that," she whispered, leaning him back against her.

"Grant an old lady her inconsistencies. When I was a child we went to the sea one summer and I walked on the sand in a long pale yellow dress with a border of delicate rosebuds. I walked on the sand in a long dress but my feet were bare and, oh, how the sand burned against my skin. Snail shell, conch shell, shell of clam, shell of crab . . . pearl, white, silver, pink . . . circle, funnel, oval, fan . . ."

Boy and woman rocked with the sea.

XII

Walter, Daniel, and the hound waited at the edge of the woods surrounding Miller's pond for Claud, who had agreed to meet them. Finally he came and extended a hand to Walter to whom he had not yet been introduced.

"I'm Claud, Claud Sarum; we've not met in the confusion. The boy belongs to me and the Englishman's my half brother—we had a mother in common. The gaunt beauty is his wife. We're hard to sort out, particularly arriving as we have like a mixed bouquet which must be pruned, snipped, and arranged before it proves decorative."

Daniel wondered why Claud had resented his simple invitation for a walk. There was going to be unpleasantness and he was sorry that Walter would have to be involved.

"Take roses, for example," said Walter, as though continuing a conversation—which had never taken place. "Or take the leaf there," he toed a scarlet leaf, "why is it red? Why not some color we have never seen before?"

"Because our perception has insurmountable boundaries. We can conceive of three dimensions of space which are conditioned by a dimension of time, and we see a limited spectrum of color. That's all. There ain't no more," Daniel explained indulgently.

"Oh Christ, nothing new, nothing new in all my four score."

"You don't know it, Walt, but you're an optimist," laughed Daniel. "Eighty years is well beyond the average life expectancy."

Claud refused to be ignored. "My wife used to talk like that," he announced. "Always asking why things can't be what they are not."

"My Lela still does," Daniel replied, hoping to turn the conversation. "Sometimes I do too. I think I caught it from her. It's early for dead leaves."

"Are you divorced, Claud?" asked Walter, choosing to meet the situation head on.

"No. Last spring she took a hunting rifle and . . . 'blew her brains out' . . . is, I think, the precise American idiom."

"Stop it, damn you!" muttered Daniel.

"I didn't know. I'm sorry." Walter turned away and walked down a path after the hound, who was saluting every other tree trunk with his lifted leg.

Claud observed Walter's abrupt departure with triumph. "Well," he confronted Daniel, "it's nice to know you didn't feel rehearsals of our long sad tale were necessary preparations for your other guests."

"Oh, I felt they were necessary all right. There simply wasn't time. Why must you lay it out like that—embarrass him, make him feel less than human, less than adequate, because he hasn't got a wife, because his nonexistent wife hasn't gone and . . ."

"Hah!"

Claud's hysterical laughter echoed in a spiral around the trunks of trees, plateaued on a high pitch, and sustained itself for an unnatural time.

"You can't even say it!" He was still laughing. "Daniel, my friend, there she was . . . supine," he howled, "knees aloft, the stock of the gun between them like . . ."

"Stop it!"

Daniel pushed, his hands on Claud's shoulders, and flattened him against a tree trunk. "Act like a man, can't you? You make me sick!"

Suddenly Claud's voice was calm and his eyes were gay: "Don't give me any cant about manhood, sufferings of surly silence, self-conscious, virtuoso displays of demonic self-control. I never swore the vow; I never earned the badge."

He laughed again, his head thrown back, and then, as Daniel released his hold on him, he slid down the tree trunk, sinking to the ground, crouching, his buttocks stretched uncomfortably over the ridges made by the roots of the tree.

"Stop it! God damn you, stop it!" Daniel shouted.

"Leave me. Just leave me."

Daniel moved off along a path which skirted the pond. It was edged by a low wall of carelessly placed stones. He walked slowly counting the stones. Stone steps led down to a brook which fed into the pond. Stone gave way to planks of sagging wood—a bridge. He sat on one of the planks, swinging his feet over the stream, contemplating the water.

He had failed with Claud, he knew. It was inevitable; he would always be impatient with emotion which dragged out after the event of its cause like the tentacles of medusae. (He had seen them the week before in the sea. It was a strange coincidence that Matt should have written about them a day or two later. They were beautifully grotesque, pulsating things.)

He could not put his hand out to Claud, could not allow a free flow of feeling.

But was that all, he asked himself.

Lela and his work, they were enough. But there was some discomfort still.

Suddenly he knew it was the makeshift wall, the loose steps, the decrepit bridge. Someone had not cared enough to make solid structures.

There swimming toward his dangling feet was a beaver. "*Castor candensis*," he muttered.

Back and forth the creature swam as he gathered sticks and mud, repairing the dam which formed a pool around his large one-room house with its underwater entrance hall.

"You *are* busy," Daniel chuckled, delighted to have established, in time present, the necessary evidence to support the aged assumption in the familiar simile.

He remembered that beavers mate for life and the fact aroused in him certain thoughts (if not precisely thoughts, at least feelings) about the limitations of mortal life which were further limited by certain inevitable but irrevocable decisions such as marriage. Nevertheless, Lela was quite good, quite beautiful in her own way. His wife and his work, they were enough.

He stamped across the planks, enjoying their hollow sound.

"Plosive push of wings . . . pppppppppphhip . . . pheasant? Partridge? Pretty enough for any symphony. What do you say to that, old man, gray dog, slouching, lounging hound with yellow eyes?"

Unused to sudden birds or soliloquies, the dog stood bewildered. Walter walked on singing:

"Ooooooh Blue, you good dog, you.
   Blue's feet are big and round,
   He never let a possum touch the ground.

Come here, Blue, you good dog, you.
Gonna take my gun, gonna take my horn,
Gonna get me a possum in the new growin' corn.
Ooooooh Blue, you good dog, you.

"Well, old man, slouching, skulking, serious hound with yellow eyes, how like you my ethnic, legendary, primal chant? Would you like another? How about the black man's burden in the fields of snow, key of C sharp?

"Take my hammer,
Back to the Captain . . ."

Daniel appeared from behind a screen of trees and shouted:
"For Chrissakes, stop roaring!"
Walter shouted back:
"Sirrah, you malign my voice: my golden tones, my full-throated ease, my lyric gift!"
"All true, black nightingale, but the last. Who am I, mere I, to deny your lyric gift? I admit, here and now, in the presence of the so-called almighty God and all his alleged host, that you tell the sweetest, most lyrical lies I've ever heard. That is the verily-I-say-unto-you Truth."
"White man, you got your nerve—lies, I never."
They joined lustily in a stanza of "Water Boy," which Daniel suddenly interrupted:
"I left Claud in a bad way. Let's get back to him."
They reversed direction.
"Interesting chap, that. Schoolteacher too?" asked Walter.
"No. Archives. Something to do with archives. Keeper or librarian. I'm not very clear about it."

Walter pondered the subject.

"Tapered fingers and incomprehensible filing systems. Somehow he doesn't seem like the type."

"He's not. In it but not of it. Very good at the job, but doesn't care about it. That's half the problem. Nothing to fall back on. Nothing to put himself into. He never cared much for things. He cares less now. He used to be polite, very well bred, as they say, used to be amused by things. Now all that's gone. Of course, I oughtn't to talk. I don't really know. We never saw much of them while Rachel was alive."

Walter was silent. He did not understand Claud's grief, his bitterness. To live was simple: to move and not to be involved. He believed that emotional involvements with other people ought to be declared venial, if not mortal, sins. That an obviously intelligent, mature man could allow himself this excessive alliance, this wife, so that the simple fact of her death disallowed the morning sun its usual brightness, shocked Walter with its strangeness.

Claud sat still and half asleep in the clearing, hearing only the wind. Finally he opened his eyes to a regiment of new pines; each tree stood unbelievably straight, and the symmetry of the whole was marred only here and there by a crooked silver birch, unfit for service but exceedingly welcome to the eye.

XIII

THE LAST RAYS of the afternoon sun struck through the cave of Woodward. The keeper of the cave held his empty glass up to them and cast a prism on the floor.

"All right, Lessing, you say you do not believe in the existence of the human soul and I am willing to grant you that yours is a reasonable disbelief. Let us begin again. I will rephrase. If you believed that you did indeed possess a soul and if you believed in all the attendant cant about its immortality, what would you be willing to sell it to me for? I shall play Satan and Mephistopheles for your amusement; these are the obligations of the perfect host."

"I would hypothetically sell my hypothetical soul for all the kingdoms of the world, of course. I am not such a fool as Christ," Neil replied.

"Satan was the fool, not Christ. What little imagination he had, and you too. Why the kingdoms of this world? I offer you that which is not world—anti-world: spaceless, timeless, egoless—I offer it to you now. Step right up, my children, and sign up with Father Seth."

"You're on!" laughed Neil, swilling the rest of his drink and taking the pencil and paper Seth offered.

"I, Neil Lessing, do hereby sell my soul to Seth Woodward

in exchange for . . . But I really don't know for what yet, do I?"

"Illegal tender, my boy, very illegal tender. Just sign your name. You can fill in the details later."

"Don't, Neil please don't. It's an awful kind of joke." Gail put a restraining hand on his arm.

He turned on her and sneered, "What's the matter, Alice, is the Mad Hatter beginning to frighten you?"

"A tea party isn't exactly what I have in mind," said Seth, "but that's a damned close guess, I do admit. Come on, Lessing . . ."

Neil signed his name. Seth grabbed the paper and danced toward the kitchen caroling:

"Love and joy come to you, and to your wassailer too . . ."

"I'll come too," cried Sonja, leaping up. "I'll be the voluptuous white rabbit," she leered, hopping after Seth, lifting her breasts with her hands.

Seth returned bearing a silver sugar bowl.

"Now then . . ." he said, demonstrating a cube of sugar clasped between silver tongs.

XIV

"MAGNIFICENT! Where did you get it?"

Walter crouched down to admire the architecture of a nine-foot-long table as Lela covered it with bottles, decanters, glasses, and plates.

"What? My overladen board, you mean?"

"The very same indeed."

"Daniel socked it together one afternoon. All bolts and screws and solid oak, which, he assures me, I and he and you may, if we wish, jump up and down upon."

"Good. Good. Oh, very good." Walter worshiped the bottles with his eyes.

"I'll leave all this in your capable hands. The idea is that we should eat and drink very informally in here; that is to say, blend cocktail hour and buffet and all mellow into conversational civility. You understand what I have in mind?"

"But of course, dear girl, leave it all to Walter's black magic." He began to arrange glasses and caress labels with aesthetic tenderness.

Lela stepped back to survey the living room. It was not half bad. It lacked, she knew, grace, proportion, the sense of being well fit out; but it had, she felt, a perfectly legitimate claim to comfort and lack of pretension. There were not enough chairs, but colorful cushions invited from the floor.

"Hold up a minute, Beth, and let me take something!"
Daniel strode into the room behind Beth, whose arms were
filled with salads and breads.

"It's all right," Beth gasped, gratefully depositing the food
on the table and adding, without taking a breath, her dis-
satisfaction with the fare: "Nothing hot; we should really
have something hot."

"A fire," suggested Lela, "Daniel will build us a fire."

"It's too warm."

"No, no, it will cool down quickly without the sun. Look
there!" Lela pointed out the window. The low and sullen
sun pushed cold red rays against the glass.

"All right, a fire then! And if anyone finds the heat too
much, they can go out on the veranda. May the sea freeze
them! Logs! And then a drink!" Daniel trumpeted, trailing
his fingers down his wife's back as he left the room.

The fire was lit and the room filled. It grew dark but they
did not turn on the lights. Now a shadow, now a face was
caught by firelight. The sounds of conversation grew gradually louder.

"Try the shrimp; they are, what you might call, home grown."

"Lela out with a net at dawn?"

"Don't be ridiculous! She rarely stirs before noon."

"No, no, no. Good heavens, it's much too strong. Add a
little of that."

"Well, as I was saying, you must understand it's not that
we weren't flattered, in spite of our comparatively lowly and
provincial station and in spite of not having the proper
clothes, by an invitation to spend a weekend with TITLES.
Nor is it that we disliked them. To the contrary. It's just

that they were obviously having difficulties. The timing was poor. There we were, both a burden and burdened."

"Yes, yes, but do tell me about their . . . difficulties . . . as you put it."

"Well, my dear, she castrates him daily before breakfast, a deed both bloody and foul. Very hard on (no pun intended) the digestion of guests. I could not set teeth to my hard-boiled egg; the analogy was too direct."

"Oh dear, Walter, no, though I do thank you for the thought, but I do believe I've had more than enough of *that*. Food, please, quickly. Before I make a worse ass of myself. A plateful of anything, anything at all; it doesn't matter."

"London is dead; Alexandria, a lie; New York, a cliché. And Copenhagen is sterile. But Hong Kong . . . Hong Kong is a different kettle of fish. Hong Kong is . . . but why do you laugh?"

"It's such a peculiar noise: Copenhagen."

"But I don't understand why you feel it so deeply; from what I understand, you didn't get along with her that well while she was alive. Let it be over."

"Can't you understand, you bloody fool, it isn't grief! I'm not mourning a vision of a pale and faithful wife driven to her doom. It's nerves! Can't you see that? Nerves! Suddenly these last two days, I can't seem to get the lid back on the box. Mark, my son . . . now suddenly, I can't bear the sight of him! God, what's the point of talking!"

"Have you seen my wife?"

"No, not in a long time."

"Beth, is that you over there?"

"Yes. Perhaps we should have some lights on."

"No!" chorused the others.

"That's all right. I just wanted to know if you had seen Lela."

"She's taken Mark to bed."

"Good God! What a way to put it."

"You know what I mean."

In the room he was to share with his father, Mark awaited Lela. Finally she came, settled next to him on his bed, and spread before him the block-lettered manuscript of her story.

"Is that for me?"

"Yes."

"When you're done reading it to me, may I take it?"

"Yes."

"And this is the only one?"

"This is the only one."

Lela began to read.

> The garden in which Euzilpha and Carduff had spent their lives was bounded by a low but thick stone wall. So it is with many gardens. Although they lived together, Euzilpha and Carduff did not always understand each other. So it is with many small boys and girls.
>
> The day was like any other day, except that the sky was green and the trees were blue.
>
> Her eyes squinted shut, Euzilpha tiptoed cautiously down a path, sometimes stumbling against a bush or a tree trunk.
>
> "If you were going to tell a story about us, how would you begin?" Carduff shouted, looking down from the great height of the second lowest branch of an admirable blue tree.
>
> Euzilpha opened her eyes and looked up at him with annoyance.

*"Why must you always interrupt when I am pretend-
ing to be someplace else. It is a game of PAR-TIC-U-
LAR importance. Anyway, I'm not."*

"Not what?" Carduff turned upside down and hung
by his knees, finding that a superior position from which
to discuss.

*"Not going to tell a story about us. How did you get
up there?"* she asked, lying down flat under the tree, finding that a superior position from which to converse with
Carduff when he was upside down.

"I really don't remember."

"Well then, what are you doing?"

"Being pensive. How shall I get down?"

"What's pensive?"

"I don't know exactly, but that's what I am being."

"A very odd day," Euzilpha observed, stroking the blue
tree trunk.

Lela paused while Mark turned the page for her. He
shifted against her impatiently. Her voice moved on . . .

"Right in the middle of St. Giles's Circus . . . The car
was completely wrecked, the chauffeur dead; but there, there
he was, in the back seat with his two black Janes, a white-
haired cadaverous cadaver (looking like a bad photograph
of the Duke of Windsor ailing)—his skeletal hand still
squeezing the black nipple of the black breast of one of them
(it was not the Duke, you understand, but someone who
looked like him; I know how you English are about
royalty) . . ."

"But surely the nipples of Negroes are not black, Walter!"
Anne hooted.

"Ah . . . ah . . . ah . . . let us have no skepticism until
I have done. And those black Janes, related however dubi-
ously to the dead false Duke, were still alive, and amply pro-

vided for by him. They lived happily ever after (for despite
death duties, the false Duke's estate was large), in a house
with nineteen rooms and a cupola. And that is what I know
of London, to answer your question. I much prefer Hong
Kong . . ."

"Never mind Hong Kong!" Matthew interrupted, emerging
from the darkness of the rest of the room. "How are you
getting on with him, Anne? He can be impossible."

"I don't believe a word of what he says, but I'm enjoying
him thoroughly."

"You should always sit by firelight," Matthew saluted her,
for London ladies had such charm, and this one was supcrb,
leaning forward as she did, very gay, very tense, her pale skin
tinged by the firelight. Go where he would, across the ocean
or across the room, thcrc was a world of women. It was
fantastic. He wanted to laugh the sky down. Instead he
said:

"Beth wants me to reassure you that he really does enjoy
sleeping on floors. It's a matter of temperament, not race."

"Oh, in the name of all that's honest, do *reassure* her; I'm
not at all concerned where Walter sleeps."

"Well, I'm not sure I like that," Walter protested, as Anne
laughed expansively and finally took the glass of wine which
Matthew had brought for her.

"Has he explained to you about the gulls?" Matthew
seated himself upon the arm of Anne's chair.

"Gulls? No. Not a word."

"He hasn't explained it to me either. Come on now, Walt."

"Certainly not. You must be patient. Before the moon goes
down, when the wild waves whist, we will all foot it featly
here and there on the yellow sands and the black rocks to the
bonny tune of the gulls. Oh yes."

"Mad."

"Mad."

Anne turned toward Matthew. The firelight caught and played with the movement of her lips.

"Have you seen my husband?" she asked.

"Yes, just a moment ago, in the dining room with Daniel. They are deeply absorbed," Matthew said.

"I daresay Richard is picking poor Daniel's brains unmercifully. You see, he contemplates an essay on the poetry of science."

Matthew watched her wryly, for it was a wonder to him —with the fire lighting up her face so exquisitely—that she could talk of poetry, science, and husband. It was an unnatural wonder.

Anne answered his look with irony: "But of course," she said, "As a poet you disapprove."

> *And so after their long journey, Euzilpha and Carduff returned, having decided that the forest was indeed a very unpleasant place. They climbed once again the low stone wall and cried with joy. For there was the garden, and the trees were blue and the sky was green.*

"The end," read Mark.

"And time for Mark to sleep." Lela arranged his blanket and turned off the light.

"Thank you, Lela."

"Good night, Mark dear."

She met Daniel in the hall coming to tell her that Beth had been persuaded to play the harp. Together they went back to the living room.

Richard lounged on the floor near his wife's chair, puffing on a pipe, taking her hand, looking handsome, flattered by firelight, looking quizzical because she was laughing at him.

Walter had joined Mrs. Macleod, who sat peacefully in an armchair, sipping wine, staring at the fire.

Claud sat by the window, looking out at the sea, but he saw instead the reflection of the fire, the room, and the people.

"Can you manage in the dark, dear?" Matthew asked his wife.

"This will be fine," she answered, poised to begin.

He leaned against the mantel, looking at her with pride, for he liked this best about her, that she played the harp. She bore him children, she was often angry, often worried, generally felt unsafe, and yet, still she played the harp. She began, and as her hand struck the strings, he rhymed to himself: The fact of being a harpist—now—taut strings and hand arched intense, rebound with sound when they meet, strike quiet and become complete.

Intrigued by the composition of shadows cast by the fire, Anne did not give the music her full attention.

Walter listened to the harp and its counterpoint, the capricious syncopation of the fire, and the distant regular thud of the waves. He put his hand over Mrs. Macleod's hand.

An arm around Lela, Daniel listened with careful joy to the inevitability of the unfolding pattern. "This is good," he murmured.

XV

AT THE WOODWARD CAVE Neil and Gail Lessing sucked sugar cubes self-consciously.

The walls of the room gave way, like the sides of a cardboard box, and disappeared. Gail was alone. There was an eye before her, larger than any single object she had ever seen. It came closer. The plastic surface of the scarlet pupil pressed against her. She was within the eye. She was drowning in red jelly. Membranes strangled her; she could not breathe.

Neil laughed with joy. It was all so simple. One had only to love. He loved. The skin of his hand dissolved. The blood of his hand evaporated. The bone of his hand became dust; it rose, it disappeared.

XVI

CROSS-LEGGED upon a cushion, Walter raised his flute and was answered by Beth's harp. The ashes had been stirred and new logs thrown upon the fire. The room was warm.

Lela and Daniel, upon a ledge of rock beyond the view of the house, breathed deeply the crisp night air of the late summer sea, enjoying the sting of cold salt. Shutters creaked in a light wind. Points of light from ships at sea blinked like matches in an amphitheater.

Daniel pulled her down across his lap and kissed her, loosening her clothes and caressing her until she protested.

"Stop. You had really better stop *now*."

"Why the hell are there a dozen people in the house when I want to take you to bed? Why do I have to sneak out with you and grapple with your clothes like an adolescent in the back seat of a car?" he groaned.

"Oh you enjoy it, you know you do," she laughed, kissing him and holding his hand still against her breast.

There were not twelve people; there were only ten, she reminded herself, for the Lessings never had escaped from the cave into which she had banished them. She destroyed the thought of them by releasing Daniel's hand for a moment.

"Good," she murmured, for it was. Out-of-the-ordinary good. Again she stilled his hand.

He laughed at her, withdrawing his embrace, straightening up again to look out to sea.

She too laughed. For it was splendid, who could or would deny it—feeling his flesh and bone as she did, with every atom of her flesh and bone; the explosion of sensation could not be described; it needed reverence. But what was it all about, after all? Pleasure, of course, pleasure of the self, but that pleasure diminished unless there was pleasure shared. Feeling it so right and so intense, she often told herself that it was unique, that they had what few others had. That was no doubt absurd; what they had—(now her mind could assert it with clear reason, for he was not touching her, and the weather was cold against her skin)—what they had was merely a sexual courtesy common to the usual love, the ceremonies of the ordinary bed.

He was looking off into the distance; they were not going to speak, not going to move. That was bad, for the image which she dreaded was about to rise. (It had been just beyond the nearest minute since noon when Anne had confronted her across the dining room table, and she had shouted back, "Rachel, Rachel, Rachel!")

There Rachel was, walking by half moonlight out into the surf, neither proudly nor humbly, but with a certain dramatic determination. One could never tell with Rachel where the play ended and life began, even then, on that spring night so many years ago, when she had waded naked into the sea. Absurd and splendid, she walked deeper and deeper.

"Going for a bath or a baptism?" Lela had shouted, hoping to mock her back to shore, and resenting the fact that she had to play keeper to Rachel's madwoman.

"If you don't come back now, I'll have to come in after

you. Not because I want to—God knows, I don't. The water's cold and I can hardly swim. I like life more than you, a
thousand times more!"

"Then don't bother. Stay where you are. No one will ever
know!" Rachel struck deeper; the waves covered her shoulders.
But of course it was necessary to bother. Plunging frail and
naked into the sea after another fool was just the sort of thing
life required. Plunge she did, swimming in a hysteria of motion, each muscle tensed against the assault of frigid water.
She stood, finally, neck deep but still several feet from Rachel, who floated arrogantly out.

"I can't any further!" Her lungs screamed in agony for air
as she toed the elusive sand for a firm hold.

Insolently, indolently, but also weeping to the moon, Rachel backstroked toward her.

"You pity me, don't you?" Rachel accused, as they waded
back to shore.

"Pity you, pity me, pity us all, mere flesh in a cold sea. You
and your insane posturing . . ."

"But you never know where the posture ends and the in-
sanity begins, and so you dive in after me like a perfect idiot.
Oh Lela, I am really in love with your absurdity!" Rachel collapsed, hysterical, on the sand. Clasping her arms around her
body, she rocked backward and forward, chanting, "Touch
me, touch me, touch me."

Lela saw them clearly from the distance of ten years. They
were figures on a beach locked clumsily. What had she felt?
She could not remember either sympathy or desire, although
she must, indeed, have felt them. She could only remember a
rather cold, a rather cruel curiosity. She saw herself rise and
be quit of it, saying, "Rachel, put on your clothes before you
catch cold!"

Daniel brought her back to time, laughing down at her.

"Lela, whatever are you thinking about?"

"My dear, it is far too long to say, and you'd never believe it anyway. And you? What were you thinking?"

He recited:

"That the entropy of an isolated system can spontaneously decrease, in spite of the second law of thermodynamics. However, such a phenomenon is invariably short-lived. Thus, I sometimes know where I am and what I am doing, but never for very long."

"Oh, come off it! I don't believe you, not a word of it. No one *thinks* such a language."

"I was thinking that in different words perhaps—but I was thinking just that." He bent down and kissed her.

"You are altogether too many for me," she laughed.

"Never enough of too many, my darling, never enough."

"Shall we go in?" she asked.

"No, not just yet. It's so good here. Unless you're cold . . ."

"No, I'm fine."

Now there was before Lela a room, three stories up and bounded on three sides by windows. It was like a boat sailing among the swaying boughs of trees, the skeletal dance of bare branches in winter.

Only the bed and dresser remained. An open pomegranate spilled its seeds onto the surface of the dresser; its juice ran along the oak grain.

"I called the Salvation Army. They carted it all away, away. I could not bear the clutter. This terrible room. How I hate it. Do come here to me. I have had an awful night." Rachel stretched out her arms.

She had not gone to her. She had called a doctor, and he

had recommended rest and an end to . . . indulgence, he called it . . . emotional indulgence. Rachel had laughed at him but done as he suggested.

Soon after, Rachel had married Claud and unto them a child was born. Lela had married Daniel. They too would have a child; upon that she was resolved. Here she was, alive, and Rachel, a ghost, whose being or non-being she controlled by the will of her mind, which now said—no—as Daniel stiffened, wrenching back his arm and shoulder, and sent a stone spinning into the sea below them. She turned on her side, circling his waist with her arms and pressing her face and breasts against him, for she was cold and he felt warm.

He rubbed her back and arms for warmth and for sympathy; he knew she had been thinking about a child. She had been more than usually restless lately. There would soon be a child. No . . . he would have to tell Matthew no. Matthew wanted them to purchase the summer house jointly. Matthew said the property alone was worth the price, and he was right. The location was choice and would double its value in the next few years. But there was no aunt's legacy for Lela and him to fall back on; they hadn't the security of the Steads. No. (In his mind he rehearsed telling Lela, for she loved the place and would be disappointed.) He had to think of the possibility of a child. For a moment he did, wondering with what violence it would challenge the daily calm. He wanted children, of course, but still he wondered. Impulsively, he wound his arms hard around Lela.

"Remember Bundoran?" he asked.

"Yes," she muttered, her voice muffled by his body. "Bundoran where we met the Australian lady. The only woman I've ever been jealous of."

He laughed, delighted, rocking her back and forth in his arms, for it was like her to know that in all of their marriage there had been only that one, momentary threat.

He had been thinking all evening about their trip to the coast of Ireland two summers ago, for then too there had been a decision to be made about money, and a seascape. The problem had been the usual one: the fat and the lean, the munificence of industry and the parsimony of academia. A company building missile components had attempted seduction by offering him twice the salary the university was paying him. He had decided no, had taken instead a part-time consulting job to bolster the university pittance. He did not regret it; they had everything they wanted, and his soul and much of his time were still his own. He had congratulated himself anew that very afternoon after his first look at poor Lessing. Lessing's shoulder was permanently dented from the pressure of the wheel.

"I wonder where she is now?" Lela murmured.

"The Australian?"

"Yes."

Daniel wondered too. He saw her, sitting solitary at a table for one, in a frayed tweed coat, tall, timid, wounded. A recent widow was Daniel's guess. Lela's idea was more poetic but less likely: the sudden loss of parents or a parent after a too sheltered life. Whatever the cause, her grief was apparent and her timidity; for she never spoke, not to anyone, until that last night when, as he and Lela walked off to say farewell to Donegal Bay, she hailed them from the columned porch of the Great Southern Hotel.

"Let us find a path down to the sea!" she cried with shrill gaiety full of effort.

And so they walked along the cliff road. The wind was bit

ter and the waves leaped like ghosts, threatening, arms spread wide.

"There must be a way down somewhere," she called, leading them on down the road, in spite of the weather, and into a dumping area—about three square acres of Irish garbage with a fine view of the sea. Evil birds and the scuttle of rats— but still she pushed on, looking for a pass down the cliff face to those ghost waves raping the sand.

Suddenly the wind let go with a roar and the sky spilled seed as if it had an apocalypse in mind. Lela turned tail.

He laughed to himself remembering so clearly how she looked—her wet skirt hiked up, slapping against her thighs— sprinting back down the road toward a pagodalike structure about a quarter of a mile away.

But the Australian was not deterred, not by skyfall, windroar, or the end of the world. On she went, deeper and deeper into the mountain of rot and decay. Her green tweed coat swam ahead of him through the rain, and, of course, he gallantly followed; one could not leave a woman to drown in a garbage heap, not even on the Day of Judgment.

He caught up with her as she confronted an ancient Anglia parked on the side of the road. The rain streamed down the windows. The figures in the back seat looked like divers in a vast aquarium, but their movements were clear. Irish lad and Irish lass banging away in the middle of the midden with rats and rain for company. The lad had dropped his trousers; the lass had obligingly lifted her skirt—no more ceremony than that. They grappled on the seat, narrow as a coffin.

The meek Australian stood aghast and agape, flanks quivering, until he dragged her on down the road. Fresh from whatever tragedy it was, she stood there in the middle of garbage and fornication, looking for the sea.

He forced her away from it, and she turned to him and said, "But you see, I don't think I can take care of myself. It is very dreadful. Whatever am I to do?"

Her question was academic and he could not now remember exactly what he had replied. Something about the world being a pleasant enough place . . . sea, sun, moon, stars, and an occasional person . . . the automatic empiricism of the practicing pragmatist. Then he had taken her in his arms as if for proof. So much sophistry, no more, in rain and stench. A feeble performance, he told himself. That had been the end of it. Presumably the Australian went back to Australia; he had been down and out with a bad cold for a couple of weeks. Sometimes, watching Lela, when she seemed particularly competent, complete, self-contained (so she had seemed today during lunch), he thought he had no idea who she was and told himself, "That other needed me."

However, the course of their lives was set and it was good, oh yes, for the most part it was very good.

"I am acquainted with the more complex algebras." He spit it out aloud.

Lela ignored it, knowing that there was nothing she could say. Instead, she sat up, clasped her arms around his neck and growled in his ear:

"I want wine."

"That you shall have."

"And bed."

"That too. In spades."

He helped her up, and they climbed over the rocks and walked back to the house.

XVII

THEY DO THAT very well, Claud thought, as Lela and Daniel passed him, now holding hands. Claud sat on the edge of the veranda, shivering in the dark, embracing a pillar with one arm.

"It goes on," he said, as they disappeared into the house. But, of course, not even a sane God overseeing a rational universe could be expected to say, or even know, why. Was it pity or envy he felt? He did not know.

In the living room the concert was over. Jean Macleod and Anne Bennett were huddled together near the fire, conspiring like sibyls, their presences dimmed but hardly eclipsed by the darkness of the room.

"They seem so perfectly mated," said Anne, as the Relds passed, "the quintessence of marriage; all harmony and sudden sex at noon."

"That may be true," Mrs. Macleod replied, "but I thought today that there was something not quite right, not quite usual with Lela. But perhaps it is myself; not Lela at all." She sighed, watching Lela, who stood by the long table at the end of the room as Daniel tipped a decanter.

"Have you tried our American wines, Anne?" Lela called, smiling at them.

"But of course, and found them of rare vintage indeed."

"Now you're being elliptical." She walked over to them, glass in hand.

Daniel watched the shadow of her progress through the bulb of his wineglass. She appeared convex and two dimensional.

"Here, Anne, now take a sip." Lela offered her the glass.

"Dear girl, I've been drinking it all evening."

"Well then, Jean, you try."

"Ah, but I've been sipping at it too. Now tell me, what is its name?"

"Buena Vista Ultra Dry."

"Good heavens, how foreboding," Anne exclaimed.

"Beneficent for diseases of the sinus nonetheless," Lela countered. "We Americans are infamous for chronic disorders of that sort—like a tribal cleft palate."

"Go away!" laughed Jean. "You're being claimed." She waved to Daniel as Lela went back to him.

"The fire is dying; something must be done!" Anne got up and collected newspapers from a pile by the fireplace.

"Your *Times*, not mine," she mused, glancing at the top page.

Matthew presented himself suddenly.

"Here, let me do that. Sit down!"

He took the papers from Anne and, perching on the arm of her chair, examined the top page. She leaned over and read with him, running her thumb along the first line of the headlines in each column.

"Nouns and verbs, nouns and verbs, nothing but nouns and verbs," she announced, proceeding to enumerate aloud:

"U. S. Bombers Cut—Rising War Worries—Five Thousand Warheads Stored—Thousands Protest—and look there, at the picture, the placards the marchers carry: noun and verb again—War Erodes, War Erodes . . ."

"War and again war," sighed Mrs. Macleod, "hot, cold, hard, soft, loud, quiet, but war nonetheless. I sometimes think we—all of us make it happen."

"Oh I do so agree," said Anne.

"Yes." Matthew stared at the dull glow of the fire and crumpled the paper to feed it. "It is a kind of collective orgasm in which each of us, quite unconsciously, finds relief, finds expiation for his minor guilt in the more general enormity. We exorcise our petty distortions of spirit in this . . ." he waved the paper at her and then tossed it into the fire. "It's like some black rite necessary when all other rites fail."

"Yes, that is exactly it," Anne put her hand over Matthew's and clasped it, "that is exactly what I should like to paint, to abstract and put into form. How all our relations are wrong —no balance, no harmony, no rightness. From this house here, from that house there, all over the world, there rises, like thin strands of smoke from chimneys in winter, each minor dissonance, which can only be resolved when the separate discords are absorbed in a greater cacophony, a noise so loud that it deafens before it displeases, a noise louder than the songs of the angels in heaven or the howls of the hounds of hell or the wails of all the dead that death has undone."

"But I am confused," Jean Macleod interrupted, while Anne caught her breath. "I do not think I quite catch your meaning."

"I understand that," Anne confessed, "I know I'm not making much sense, and, what's worse, not even trying."

Matthew also recanted, very gently and very politely:
"It is all rhetoric, an empty egg carton with its cardboard

jaws yawning open—so much form without content. Was it Freud or some lesser saint who so truly proclaimed: 'Language is disease.' Please do excuse me, Jean, and you too, Anne, I've had too much whisky. Distilled spirits do not, of necessity, yield distillations of spirit."

They silently watched the fire, as Matthew added logs and prodded them into a blaze, until Anne bent forward intently and spoke again:

"But there is in all of this an idea, something I believe. Without knowing it, even the most passive of us needs and wills these things—even you, Jean—and so the events take place. I believe that all events are the extensions of ourselves and our desires. What seems objective (fire, walls, people) is simply what we invent. Reality consists of our fantasies, the fictions we select, the myths we create and perpetuate."

She took a long sip from her glass, leaned back, and again spoke:

"Permit me to be whimsical to demonstrate the point. Here we are now; for whatever our separate reasons may be, we have chosen to dream the same dream. Perhaps all human life is such a dream, and we are all merely stones—there, there on the beach," Anne gestured in the direction of the sea beyond the window, "stones on the beach bored with that condition, which have sought and found another form, and, with the conviction of our stony imaginations, have fleshed it out entire: a universe, replete with unseen solar systems, which grows and changes with the intake of every stony breath. There is only one question: do we dream our life or do we live our dream—and the question itself is meaningless."

Anne paused, drew a deep breath, and laughed at herself. She was a bit tipsy and it was a delightful feeling.

"But why should so many stones choose to be people?"

Mrs. Macleod asked dryly. She suspected she was having her leg pulled, but these were serious subjects, and she did not think they ought to be treated with levity, if indeed levity was what Anne meant. She badly wanted another glass of wine to ease the strain of continued encounter.

"But why shouldn't stones choose to be people?" Anne giggled.

Jean persisted seriously:

"But when I said that we make it happen, I had in mind something far more conventional . . . the religious idea that we are all flawed . . . and so we are punished . . . afflicted . . ." she paused but Anne made no move to answer.

"In a way I envy you," Jean continued, "I have traveled a great deal. I have felt. Yes, I have felt most of the deadly sins at one time or another, but I have come to no daring conclusions, nor have I been able to dismiss the questions with laughter or unconcern . . ."

Matthew interrupted her:

"And I envy you. Your serenity appalls me, and that it should have anything to do with the alleged afflictions wrought by an angry God, or the Seven Daily Sins seems to me incredible."

"Perhaps my serenity is not real; perhaps it is, as Anne has suggested, your fiction, what you choose to imagine about me."

Suddenly out of the darkness Walter presented himself and a decanter and filled Mrs. Macleod's glass. She sipped and, staring into the fire, spoke again:

"Several months ago I arrived in Beirut and no one was there to meet me. Mail had been delayed, for a minor official had been kidnapped and all the processes of the bureaucracy ceased with sympathetic paralysis. I was not met, and of a sudden discovered I had forgotten my Arabic. Looking back, such a lapse seems unaccountable, but I could not remember a word. I could not speak to anyone, nor could I read the phonebook. I could not call for help. And so I sat upon my luggage, while strangers circled like carrion birds cawing strange noises, the meaning of which I could not remember. I sat and calmly smoked a cigarette. They chattered around me, admiring, I suspect, the stoicism with which I accepted my desertion. Actually, I prayed for death, for the sun was hot, I was alone, and I had no words."

They were all silent, watching in their minds an old lady with white hair sitting under a Middle Eastern sun. Finally Matthew rose and excused himself.

"I must go track down my wife. Have you seen her, Walt?"

"Yes, over this way." They moved away from the fire.

Anne spoke gently:

"Please, if you are tired—it has been such a long day—don't feel that you must stay here keeping me company, Jean."

"No, I would rather stay for a while. Lately I have not been sleeping well."

"Ah, I sympathize. I've been an habitual insomniac all my life. Wretched disorder."

"Yes, I quite agree, although this is my first experience with it. Perhaps, it is natural. They say one sleeps less as one grows older."

"Nonsense," laughed Anne. "Lela tells me that you are the youngest in spirit of all the people she knows."

"Lela has not seen me in a number of years."

"How did you meet her?"

"It was about ten years ago, the year my husband died. He

was teaching for a semester at the college at which Lela was a student. She typed sermons for him one day a week."

"Lela?" Anne was incredulous.

"Yes, Lela," replied Mrs. Macleod. "It was a job, not a declaration of faith. I have traveled since then, but we have always kept in touch."

"You may have known my sister-in-law Rachel, then."

"I met her only once. Quite a handsome girl. Lela wrote me of her death. I am most terribly sorry; I suppose it's disrupted all your lives. It must be a dreadful business for your nephew. He's a beautiful child."

"He is also a strange child. He hardly ever speaks, you know, and he's extraordinarily unemotional. I saw you with him out on the rocks. It was a unique interlude for Mark. He rarely gives or takes affection. I once told him he was either a coward or a nihilist. Hardly the language to use with an eight-year-old."

"Hardly."

"Yet I think he understood. He told me not to worry and bestowed upon me one of his rare caresses. He usually reserves them, you know, for Lela and me; it would seem he has added you to his harem of mother substitutes."

"I'm flattered."

"So, I dare say, are Lela and I. He gives one the sense that he is gifted and so we are flattered that he chooses to notice us and perhaps even to care for us. At the age of eight, Mark has mastered the very difficult, very complex gesture of blessing. He accomplishes it with grace and without condescension, but one is always aware of his godlike indifference. I do homage to the child but, at the same time, quite frankly, he frightens me. We consider taking him with us back to Eng-

land, for his father seems quite incapable of coping with himself let alone with the boy; but the prospect appalls me . . ."

"Oh, but you make far too much of the child," Jean interrupted impatiently; "he struck me simply as a poor mother-
less little thing needing love. Why make him more complicated than he is? Surely the father would prefer the child to
stay with him. Surely he is not your responsibility."

"Oh God, I don't know. I find questions of responsibility
difficult. I want to be free of them. I want to go home to my
hills and lakes. From my studio window I can see the Lion
and the Lamb, or so we call the crags of one of our small
mountains. I want to work and be left alone. It is there that
I am most content. There I can neither harm (for I am not
stable and I would most certainly harm Mark), nor be
harmed. I want to live to myself, simply, without complication, although I know it is cowardly to desire such simplicity."

Jean leaned toward her anxiously:

"Yes, to live that way is too simple. Surely we ought to involve ourselves. I have lived for myself alone, have traveled,
have watched, only . . . now I am not content, or, perhaps,
it is closer to the truth to say contentment no longer seems
enough. Landscape begins to pale and sometimes to frighten
me."

Anne spoke and it was clear that she had not been listening:

"A few weeks before she died, Rachel wrote to me and
I . . ."

Mrs. Macleod rose abruptly. She was tired and it was impossible to talk to another human being. Anne did not listen; she herself did not listen. One was alone and could only
make the best of it. She heard her own voice as she excused

herself—shrill, petulant—a tired, spoiled old lady, that was what she was. A snowscape swept across her mind; it was punctuated with small houses from which there rose separate spirals of smoke.

"Sleep well," murmured Anne to Jean Macleod's departing back.

In the center of the living room, Matthew, Richard, Walter, and Beth formed a ring on the floor. Walter held them enthralled; Anne could not hear him, but his gesticulation alone was an enchanting mime which the firelight caught and cast upon the far wall. Richard broke the circle and joined his wife.

"What doing?" he asked, stretching himself on the floor by her chair.

"Getting tipsy, I fear, and, as a result, frightening sweet old American ladies away."

"Nonsense. You've not had that much to drink."

"You do keep a sharp eye on me, don't you?"

"What thinking, my love? I could feel you begin to brood all the way across the room."

"Nothing in particular. Just watching Walter's hand make shadows."

"Yes, Walter Bridge is a marvel; but I don't believe you. There is something."

"Don't badger me," she snapped. "If I tell you, you'll only be upset with me."

"Nonsense." He lit his pipe with a splinter of wood from the fire.

"Very well then, I was thinking again about Rachel's letter."

"My dear, you must forget about it; you simply must."

"There, you see, you are upset. I think I'll go on up to bed.

Perhaps you had better look for Claud. He's been gone for hours. Out there." She pointed toward the sea. "I'll see you soon." She laid the back of her hand against his temple and then left the room.

Claud still sat upon the veranda, looking out to sea. Approaching him, Richard felt again the pity he had so often felt when Claud was a child. Claud had always had some grief about him. Orphaned at an early age, his life had consisted of public school, university, obscure librarianships in London and New York, and finally Rachel. All of it had led to Colton Mark, and finally, these last two days, Claud was in revolt, saying his long self-contained no. Colton has armed himself, as if by instinct, thought Richard, remembering the uncanny aloofness of the child, his daily reluctance to speak or to feel.

Richard tapped his brother on the shoulder and asked him if he were cold.

He sat next to him on the edge of the veranda and spoke calmly and sensibly for fifteen minutes. He hoped that he had made clear his fondness and his wish to do the right thing. Finally Claud answered:

"But of course, you're quite right. Do something . . . yes . . . I must indeed do something. As you say, I cannot go on this way." His sarcasm severed whatever tenuous filament of platitudes Richard had diffidently woven for the purpose of connection.

The wires are down, all the circuits are out, we are completely in the dark, thought Richard, picturing the fall of high tension wires over a deserted field. He relit his pipe. Claud would persist in his childishness, that was clear, and there was nothing whatever to be said to him. Naturally one

had to try to keep civil and not be bored by his adolescence—
or exasperated. Claud would come to his senses sooner or
later; he was, basically, a sound fellow. Meanwhile there was
the child, and that was a duty. But how was it to be managed? It was a delicate situation. Colton might easily be
harmed. School, perhaps? A tutor and travel? That would be
expensive, but it could be managed if necessary. Home with
them to England and the semblance of family life? Anne
would certainly make an effort, and she might just pull it off,
if Claud could be trusted to come round in a reasonable
length of time. She had managed beautifully for four months,
had entertained Colton, humored Claud (not an easy task),
overseen domestic procedures—but that was in New York
and there she had the freedom of the city when the apartment became impossible. Grasmere would be different. The
danger signals had already appeared: she was overtired, had
begun to feel guilt about Rachel, had begun to brood, to wish
to separate herself from him, from everyone. No. They could
not take the child with them. Anne needed rest, needed solitude, needed to be able to see her mountains, needed to paint.
This Richard knew. Something else would have to be done
with Colton.

Claud interrupted his thought:

"Perhaps I'll give up my leatherbound, thermostatically
controlled existence—such insulation against reality can
hardly be healthy—and do something different. How does
that please you, brother?"

The cold hysteria in Claud's voice startled Richard, giving
him, momentarily, the sense of himself as a traveler who had
stumbled into the wrong, the unreal part of the forest inhabited not by the people he knew but by distorted sem-

blances of them. For the moment he was convinced of the madness of everyone. The moment passed. The fragments shifted back into the usual design.

"A change might be the very best thing in the world for you," he told Claud. "Have you anything specific in mind? Teaching, for example? I'm sure you could get a place at an American university. Matthew or Daniel could see to that."

"But, of course. Teaching!" Claud brandished heavy-bladed irony. "How stupid of me not to have thought of it! However the Establishment must be rejected. Something with more éclat would be more promising. These new universities of the left, for example—I've just been reading about them today. They reject the bourgeois limitations of the usual institution. I think I'd do very well, lecturing in a garret on the East Side. I could take as my subject the exposure of the decay of the western world—'Decadence I have Known, from Piccadilly to Rockport'—a subject requiring experience and eloquence. And my knowledge of it is superior, is it not, brother?"

"Frankly, Claud, you're not making much sense."

"You must understand, Richard, it isn't that I espouse Marxism. It is simply a matter of my dispassionate observation—a state of mind and a field of experience which qualify me preeminently to lecture the enlightened few on the most recent subtlety of the human condition."

Richard was finding it difficult to possess his soul in patience. "I can't separate substance from platitude in what you say. What are you getting at? Come to the point, man!"

"Do you pretend not to know what I mean by decadence?" Claud challenged.

"Stop talking nonsense."

"Surely, Richard, you of all people ought to know exactly

what I mean. We've been living virtually within the same four walls for four months; don't think I don't know all there is to know—about you and Anne. Poor Richard," he mocked, "poor brother, sick with desire and fastened to a . . . dying animal—is that how the poem goes? Of course, one can hardly call Anne a dying animal."

"Hardly!" Richard echoed angrily. "What the hell is the matter with you? My wife has given up four months of her life for you and your son. How dare you?"

"Anne's goodness and virtue to poor, downtrodden relatives is a bit wide of the mark. We were discussing decadence, brother. The gentleman desires, but the lady refuses, and refuses . . . and refuses. The gentleman acquiesces with perfect manners. I call that decadent. Dammit, why don't you simply take her? Do you both a world of good." Claud laughed heartily, throwing an arm around his brother's shoulders which were rigid with anger.

Richard wrenched himself free and stood abruptly.

"Take your hands off me. You disgust me. I don't want to hear another word about Anne from your filthy mouth."

"The subject is sacrosanct, heh? Perhaps I'm mistaking decadence for disease, is that it, Richard? After all, one must forgive all things, endure all things in the name of disease. Is she frigid, Richard? And that is a genuine question, a direct question, brother."

"I'm warning you, Claud . . ."

"I must confess I don't fathom it, Richard, for underneath all your intellectualized modernity, you have such a strong sense of blood, the family line and all that. I should have thought you'd have discarded the lady years ago and found yourself a healthy breeder—good solid country stock. Mother would never approve—she's turning in her grave, to be sure, for she was the true, archetypal believer in the ethics of the barnyard. In the fifteen years between you and me, the first and the last, she conceived and carried five times, and each time it died in her womb, and still she went on with it. When she wore out your sire, she took another, and finally obsession was rewarded; I lived. In the end, it killed her . . . a tumor the size of a foetus. I remember how it horrified me (I couldn't have been much older than Mark): that huge thing in her. Oh, but with what pride she carried it, do you remember, Richard?"

Richard sat down next to his brother again, for he did remember. He had not known that Claud had understood. He had been so young and they had all tried to keep it from him. She had been convinced until the very end that she was pregnant and could not be persuaded otherwise. He could hear her now, half dead with the thing that was eating inside her, boasting to the vicar's wife: "Fifty-two years old, and still doing the Lord's most precious work!" It must have been hard on the little chap, yet Claud had never said a word, never in all these years. Richard could no longer be angry with him. He spoke gently:

"She was good and just; her strength was superb."

"Precisely my point, brother Richard, she was superb, strong enough for several generations. But here we are, you and I: the rich strong blood has turned thin, fanatic, and inclined to crisis."

Richard was silent. He saw himself a young man; his mother lay before him on her deathbed. He stared at the perspiration on her forehead but did not touch her; he could not bring himself to the faintest suggestion of a caress.

What was it that kept him from so simple an act? Disgust or fear or dislike? He could not remember what he had felt. She had called him to her, her eldest son. He had done nothing for her.

"We fail," he muttered aloud.

Suddenly Walter plunged out of the house, across the veranda, and onto the rocks, followed by Matthew and Beth. He carried the tape recorder.

"Come winged saints, descend!" he shouted, spreading his arms to the moon. "Gull into God; God into Gull, descend!"

Beth and Matthew spread open cans of food along the rock edge; Walter threw a switch and pushed a button. The machine played back several minutes of raucous noises, assisted by Walter's own imperfect rendition of gull calls:

"Kak-kak-kak, kyow, kyow, kyow," he screamed in imitation of the gulls recorded by the machine.

"Herring gulls, laughing gulls, come," he cried.

"Great black-backed gull, descend!"

He switched the machine to "record" and waited.

Moments later, to the surprise and amusement of everyone, gulls did, in fact, descend, in the wake of a late fishing trawler on its way back to the harbor of the town. They skated and skidded around Walter, hawking after the cans of fish, until they were dispersed by a larger bird which wheeled in upon the rocks, alternately barking and croaking.

"Ah," proclaimed Walter with mock reverence, "here is the great black-backed gull. He is cruel but full of courage and has been sent to decrease the numbers of lesser scavengers."

He gathered up his machine and turned his back on the rocks, leaving the rasping gull to his prize, crying over his shoulder as he retreated to the house, "It's all yours, O Great Gull!"

Matthew wrapped Beth in his jacket and led her down the rocks. "Whatever would we do without Walter?"

Although she was very fond of Walter, Beth was not entirely convinced of his indispensability on this particular weekend, and so she remained silent.

Matthew waited for her to tell him that she was again pregnant. Although she had not so informed him as yet, he knew—from the shadows under her eyes, from the heaviness of her breasts, from the ponderously cautious way she moved, as if anticipating the weight which would soon grow within her.

She was not altogether certain he would be pleased and so came out with it quickly and nervously:

"There's to be another one."

"So I've gathered," he said, laughing. "Will it be too much for you with those four other louts hanging around?"

"Oh Matt!" She could tell that he was pleased and she was relieved. "Even these few short weeks I've missed the children dreadfully. Why must we send them off? Particularly when we have this house. Let them stay with us all next summer. Please, Matt."

"No. The separation is good. They learn to be themselves; their own people. Besides, you know how it pleases your mother and father to have them. They certainly must go away for a while next summer, for you'll have the baby to cope with and be needing rest."

"Here, feel," she said, placing his hand against her.

"Elizabeth, Elizabeth, silly Beth, it's much too soon to feel anything." He kissed her, but even as he did, he vaguely wished to be away. He sensed her fecundity and was a little repelled. Nevertheless, he knew revulsion was a prelude to his desire. It was something he always felt while she was pregnant.

The child would be his. He had not claimed the others; they were Beth's concern. With the others he was mild, he was just; they cared for him and found in his male detachment relief from Beth's powerful giving and receiving. However, he was resolved to make a passionate connection with this new child.

"Let's go in; it's too cold for you here," he said, helping her up and guiding her back to the house. He found himself wanting to give her pleasure more than he wanted to satisfy himself. He wanted to begin to expiate his part in the coming struggle for possession of the child before the war itself began.

Catching sight of Claud, who was still hunched on the edge of the veranda, Matthew tried to convince him to come inside. Claud refused.

Beth surveyed the disheveled living room with distaste.

"Naturally the Relds have gone up without doing a thing."

"It can wait until morning," Matthew said, as she began to collect glasses. He switched on a lamp for Claud and together they went upstairs.

XVIII

AT THE CAVE of Woodward, the party was almost over. Gail lay upon the avocado couch, sobbing hysterically, her eyes wide and dark with panic because she could not catch her breath.

His back to her, Seth stood staring at the room reflected in the panel of glass.

"Silly, silly, silly bitch. You are miles away; miles and miles away. Down there somewhere."

In the next room, on the bed beneath the suicidal film star, Neil struggled wearily as Sonja undressed him.

"But I tell you I can't," he laughed. "I simply can't. I'm much too sick."

"Yes you can, darling, of course you can."

He felt her mouth on him.

"You see, it's simply no good," Neil protested.

"Give me your hand then. Quickly. Please."

As her thighs closed over his wrist, spasms of nausea erupted.

"I'm going to be sick," he said.

XIX

LELA AND DANIEL lay listening to the silence of the summer house. She drew his head down against her and covered his exposed ear with her hand.

"Like a stethoscope," she laughed.

He was closed and hollow and the canter of her heart crashed its echoes against his skull. Then the slow mounting thrust of his blood marked the rhythm but subdued the sound.

He drew his hands down her belly, along her hips, to the soft inner skin of her thighs. She marked the slow advance of his hands impatiently. He deliberately delayed the pace.

She began to move beneath him, pushing her fists against the small of his back, pressing him deeper and deeper within her, finally encircling his buttocks in the vise of her legs.

He submitted to the paralysis for the moment, feeling the mouthlike clutching of her spasms, then he broke her grip and exploded within her.

They lay still again. Lela tried furtively to smooth the tangle of sheets, while Daniel traced her body with his hand.

"Perhaps we won't have any of our own," she said.

"Own what?"

"Children."

"There's time for that. You're still an infant. And even if

we don't, will it be so important? Will you mind so very much?"

"No, not right away," she admitted. "But later I should have the feeling that I had missed something important, that I had been left out of the central rhythm. You would mind too, you know, perhaps even more than I."

"You may be right, but good God, Lela, let's not worry about it tonight. There's time. It will probably happen quite naturally, without worry, fuss, talk."

"I haven't your faith in nature," she sighed.

"It's me you haven't faith in, or yourself. Can't we just rest now?"

"Could we have the door open a bit?"

"Damn you, wench!"

"Enough?" Daniel asked, naked and yawning by the open French door.

"That's fine. Come back quickly, idiot, you'll catch cold!"

"Sirius," he noted from the balcony, "eight point eight light-years away."

"How far is that?" she asked.

"Fifty trillion miles, give or take a few. Give a few, I would guess."

"Someone else's sun."

"Perhaps. You're sure there's nothing else milady wishes: water, blankets, caviar, an opium pipe, marshmallows?" he suggested, throwing himself on the bed.

"It might have happened tonight," she whispered.

"Doubt it. Wrong time of the month."

"True," she agreed.

"All right, Lela, I give up. What is all of this?"

"Mark."

"What about Mark?" he asked impatiently.

"Maybe we should take him for a while. Claud obviously can't manage and the Bennetts are planning to go back to England soon."

"No!" he pronounced.

"Why so emphatic, fond lover?"

"You know why. Something unnatural about both parents —particularly his mother. I don't suppose suicide has got into the bloodstream, but he's hardly a normal, healthy youngster. Not the sort of child I want; not the sort of responsibility I want."

"Oh Dan, be fair, you can hardly expect him to be all peanuts and ice cream after what he's been through."

"I don't expect anything of him. I simply don't want to have to cope with him. He'd prove too much for both of us. You'd be out of your mind in a week."

"You never did like Rachel, did you, Dan?"

"No. I never did like Rachel. Now that I've confessed, may I please have permission to go to sleep?"

After several minutes of silence she spoke again:

"We should have called them."

"Who?"

"The Lessings!"

"Lela, if you're hell bent on a curtain lecture, surely out of a world of people you can find one or two pleasant ones to talk about."

"What was that?" she cried, sitting up suddenly.

"Just a shutter somewhere at the back of the house. The wind's picking up. I'd better close that door."

Standing on the balcony once more, Daniel looked down, catching a glimpse of Claud's legs stretched out along the edge of the veranda.

"Claud, go to bed you fool," he called down to him.

Claud jerked awake at the sound of his voice.

"Cold. Must go in," he muttered.

Putting one arm around the pillar, Claud pulled himself up, steadied himself, and walked the length of the veranda, counting his steps and taking care not to look down. At the door he paused, leaning against it, commanding himself to breathe deeply.

He was dizzy, intolerably dizzy, and it wasn't the drink. He'd been having it off and on for nearly two weeks. He was . . . vertiginous . . . that was the word.

The sweet, sacred ground was solid again. He got himself across the living room and into a chair.

Yes, it went on. And what was *it?* Birth and union and death, he supposed. Birth—to have a son, for example—was only the ambergris (an infinitesimal amount of substance which, when perfected, is valuable), the least secretion from the vast drifting monster, marriage.

And death? Just the week before he had met a religious on a park bench, S. J. and happy in his shroud, who told him that death was simply to cease to breathe, not necessarily to cease to live; however, as he, and indeed almost everyone but the Society of Jesus, knew, it was quite the other way round. Death was to cease to live, but not necessarily to cease to breathe.

Birth and death were thus defined and disposed of. Union remained. Claud closed his eyes and thought of his own. His marriage to Rachel was revealed in a series of static pictures.

Courtship on a rare day in July. The grass in Central Park needed mowing. Mosquitoes were plentiful. Sunlight on a dirty swan. The lady was handsome; the gentleman ardent. The flowers opened, the bees sucked, he proposed, they kissed. Shortly thereafter they had moved into five rooms in a brownstone.

Pregnancy in September. The late autumnal sun dappled the filigree frame of the mirror as Rachel strutted naked before it, kneading the first fullness of her womb with angry hands and shouting obscenities at her reflection.

Marriage in name. After the birth: the relief of a room to himself, a uniform pushing a perambulator, Rachel's cold but usually polite face at breakfast and dinner, her hands painting vases, their tremor adding vibration to the colors.

R. I. P. A stack of books against a wall in the empty hallway.

That was the whole deck of cards. Claud stood. The dizziness was gone. He groped up the stairs in the dark and stumbled into the room he was sharing with Mark. He looked down at his son and wondered what he thought of it all.

With Mark, Rachel had been neither warm nor cold, but simply separate. She was never tender with him, but usually kindly. She often brought him gifts, but rarely spent any time with him. As he grew older, he seemed to regard her as a generous and lively visitor, always welcome, but never really missed.

Claud suspected that his son's mourning went no further than an infrequent curiosity as to why the visitor never came anymore. The boy's life had not been torn up; no artery had been severed; he had, after all, been brought up by uniforms. Women and relatives could nag all they liked about what was to be done with poor Mark, but the solution was simple and clear: another housekeeper and the usual routine. He would send the meddlers back to England directly he woke. Now he would sleep. Claud began to undress.

Mark heard his father moving around the room, but he was more than half the way from waking to sleep and did not rouse himself fully. Mark was watching himself come home from school on the very last day he had seen his mother. It was very clear before him, as though it were happening again, but he was not there, he was here, in the bed, watching. The bus let him out at the corner and he walked down the street toward the house—his house, although they only lived in one part of it. He had on his school jacket with the picture of lions on the pocket. (He remembered putting it on for the first time and thinking it very beautiful, but then, on the first day of school, when he discovered that all the boys had the same jacket, he had been disappointed.)

He was walking home and doing all the things it was necessary to do. First it was necessary to take only three steps in each square on the sidewalk. Then it was necessary to watch carefully and never, absolutely never, step upon the crack between the squares. "Step on a crack; break your mother's back." Halfway down the street, the spiked railings which surrounded the house began. It was necessary to count the spikes by touching them with one hand while still taking care of the cracks and the number of steps. Seven, eight, nine—the last railing and the last square of sidewalk.

Mark watched himself raise his right foot, very carefully, very deliberately, and stamp it down directly on the crack. He still did not know why he had done it. It was a terrible thing. Running up the stairs to the apartment, he prayed that she would be there (for she was not often there in the afternoons) and that she would be all right. He threw open the door and there she was, stacking books against the wall in the hallway. There was nothing whatever wrong with her back. How happy he was. (And yet, as he watched himself, he knew he had been just a bit disappointed too. What if he had been able to do something like that, just by stepping on a crack? It was a horrible and a wonderful thought.) He ran to her, throwing his arms about her waist.

She explained that she had told the lady who took care of him and the house to go home and she was straightening his father's study. It was, she said, a kind of game, and he could play too. She had a way of laughing he had never understood. She explained the rules of the game. He was to bring all the books from the shelves in the study into the hall and put them in piles on the floor: all the large, dark books in one pile, the middle-sized ones in another, and the small ones with pictures on the covers in a third pile. That was his job. Huffy, puffy, she called him; for it was hard work.

There he was, running from the study to the hall, while she stood on a stepladder, placing the books (large ones on the bottom, small ones on top) in one enormous column. The column always fell. Once she got it very, very high—over her head—but she wanted it still higher. He held his breath; she placed another book, very carefully, very gently. Down crashed the whole column. He just got out of the way in time. One of the books fell apart and its pages lay scattered on the floor. The game was spoiled, for he knew that his father would be angry.

She said a word he had never heard. Sisfus, he thought it was. He asked her what it meant, but she did not answer. He crawled on the floor, gathering the pages, hoping to collect them all and place them inside the cover again so that his father would not notice.

He had picked up one page with a picture of a bird on it, a

strange bird with four feet like the feet of the lions on his jacket. She had begun to build the column again. It would fall; he knew now that it would always fall.

Then his father was there, standing in the doorway.

"Father, what is this funny bird?" He had forgotten that the book was broken, lying all over the floor, in his wonder at the bird.

"What the hell is going on?"

"Well, well, well, you're home early, for a change. Don't tell me the library drinking society has forgone their nightly libation. Just think, right this minute, all over Manhattan displays of heroism are being enacted as you all come home to face the wife and kiddies—cold turkey."

"I asked you a question!"

"Cleaning your study, milord. That's just what I'm doing. Getting rid of the clutter—these filthy books; I cannot bear this beastly clutter a moment longer."

"Mark, go to your room!"

Mark saw himself going to his room. Then the picture stopped. There were voices, but he could not remember what they said. His mother had gone away then and he had not seen her again.

Mark opened his eyes. His father was a dark form sitting on the next bed. He closed his eyes quickly.

"Libation" was an odd noise but it meant something. All noises meant things, even noises which weren't words. "Libation"—"Sisfus"—the bird with four feet. Those were the things he had not known and he still did not know them. But that was only one day. He was eight years old. There had been thousands of days and thousands of words and pictures he had not known about, but he had forgotten most of them. He could feel himself falling asleep. He turned over and hooked his arm through the crook of his knee. It was necessary to do that before sleeping.

"Sleeping, Mark?" Claud asked softly.

Mark did not answer, for he was thinking, as he fell down, down into sleep, that, although he still played the game sometimes, it wasn't necessary. He could walk anywhere he liked, on all the cracks in all the sidewalks in the world. It didn't matter anymore.

Mark dreamed that he was climbing a spiral staircase. The steps were books. A bird with four feet peered down from the top and laughed at him.

"Lucky little chap," murmured Claud, lying down on his bed, and noticing light through the crack in the door. It came from the room directly across the hall, he decided, his brother's room. His brother had been sleeping for hours; he was sure of it. Richard's ability to fall instantly and profoundly asleep, regardless of time, place, or circumstance, was a family joke. Anne was having a bad night of it, Claud deduced.

"My sister-in-law, madwoman and meddler," he muttered.

Nevertheless, he was fond of Anne and wished she could rest. For a few moments he practiced long-distance hypnosis, telepathy through closed doors. With the concentration of all his mind he instructed Anne to sleep, until he himself lost consciousness.

XX

The Bennetts had left the balcony doors open. Dejectedly, Anne listened to the clock chime twice and wished she could sleep. She had been sitting in the armchair next to the open French doors for a long time, hearing the murmur of the conversation in the next room (finally Daniel had closed their door) and the regular crash of the surf against the rocks. She had tried to read. Richard lay inert, expelling an occasional decorous snore. Their open suitcases yawned forth tangles of clothes and cellophane bags on chairs and tables all over the room.

"What a horrid muddle," she said aloud, half hoping Richard would wake. "Belongings scattered over two continents. I abhor suitcases," she hissed in the direction of Richard's bed.

She plunged her hand into one of the least objectionable knots of nylon stockings and silk ties and felt for the bottle of sleeping tablets.

"Oh God," she groaned, clenching her teeth and fists with the sheer exasperation of not being able to sleep when she was so tired. She plunged her hand in again, came up with a long blue envelope, and went back to the armchair.

For one thousand and one nights—she asserted silently—she had been lying down to sleep on beds of thorns, on hill-of red ants—since early childhood. Her nerves were bare. They were forever being rasped raw by bedsheets. The pity and pain of it brought tears to her eyes.

Richard turned in his bed and breathed a long peaceful sigh.

"How can you?" Anne reproached him silently.

She drew out the letter: several pages of onionskin with Rachel's script moving downward across them. Although there now could be no doubt that the letter was heartfelt, a genuine appeal, Anne still found herself reacting to it as she had when she first received it. It still seemed to her to be the cheapest sort of exhibitionism, despicably self-indulgent, obscenely self-revealing, unforgivably self-pitying. These were common sins, of course (Anne recognized that she, herself, was guilty of at least one of them during most of the hours of every day), but they were repugnant on paper and at such public length. After all, she had hardly known the girl. Anne particularly disliked the assumption upon which the letter was based, the assumption of kinship. Claud had no doubt told Rachel that his sister-in-law was susceptible to what were called, euphemistically, difficulties (and he had probably added that Richard "bore up" beautifully). Rachel had consequently assumed an empathy, a "feeling with" which did not exist, could never exist.

"No," Anne replied to the letter silently, "I do not know what it is to be a twenty-nine-year-old American woman, alone in a hotel room in the vast city of New York, at odds with my husband and bereft of my son. Nor do I even care to know—which is, no doubt, to be less than human. Finally one wants to be left out of the mess of other people's lives." Anne pictured with distaste a half-eaten dish of floating island.

She paged through the letter, reading random sentences. It contained a catalogue as monotonous as the biblical begats. First there was a delicately phrased alphabet of marital misfortunes (from adultery to misunderstanding). The effect of this was a kind of well-bred sordidness. Anne judged that most of it was more fancy than fact, more Rachel's fault than Claud's. Claud simply did not possess the psychic energy necessary to perpetrate domestic disaster. The second part of the letter catalogued personal symptoms (from nausea to photophobia). Whether real or invented, the list had what Anne guessed to be textbook accuracy. Here Rachel threw her restraint and her prose to the winds. She had apparently labored under the misapprehension that her condition required the pathos of poetry for its proper description. Her metaphors were appalling.

"The sun rips my eyes," Anne read, wincing with embarrassment. She quickly turned the page.

The letter concluded with a lengthy description of the hotel room to which Rachel had run and the view from its window. Each article of furniture was enumerated, for Rachel claimed that the furniture moved; the dance of electrons, she called it, a molecular fugue. Her window looked out upon the ordinary terror of New York, the hysteria of traffic and neon signs. Anne agreed that it was hardly the landscape of peace. Nevertheless, eight million people survived it.

Anne read over the last page of the letter carefully. With relief she found herself not guilty. Rachel had given no indication that Claud did not know where she was, that he was, in fact, looking for her. The letter seemed to imply quite the opposite state of affairs, that Claud had encouraged, if not demanded, her departure. She had not contacted Claud, because, three thousand miles away, she had seen only the profile, not the full face of the situation. Surely an intervening ocean diminished one's responsibility.

The letter concluded with the phrase "you will understand."

"Not a bit of it," Anne muttered and wondered what she could have done. Cabled a reply, perhaps. She composed one in her mind: "Dear 'you-will-understand,' go home to your husband and child." Hardly satisfactory. She could have telephoned Claud, but at the time such an act would have seemed a betrayal of Rachel's confidence—not that she had really given a rap for Rachel's confidence.

No, she could not be blamed for ignoring the letter; one could not take it seriously. It belonged to the genre practiced by precocious adolescents who were overly influenced by Dostoevski and his French descendants. Her young cousin who was going up to Cambridge in the fall had written similar dissertations on despair when he was sixteen years old. Anne remembered them well, for they were discovered by the boy's mother, who had been most upset. After consultations with various members of the family, his parents had sent him to Italy by way of a cure. The cure had worked, and now he was a fairly ordinary young man.

Anne put the letter back into its envelope, accusing herself even as she excused herself, for she had been—and, indeed, was still being—unsympathetic and callous.

One got on as best one could by oneself. That was the way of it. One held on to the look of things during occasional moments of grace. Anne suspected that half the world got on with it in just that haphazard way.

She switched off the light, climbed into bed, and settled back to try one of several magical incantations she had devised for the calling of the elusive powers of sleep. With a one-inch ordnance survey map in her mind, she began to name the lakes near her home, moving her lips without speaking.

"Working from south to north and from west to east: Windermere, Esthwaite Water, Coniston, Rydal Water, Grasmere, Wastwater, Hawes Water, Ullswater, Thirlmere, Derwentwater, Buttermere, Crummock Water, Bassenthwaite, Ennerdale . . . Fourteen. One missing."

The fifteenth lake continued to elude her, and the effect was more irritating than restful. She commanded herself to change the subject, and invented a climb to Helm Crag on the first day of spring.

She swung open the casement window; lilacs invaded the room; the cold damp house drank the new air in long draughts; winter was over. From the window she could see Richard in the garden, scattering seeds of summer savory among the rocks along the edge of the pond. He straightened and stretched into the sudden sun.

For the first time in months the crag stood out clear against the sky; no mist obscured it. Carrying an apple, her mackintosh, and a stick with a gnarled head, she walked down the path, waving to Richard, and feeling a bit guilty for not asking him to join her.

She turned left on Easedale Tarn Road, saluting a line of Girl Guides quick-marching to the local hostel, marshaled heartily by a long woman with a whistle and knees like ivory doorknobs crowning her long green woolen stockings.

"Your left, your right, your left," the woman croaked lustily.

"Your right, your left, your right," the girls answered thinly.

The old shank of a sheep had probably not let the poor things have their breakfast yet.

The sun was holding; it was keeping fine. She reached the narrow wooden bridge upon which Mrs. Barton-Dawes of Ambleside, who weighed fourteen stone and took the air for her health, was once marooned. Weeping and sweating, she had stood paralyzed upon it, while it groaned and swayed in protest. Finally Richard had charmed her off, by claiming that he himself with all his weight had jumped up and down upon that very bridge on many occasions, risking neither life nor limb. Dear Richard had gallantly kept his face straight as befitted the severity of the situation. His wife had proved weaker; she had gone off behind a bush to laugh.

Now she was over the historic bridge and past the sign, "To Easedale Tarn," which had been upside down since All Hallow's Eve. She pushed through a gate and into a meadow, sinking ankle-deep in mud. There was hardly a piece of turf above water and the sun seemed to have cooled, but she persisted, for the crag stood directly above, a half mile up. She began to ascend the long steep pitch very slowly, climbing sideways, pushing her stick into the turf, pulling herself up, and counting the cairns as she passed them. Finally she achieved the shoulder of the slope. The crag was still a long and difficult distance above her. She threw herself upon the wet grass to rest. The mists were closing in; looking down, she could not make out the path beyond a few yards. The mist turned to rain. She buttoned her mackintosh and clumsily got to her feet, accidentally kicking her walking stick. It tumbled down the slope before she could retrieve it. That was bad luck. What would she do now?

Abruptly, Anne sat up in bed, stating in a loud voice:

"I am still awake!"

Richard grunted himself out of sleep. "Good heavens, how you startled me," he complained.

"How do you sleep like that?" she asked. "I've named all the lakes but one and climbed Helm Crag."

"Oh have you really? Poor darling, you must be exhausted. How was the view?"

"Very poor. It rained, the fog was horrid, and I lost my stick. I left myself sitting there on the slope. I'm too frightened to climb down. You're in the garden and no help at all."

"Not in the rain, I'm not. I'm in the house worrying about you, pacing the floor. Soon I shall come after you. So, you see, there's nothing whatever to worry about."

"Perhaps not." She got out of bed and went over to him. He took her in his arms and together they lay down.

"Do you remember Mrs. Barton-Dawes?" she asked.

"Let me see now . . . the wife of the printer in Keswick?"

"No, the wife of the estate agent in Ambleside," she corrected.

"Ah yes, now I do remember. What is that amusing phrase Daniel uses? As broad as the side of a barn."

"That's the very woman," laughed Anne.

"Of course. She is the one who got stuck on the bridge to Easedale Tarn. She would not move. You, you traitor, ran off to laugh and left me alone with her.

"You were very nice to her, you know. Most gallant. Generally speaking, you are in fact a very nice man."

"I'm not sure I like the idea of being 'a very nice man.' After all, one likes to think of oneself as a bit more interesting than that."

"You are interesting; but you're also nice to Mrs. Barton-Dawes of Ambleside, and that takes a bit of doing—a certain gift. I haven't the gift, I fear, for I'm never nice to Mrs. Barton-Dawes of Ambleside. Do you know what I've been doing?" she continued, moving her lips against his cheek.

"Climbing Helm Crag when you ought to be sleeping." He curled a strand of her hair around his finger.

"Thinking too."

"I don't like the sound of that! Anne thinking bodes trouble for the universe."

"Not this time, Richard dear. I've simply come to some conclusions. I've decided that your half brother, and your half brother's son, *and* your half brother's dead wife—(it sounds rather like the cast of a melodrama, doesn't it?)—*they* are not my responsibility. I want to go home."

"Very sensible of you and quite right. We shall go home; as soon as this damnable weekend is over, I shall book us a flight. We are not my brother's keepers, particularly when he is so strongly opposed to being kept. I'm rather tired of his rudeness. He's more of a child than Colton."

"Brothers . . . Brotherswater. That's the lake I could not remember. Imagine my forgetting that one!"

"It's a very small one and easily forgotten. They say it was named after two brothers who were drowned there."

"Do they walk?" asked Anne with a mimicry of horror.

"But of course. They rise every second Tuesday and haunt the shores. Once when I was very young and strong I walked from Patterdale to Windermere and stopped to rest by Brotherswater. Unfortunately, it was too early in the day for ghosts."

Embracing him, she whispered, "Oddly enough, I never

think of you as anything but young and strong. I feel myself old, haggish, much the worse for more than half a lifetime. But you seem untouched."

"Anne, dear, for 'a mature woman of the world,' as they say in the cinema, you are an awful tease."

"I don't mean to tease, not a bit of it," she answered, feeling, with relief, her body begin to respond to him after it had been silent for so many weeks.

It was a laughing matter, she thought, a comedy. It could not be taken seriously. One day it seemed that she stood on the north pole and he on the south, with seas, nations, and glaciers between; the very next day here they were, together, with not even flesh dividing them; and she would never know which was the truth, and which, the lie—no, never, until some last and final day, when, hopefully, all the sliding panels, false bottoms, secret compartments, marked decks, and sleights of hand would be revealed.

XXI

OUTSIDE on the balcony Walter slept soundly within the layers of his sleeping bag until the alarm on his wristwatch buzzed. Five minutes later the clock in the town chimed five. Walter switched on his flashlight and pulled on his trousers. The sky grew lighter. He paged quickly through his dog-eared copy of *The Old Farmer's Almanac,* and read from page twenty-four: "Saturday, August 27. Sunrise: 5:03 A.M. Sunset: 6:27 P.M. Length of day: 13 hours, 25 minutes."

He was just in time. He removed his flute from his bedding and softly piped until the sun was safely over the horizon. Even as he did so, he wondered why such idiocy possessed him even when there wasn't an audience. The idea was unoriginal anyway; he had taken it from a movie.

He packed up his sleeping bag neatly and moved quietly into the house and down the hall. He had left some of his things in the room in which Mrs. Macleod now slept. He hesitated outside the room, tried the door, and softly opened it. The shades were drawn and he waited a moment for his eyes to adjust to the dark. Mrs. Macleod gradually came into focus. Coffined within a sheet pulled up to her chin, she lay flat on her back in absolute repose.

Walter slid open a dresser drawer and felt inside; it was the wrong drawer. He tried another; it scraped open.

"Oh!" shrieked Mrs. Macleod, bolting up in bed, clasping the sheet to her neck.

"What do you think you are doing?" she asked severely, recognizing Walter.

"Well," he answered, somewhat at a loss, "I think you have my underwear."

"Whatever would give you such a strange idea?" she asked.

"Surely you are wearing it." She had determined with relief that he was more or less clothed.

"My clean linen, as it is called. I left it here yesterday morning," he explained.

"Then you had better claim it."

He rifled through the drawers. Mrs. Macleod yawned elaborately.

"You're not thinking of going back to sleep, are you?" he challenged.

"As a matter of fact, the idea had occurred to me. What time is it?" It seemed to Mrs. Macleod that for days she had done nothing but ask the time.

"Precisely sixteen minutes past five. There are only thirteen hours and . . . twelve minutes left of the day." He regarded his watch sadly in the half-light.

She sighed deeply from the bed. "Yes. Quite right. There is, generally speaking, so little time." She sighed again, then yawned.

"Given that regrettable but immutable fact, you had better come for a walk on the beach with me," he announced.

"Surely you can find someone your own age to play with at this ungodly hour?"

"But you are much better company, truly you are." He bowed to her.

"Oh very well!" She was both annoyed and flattered. "You

really ought to be ashamed of yourself, dragging an ancient like me out of a sound sleep and a warm bed into what is virtually the middle of the night. I must dress, of course, and . . . coffee; I must have coffee."

"Good for Mrs. Macleod!" Walter cheered.

"Since we are to be playmates, you had better call me Jean."

"All right, Jean it is. We'll rendezvous in the kitchen in a half hour. I promise you the most superb cup of coffee you have ever tasted." He flagged his clean underwear at her and left the room.

"Mad. All mad," she muttered, searching under the bed with her feet for her slippers. "Quite mad. I can't imagine what I'm doing here."

When she arrived in the kitchen as promised, Walter was expertly cracking an egg with one hand. Mrs. Macleod shuddered.

"Not for me, thank you. Just coffee."

"The egg is for the coffee; I only want the shell." He crumpled the shell and tossed it, along with a pinch of salt, into the pot of steeping grounds on the stove.

Mrs. Macleod looked down into the steaming syrup and asked, "Are you sure that's meant to be drunk?"

"Not just yet—in a minute." He added a cup of cold water. "Cups and sugar are there in the cabinet; spoons, in the drawer."

Mrs. Macleod confronted "Jonah" and the knobless cabinet with perplexity. "I suppose one talks to it and it opens."

"No. You've got to use a knife blade."

"All right, as you say. Knives in the drawer, I suppose."

She opened drawer and cupboard and set the things on the kitchen table.

"Here we go," he said, pouring, and cautioning her to watch for grounds.

She tasted and approved.

"You are an expert flautist, storyteller, and cook. Now tell me what else you do."

"Nothing, as I'm sure you've already been told," he answered with good nature, for the subject neither embarrassed nor annoyed him.

"Doing nothing is quite all right as long as you keep yourself amused," she replied.

"I usually do. Every so often loafing has grown a little thin and I've gone to work—but only briefly. I always say to myself, 'Walter, my friend, your ancestors were slaves; it's time the family blood had a little rest'—recuperation, so to speak, until the next generation."

"From what I've seen of you in the last . . . how many hours has it been since we met?"

Walter counted on his fingers. "Seventeen," he said.

"From what I've seen in the last seventeen hours, you're hardly resting the family blood. You're diluting it!" she accused.

"Ah, that's because I'm restless with loafing." His voice was suddenly serious. "I shall have to be on my way to something soon."

Mrs. Macleod sipped her coffee and then admitted, with seeming unconcern, "I've loafed most of my life away."

"Women may loaf," he said, "and they usually do."

"Is that because they're superior or inferior?"

"Neither," he laughed, refilling her cup, "it's because of our society. It's in the books and on the tablets: Women May Loaf."

"Tell me, Mr. Bridge," she inquired with mock formality,

"have you very distinct ideas about the relative merit of the sexes?"

"Why yes, my good Mrs. Macleod, indeed I do. It is simply a matter of logic. Let us begin by reducing the subject to biological simplicity. The question then becomes: which sex contributes most to the efficiency and effectiveness of the process of propagation? You will see at once that the question is not very meaningful. There is one interesting difference between the ways in which the sexes serve the law of survival of the species. Conceive of it this way: one healthy male among many females—there is the possibility of an almost infinite number of offspring; however, when the proposition is reversed—one healthy woman among many men—the possible number of offspring is extremely limited." Walter stopped for breath and drank off his coffee in one draft.

"What conclusions do you draw from these astounding observations?" Mrs. Macleod inquired.

"The difference seems to lie in factors of quality as opposed to quantity. One fine specimen of male would be sufficient to repopulate the world. He could just about do the trick, if he had enough women. Most of us men are therefore expendable. Not so women (I'm speaking only in terms of propagation, you understand). The more women, the better; the more offspring the one healthy specimen may beget. Thus the archetype—spare the woman, she is not biologically expendable—unconsciously haunts all those middle-class fools who let their wives lie around all day getting fat on bonbons and bridge."

"The attitude you object to is far too modern to be archetypal," objected Mrs. Macleod.

Walter continued, ignoring her:

"Since the world's problem today is overpopulation not

underpopulation, since propagation is itself our greatest danger, the female is now also biologically expendable. It is time she was put to work, made to produce something other than children; it's time it was expected of her."

"Now, you stop haranguing me," she interrupted. "I've had a full evening of harangue; that is quite enough for one weekend. I came down here for a walk, not a lecture on population control, with the clear expectation that you were not one of those odious people who prides himself on being serious-minded." Mrs. Macleod stirred her coffee vehemently and added, "You haven't a proper respect for women."

"Don't do that," he warned, "you'll stir up the grounds. Of course, I respect women. There are some women whom I respect above all men and objects. Come along now, the early dawn is best and we are missing it." He took her arm and steered her out to the veranda.

It would be a clear day—that much was certain—and a hot one. Looking into the rising sun, Mrs. Macleod contemplated the day with peculiar dread. It would be a lovely day. She would be shoved and pushed; she would be jerked about from one thing to another (unseen hands pulled strings; her limbs moved and off she went).

"Will you be warm enough, Jean? There's a chill in the air."

Mrs. Macleod resolved not to answer. She would simply stand there and observe the rising of the sun. They can all go . . . chase themselves, she thought to herself, feeling a bit profane and a bit silly.

"Jean, what is it?" He was insistent, concerned, touching her arm again.

"Nothing, nothing. I fell asleep on my feet."

She was forced to answer. The hands pulled; the string

jerked; her mouth moved. It was grotesque. They would never leave her alone long enough to think to the end of things. People. People were always a mistake. It was much better to keep to oneself.

"Shall we get on with it?" She turned down the drive.

"Just let me find out where they keep the hound. He'd like a run." He disappeared around the corner of the house, crying, "Blue! Blue!" Moments later he returned, led by the dog straining at a leash.

"The poor fellow's been tied up all night under the porch." He released the dog and they strolled down the drive. The animal ran a frantic course ahead of them from tree to tree and then turned them onto a shortcut.

"There's where he's taking us." Walter pointed reassuringly to a small wooden footbridge which connected the promontory on which the house stood to the beach. Mrs. Macleod stumbled stoically toward it, thinking that the formality of Walter's hand on her arm was hardly sufficient support for a decrepit old woman on an overgrown path and a precarious bridge.

"You had better take your shoes off," said Walter, as they stepped from the bridge onto the sand.

"Yes, I had better take my shoes off," she echoed obediently.

Amused, touched, and a little ashamed of himself, he watched her bend over wearily, remove her shoes, and then trudge toward the edge of the sea. He had meant to be charming, to amuse her because he liked her, because among the guests they were the only ones unpaired. "An adventure," he had expected she would say about a black man in her bedroom and a walk on the beach at dawn. Instead he had needlessly and thoughtlessly disturbed her when she was tired. He had also kept her from her own company, which she no doubt preferred to that of a stranger. He had patronized her, he realized. Give the old pussy a surprise, he had thought to himself. Now he suddenly wanted her friendship and wondered what she was all about.

"Footprints on the sands of time," she mocked, laughing, as she stamped her feet into the wet sand.

She held her skirt up as she ventured a little way into the surf and stood, rather tentatively, rather fearfully, ankle-deep in ocean; the undertow warred with her foothold and she staggered to keep her balance.

He ran to join her. "Easy there," he cried, grabbing her arm as a large wave struck, circled their legs, and pulled them with it as it ebbed.

"The seventh wave is always a big one! How warm the water is. Much warmer than the air. Oh, it is lovely." She moved her arm away and grasped his hand.

I am becalmed, she thought, the weather has lifted. Her anger and annoyance were gone. She was wading in the sea, the sea was warm, and the sun was coming up.

"And there . . . what is that?" she asked, pointing ahead, pulling Walter along.

"That there is Gull Island, ma'am," he replied. "Beggin' your pardon, ma'am, but ol' Walter's gotta roll up his pants."

He stooped over and she steadied herself against the undertow by firmly gripping his shoulder.

"People hardly ever touch," he said, still stooping, looking up at her.

She knew he was right. People unrelated by blood or law touched one another infrequently. They shook hands and some mated outside the law—that was all. Nevertheless, there was no point in talking about it. That was what it was to be young: to insist upon pointless conversations.

"Do gulls really live on Gull Island?" she asked, changing the subject.

"They most certainly do. At low tide it is possible to wade out to the island and observe their haunt, or so Daniel told me, night before last." Walter pulled his almanac out of a back pocket and paged through it. "High tide at eighty-thirty this morning. No good. We can't wade out there now; much too deep."

"What time is it?" asked Mrs. Maclcod.

"Almost six. Look now, at the hound! Hey there, Blue, you'll drown!" he called.

The dog was giving chase to a gull, swimming out toward the island in pursuit of it. As he neared the small island the air was filled with a general exodus of gulls.

"If he got hold of one, would he devour it?" Jean asked, as she watched the disappointed dog paddle toward them.

"Not unless the bird were dead or dying. And if he did get hold of one, he'd carry it very tenderly to Daniel and expect a reward. He's a retriever—soft jaw."

Having routed the gulls, the dog returned to the shore proudly and presented himself for praise, shaking water all over Jean and Walter.

"There's a good dog and proud swimmer." Walter slapped the dog's flanks affectionately. "We had ol' Blue out for a long, fine walk yesterday—didn't we, boy? Dan and I and Sarum . . . Now there's a strange chap . . ."

"There! Now we have it," she interrupted, counting the chimes as they struck from town, "six o'clock."

"Yes, ma'am, Sarum lost his grip completely—didn't he,

boy? We forgave him, of course, what with his wife . . . he's finely drawn, to say the least."

"Walter, stop talking to the dog. It's ridiculous. Finely drawn, hah. You are all finely drawn. You are all using the girl's death as an excuse to indulge yourselves in morbidity —as an excuse for a lot of senseless talk, talk, talk."

"Wait a minute! This boy pleads not guilty. I knew nothing about it until yesterday; I never knew the woman. Like you, I'm on the outside looking in."

"Then let us not spoil a perfectly beautiful walk. The girl killed herself, and there's an end to it. It's none of our business—not anyone's business. All this self-flagellation after the fact is nonsense. Let us talk instead about the gulls. I was watching from the balcony last night when you recorded them. I was sure they did not fly at night. They haven't the eyes for it, do they? How on earth did you get them to come? Surely the food was not enough."

Walter was delighted that she had not seen the trawler. "It's the sorcerer's secret and cannot be divulged," he explained. "Let us sit upon the rocks and tell sad stories . . ."

"I shall happily sit, but no sad stories . . ." She allowed him to help her onto the rocks. "You change your voice every second sentence. It is most unnerving."

"I do it to startle and confuse my enemies. Unnerving, you say? I thought it made me seem enigmatic. Poor ol' Walter ain't got no style of his own."

They both looked out to sea and Walter thought aloud about Lela.

"So that's what's wrong with Lela. She's mixed up in it too. I thought I was imagining it yesterday—her nervousness. Poor girl."

"I take it Lela is one of those women you respect above all men and objects."

"Yes, even though she is almost as lazy as I am. Seriously though, Lela isn't morbid. I can't believe she's still mourning an old friend. It isn't like her."

"I'm only guessing," sighed Mrs. Macleod. "But it does seem to me that something is wrong. I suspect she feels responsible in some way. I suspect they all feel responsible, even Mr. and Mrs. Bennett, who are surely old enough to know better. They think—all of them with their dark looks and perpetually gloomy conversation—that it is guilt they are feeling, a noble emotion. It is not guilt. Hurt pride . . . that's what it is. Someone has gone and done something without consulting them. Someone has thumbed a nose at the lot of them . . ."

"Really, Mrs. Macleod . . ."

Again she changed the subject abruptly. "Why are there two?" she asked, pointing to an island in the distance upon which stood two lighthouses.

"I don't know why there are two; I do know, for Daniel, keeper of verities, told me, that they are called—not unnaturally—the twin lights."

"One concludes that these are dangerous waters."

"Not too dangerous to sail. We shall sail them this morning. You are coming with us, I hope. Such a fine day for it. 'The fair breeze blew, the white foam flew, the furrow followed free,' " he declaimed.

" 'We were the first that ever burst into that silent sea,' " she replied.

"That's the spirit, Jean! Heave her up and away we'll go!" he boomed, standing up and waving his arms. "The mainsail takes the wind, blossoming like white fire; now she leans. That's the way to trim her. Oh what a proud beauty she is. If we let her, she'd take us through the gates and into heaven itself, she would."

"Hush, you idiot, you'll wake the dead."

"I might at that." He grinned down at her. "Fill a boat with cans of food and set myself adrift. Away, away, away, letting the wind blow me. That's what I'd like. Do women ever feel like that?"

There was no answer. Mrs. Macleod gazed steadfastly in front of her. She felt the early morning sun begin to warm the side of her face. The rest of her was cold. There in the distance it had begun to snow again.

XXII

DANIEL LAY AWAKE in bed. That was the worst of these damn weekends—he never got a full night's sleep. It was a little after six. He had heard the clock chime moments before. High tide at eight thirty. They would sail soon after. He hoped that Claud and the boy would not go with them. Although the *Philemon* could carry ten comfortably, he preferred a smaller number and as few strangers as possible.

Propping himself on an elbow, he watched Lela sleep until she seemed to feel his eyes. Brushing a hand across her face defensively, she awoke.

"You ougntn't to stare at people when they're asleep; it isn't polite."

Laughing at her, he got out of bed and pushed open the balcony doors. "Beautiful! You had better come with me today; it's a perfect day for a sail. One of the last we'll have."

"I can't. I've promised to pose for Anne."

"Will she cube you? I like those cubist things."

"She's not so passé as that. Lately she's been turning people into masks. She showed me some sketches yesterday."

"Just see that she does you justice, masks or no."

"Breakfast for all those people . . . God," Lela groaned and turned over. Daniel strode out of the room, swinging a towel and whistling.

Down the hall, Beth identified the sounds of Daniel's shower. She had been awakened an hour before by Walter's aubade, and her mind had followed him with horror into Mrs. Macleod's room. No screams had been forthcoming, so she assumed all was well. Walter had gone downstairs. Mrs. Macleod had followed him later. Obviously all was well. Since then, she had lain in rigid quietude, so as not to wake Matthew. Now she would get up, for the Relds were up, and there were ten to feed. It was time to get started. She welcomed the day. There were only, at best, seventy-odd years of days, and yet she so rarely thought to welcome the day. Today she would greet it, embrace it, she resolved. This twenty-seventh day of August, this Saturday, she would mark with joy and love.

"Who is there?" Matthew was suddenly awake and unsure of where he was. Finally he recognized Beth, dressing at the foot of the bed. "What time is it?"

"Going on seven. Poor darling, you must be exhausted. Stay in bed for a while longer. I'll be out of your way in a minute."

"I want to go out sailing with Dan; you'll wake me in time, won't you?" he mumbled.

"Yes, Matt." She smoothed the sheet over him.

"Well, here we are again."

Walter held the door for Mrs. Macleod and picked up the morning newspaper. After a glance at the front page, he slammed the door behind him. Suddenly he was angry, violent. He pushed ahead of her into the kitchen and turned up the flame under the coffeepot.

"What is it?" she asked.

He threw the newspaper down on the table so that she could read the front page.

"Sunrise, moonset, seafoam, and murder less than an inch away. Life is never so simple, so poetic as we would like it to be, don't you agree, white lady?"

Mrs. Macleod brandished the newspaper in front of him, for his sudden rudeness made her also angry.

"Is your bitterness real or is this just more dramatics? Does this genuinely disturb you?"

Walter looked at her with disbelief. "Disturb me?" he shouted with incredulous rage.

"Oh yes, of course it disturbs you. It disturbs me, it disturbs us all. But does it really penetrate your life more than the usual three-column picture in the morning paper? What is it you feel? Is it anger, pity . . . do you feel with him?"

Mrs. Macleod pointed to the newspaper. She was intent upon his answer. He was black; it had just hit her with full force. What did he really feel about an outrage like this? Did he always feel a stranger? He seemed so much at ease that one soon took his ease for granted.

"What do you feel?" she asked again.

"White lady, I feel like the number one leader of the silent brass band—out there all alone with the whole world in back of me. I feel like a shadow walking around a balloon. The shadow doesn't know where he's been or where he's going or when he'll get there."

"I don't understand you," she confessed.

"That's all right." He was once again perfectly amiable. He poured her a cup of the reheated coffee. He had reminded himself that the old pussy was a good sort. She had just begun to wonder what it was like to be inside his skin. It was good of her, for she seemed to have some difficulty of her own. Now she was probably thinking that life was bad enough in its crude outlines without the refinement of color, for she was very good, very human, and, he felt, she really cared about him. There was no use trying to talk to her, though; she was a world away. "The elderly are self-involved." He had read that somewhere. So were they all. He'd go out for a sail and make a decision. West, east, or . . . south. He was already as far north as he cared to go. He'd go someplace, do something, before he bored himself to death. He'd do it tomorrow. Away. Away. Away.

Mrs. Macleod sipped her coffee in silence. Beth came into the kitchen, gave them good mornings, and consulted the newspaper.

"Sunny, warm. Seventy-five to eighty. Tonight cool, low in fifties. Tomorrow fair and warm," she read, ignoring the headlines. "We are in luck. Another fine day." She began to excavate pans and skillets from a cupboard.

"Beth, love, you are priceless and beyond compare!" Waving to Mrs. Macleod, Walter departed, calling, "I'm off to wake the dead."

"What are we supposed to make of that?" asked Beth. Mrs. Macleod pointed to the headlines and the picture below them:

Whites Ambush Negro Leader

"Alone and unarmed . . . three miles from the town of . . . beaten with chains . . ." Beth read in fragments and then scanned the rest of the front page. In the small country east of Cambodia a woman in white had set herself afire, and elephants were loose in Chicago. Nevertheless there was breakfast for ten to cook. Opening the refrigerator door, she closed her eyes, prayed, opened them, and counted the number of eggs. There were enough. She began to crack them into a large bowl.

Mrs. Macleod watched the eggs drop from their shells to the bowl. It was quite conceivable that she might live for twenty more years. An egg a morning for twenty years of mornings—three hundred sixty-five times twenty equaled seven thousand three hundred, she computed, reciting the total aloud.

"Of what?" asked Beth, whisking the eggs.

"Eggs," Mrs. Macleod replied shortly.

"Oh," said Beth, thinking that perhaps Mrs. Macleod had elected to devote her dotage to some obscure ornithological research. Perhaps she had been out hunting the egg of some rare species of gull so early in the morning. Walter had been hunting their calls; Mrs. Macleod, their eggs. They had the gull in common—so Beth assured herself, relieved that Walter's early morning call upon the old lady had been prompted by science and not by rudeness or any other more sinister motive.

"May I help?" Mrs. Macleod asked.

"No, not just at the moment, thank you anyway."

Mrs. Macleod gathered the newspaper under her arm, and prepared to leave.

"There is one thing . . . could you wake Lela? Dan's up, I know, but she sometimes sleeps on into the afternoon."

On the stairs, Mrs. Macleod again met Walter. He was squinting through a pane of stained glass.

"What on earth are you doing?"

"I thought the windows would be more opaque than they are. This one's surprisingly transparent. Look through here."

She looked. A blue tree rippled myopically.

"Extraordinary."

"Really, Jean, sweet little old ladies are not supposed to be sarcastic."

She continued up the stairs.

Walter crouched and squinted again. "Let's have a little auto-hypnosis now, you very number one Walter boy. Clear your mind and concentrate. Turn on a little of that racial memory and stir things up today. I bet it's very good for the digestion, Walter baby. Just concentrate." He squinted at a tree through blue glass.

"Nothing. Not a drum, not a chant, not a chain. Poor old Walter, you're just not gifted that way."

Suddenly, as he turned away from the window, he did see something. A deserted boxcar the color of dirty brick was perched on the limb of the tree for a moment. Then it disappeared.

"Oh man! That's what I call a vision!" Walter took the steps two at a time, laughing at himself. Years ago he had been angry with his father for some reason and taken revenge on the object nearest him, an electric train his father had given him. He had grabbed the caboose, run out of doors, and thrown it with all his strength. It had lodged among the leaves on a low hanging branch of a tree.

Still laughing at himself, he burst into the bedroom of Matthew and Beth. "Matt, can I have the car for a while?"

Matthew stirred petulantly under the sheets. "You can damn well have anything, if you'll just go away and let me sleep!"

"Keys?"

"Wherever Beth has left them. Try the top of the dresser."

"Right. I'm off." He rushed out of the room, slamming the door on Matthew's curses.

Mrs. Macleod had awakened Lela and left the newspaper with her. Lela heard Walter's commotion and wondered what he was up to, and how he was taking the headlines. He had always been scrupulous in his relations with them to avoid the subject of revolution. She knew that there was in his denial of the issue a certain condescension. He had, from time to time, been active in marches and demonstrations. She did not know what he felt about it all. From the balcony doors she watched him remove the tonneau cover from Matthew's Sunbeam and jump into the car without opening the door.

The road to the town was deserted and Walter opened the car up to eighty. He took a steep curve without braking and accelerated to eighty-five as he came out of it. A similar trick a mile and a half later was less successful. He skidded off the road, spun, and found himself facing in the direction from which he had come. Several yards away on a pile of rocks an elderly woman before an easel watched him in amazement. He waved gaily to her and roared back onto the road.

In the town, he collected the *Times* and the Boston papers and went into a diner to read them over a cup of coffee.

It was about what he expected. It had happened before; it would happen again. At least the fellow was still alive. He had known the man—not well, but well enough to know that he was not a Negro leader, no more than he himself was, for they had both been briefly committed and then quickly uncommitted to one of the civil rights organizations. The fine and opportune hand of the organization could already be seen in the newspaper account of the beating. The organization had a gift for the manipulation of press releases. Willingly or unwillingly, his friend had served the purpose, advanced the cause. There would be a march and the world would watch it. He would have to find out how the man felt about it all; that would be the first thing.

"More coffee?" the waitress asked. Walter shook his head, put a dime on the counter, and spun around on the stool. Next to him an aged derelict, conventionally blotched and rheumy, mumbled to himself a rosary of complaint as he fingered packets of sugar in a bowl.

"No, you cannot be away—old man, not you, not me, not any of us," Walter told him silently, and then laughed at himself for wanting to quote poetry to a drunk at a lunch counter.

It was twenty-two minutes past three according to the south face of the four-sided clock on top of the town hall. Walter walked a quarter of the way around the building, but time was also stayed on the west face. The north face announced seven thirty. The long hand jerked spastically, reluctantly, on to the next minute. Breakfast was at eight, he reminded himself. He was being deliberately careful about meals this visit, for they were central to Beth's life, her major concern, during weekends of guests.

Driving back to the house, he tried to remember the whole of the poem. It had something to do with alternatives. It was, he seemed to remember, a clear articulation of choices. It was a poem Matthew liked. He could not capture it and cursed all poems and gulls, all friends and old ladies.

He arrived twenty minutes later and found the company already assembled around the dining room table. They were all there except Mrs. Macleod and himself. Their empty chairs were gaps in the whole. The others were talking about the headlines and did not see him come in.

With his fork poised over his scrambled eggs, Richard remarked conversationally to Matthew, "I shall never understand your country. I simply never shall."

Matthew drained his juice and slammed the glass on the table. "It is not *my* country. I sometimes live here. I work here. I do not understand it either. Nor do I understand the things you people do in South Africa." As he spoke, he realized that his tone had startled Richard and that the man's remark had probably not been intentionally offensive.

"Sorry," he apologized. "I'm disrupted this morning; not quite here yet, if you know what I mean."

From the doorway, Walter contemplated them face to face. Claud's face said clearly, "Why don't they all shut up." Lela's said, "No one at home." She had removed herself completely and was unaware of Anne, who studied her profile carefully. Daniel presented only the back of his head. He was twisted around in his chair, trying to catch a glimpse of the direction of the ribbon flying from the mast of the *Philemon*. Beth was saying something about elephants.

Mrs. Macleod came up behind him and together they took their seats and were helped to cold eggs and toast by a disapproving Beth.

"And what are you going to do today?" Walter heartily inquired of Mark in order to avoid speaking to Beth.

Mark looked at his father, who said nothing, and then at Anne and Richard, who were not paying attention. He had no idea what he was going to do for the day. He had wanted to go for a sail on the boat, but he supposed, since they hadn't said he could go, they weren't taking him. They were not being fair; he was expected to answer a question, but he didn't have the answer, and no one was listening enough to help him. What would he do for the day? Something by himself, he decided. He could explore, or he could go fishing. Boys made fishing poles with a stick and a string. It sounded simple enough.

"Exploring or fishing," he announced, but Walter had already forgotten his question and was looking in another direction.

"Now, Master Colton, what would you do if there were elephants in your garden?" his uncle inquired.

Another impossible question. He had no garden, as Uncle Richard very well knew. Euzilpha and Carduff had a garden but not he. The elephants were in Chicago. Mrs. Stead had said so quite clearly.

"Tell them to keep out of the roses," he finally said. He knew that Uncle Richard was fond of roses.

"Well said, Mark," Anne whispered to him. "You may be excused."

He nodded to her gratefully, ran out onto the veranda, and scanned the long coast from left to right. It was necessary to decide which part of the world before him to explore.

Daniel watched the boy from the dining room window. He had wanted a peaceful and easy sail, but now it occurred to him that he really ought to ask the youngster to come along. True, he had disliked Rachel, had thought her hard. A tired phrase from detective fiction always reminded him of her: "she laughed grimly." True, Claud had always been exasperating and these late, hypocritical exhibitions of grief were contemptible. However, the boy was innocent and a day's outing could not possibly be construed (not even by Lela's maternal avidity) as a commitment to board and keep him.

"You and Mark are coming with us today, aren't you, Claud?" he asked.

"I might just stay here and nap. Not much sleep last night. It would be good of you to ask the boy. I'd appreciate it." Claud pressed his forefingers against his temples. His childish, high-pitched surliness was gone; he seemed old and vulnerable.

Daniel felt sudden sympathy. Guilt, nerves, and confusion were the destroyers; not time, events, and disease. Hardpressed, thin-drawn, high-strung: the man was not whole, he was hyphenated.

"I'd like him to come. His first sail, isn't it?"

Claud nodded.

"I'll ask him now." Daniel went after Mark, ignoring Lela's grateful smile.

Chairs scraped back. Beth and Lela cleared the table.

"The sickening droppings of a monstrous bird," said Lela, holding at arm's length a plate of leftover egg, crusts, and cigarette butts.

"Speaking of birds, is Mrs. Macleod some kind of ornithologist?" asked Beth.

"Good Lord no! Whatever gave you that idea?"

"Something she said. It's not important. I never know what anybody's saying, but I'm used to it."

"Oh Beth . . ." Lela watched Daniel and Mark from the window. They seemed to be speaking quite comfortably.

Actually the conversation was not proceeding according to Daniel's expectations. Mark's reply to his invitation had been polite but firm: "No, thank you, I have something else to do."

The boy stood apart from him at the edge of the veranda, looking out along the coast. Daniel pressed him: "We would very much like to have you. Your father isn't coming and I can use another hand."

"No, thank you," Mark insisted.

On his way to the kitchen, Daniel decided that it was Mark's phrasing which most disturbed and baffled him. He spoke like an adult, but one could not fairly accuse him of pretension. The child was uncanny; he had divined that the invitation was an afterthought, late and somewhat reluctant.

Beth and Lela were washing the dishes.

"You're coming, aren't you, Beth?" he asked.

"Just as soon as we clean up this mess."

"Get everybody down to the dock, will you? I'll bring her around in about a half hour." He kissed Lela on the cheek, adding, "Master Colton won't come."

On his way out he collided with Anne.

"Is Richard coming?"

"But of course. He wouldn't miss it for the world. If he is to be believed, his whole happiness consists of full sails and a fair wind. I haven't seen him this excited about anything in years. You be sure to look after him. Don't let him fall overboard in his enthusiasm."

Daniel reassured her with a pat on the arm.

Lela threw silverware into the drying basket. "We're almost finished," she said, smiling at Anne who wore a white foam plastic pith helmet and carried a small suitcase.

"Good. I want to get started while we still have a few hours of what passes for cool weather in America."

Beth stooped to read the thermometer outside the kitchen window. "I'm afraid there will be none of that today. The house is still cool, but outside it is already hot. Seventy-two degrees and not yet nine o'clock."

Anne took a towel and began to wipe the remaining forks. "It is an impossible climate. I don't know how any of you survive. I should have been dead of heart failure at the age of five."

"You've had New York for most of the summer. That can't

have been very pleasant. As a matter of fact, nowadays Dan and I can't bear it at any time of the year."

"Narrow-minded of you, Lela," Anne accused. "It's quite a fascinating place. None of the ease and sanity of London, to be sure, for there's no place to sit down. But unique, quite unique, and therefore worth one's time. However, it isn't a safe place, you know, and I shall be happy to leave." Anne flung the towel over the back of a chair. "There! Done!"

Beth absently rubbed the table with a sponge and read aloud from the newspaper:

"Sagittarius: a long drawn-out worry or doubt today can make you less sure to face challenges tomorrow; avoid self-indulgence."

"What am I to make of that?" she asked.

"But surely you don't . . ." Anne began.

"Of course she doesn't," Lela interrupted.

"I do so!" countered Beth. "I read it every day. I think it's fascinating. What's the harm? One doesn't have to believe it, after all. I just amuse myself. What month were you born, Anne?"

"March. The nineteenth. I do hope it's a long journey rather than a tall stranger. At my age one hasn't the stamina to cope with tall strangers."

Beth ran her finger down the column. "March: Pisces. Fortunately you have had sources of inspiration through this difficult year; seek this outlet today."

"Exactly what I intend to do." Anne patted the small suitcase of paints. "Come, Lela, let's get on with it."

"Just a minute. Let me read Lela's. April, isn't it?"

"Friday the thirteenth, I'm sorry to say," said Lela.

"Aries: sometimes vagueness has been a part of your contacts with friends or close ties; accented again today . . ."

"No shit, Sherlock Holmes."

"What did you say?" asked Anne.

"No matter. Continue Beth."

"Today keep alert to trends in alliances," Beth concluded. Anne was amused. "That has a sinister, international sound. I can just see Lela eavesdropping in the corridors of power."

"Not the trench coat type, am I?"

"Certainly not—which reminds me . . . I'd like you to wear something a bit different while you pose, something graceful. Have you got a tunic kind of thing?"

Lela leaned over the newspaper. "Vagueness of contacts and trends in alliance—yes, that's exactly what it is. There's nothing else. Daily politics. Crises on weekends. I really must get hold of the Lessings this morning."

"Now Lela, stop muttering, you haven't heard a word I've been saying!"

"Yes I have. I'm to look less awkward. A tunic. I've got a terry cloth bathing robe like that. White."

"That will be fine. I'll wait for you inside."

Anne parked the suitcase in the hall, sank into an armchair in the living room, and stared at the burnt log in the fireplace. She found it difficult to believe that it had been cold a scant eight hours ago. The house was still dark and pleasant, but soon they would go out. A moving wall of heat would assault them. Anne closed her eyes.

No sleep. All night listening to a pulse in the back of her head. Picture after picture flashing. Thoughts in circles, tighter and tighter. Arid with lack of sleep. The insides of her eyelids were raw. She slept.

Passing through the hall on their way upstairs, Matthew and Walter caught sight of her and lowered their voices.

Asleep she looked older and very tired. Nevertheless, Matthew could not keep himself from exclaiming aloud, "Handsome creature!"

"Tricky, also," Walter added. "There are those who might say that your taste for older women is symptomatic of a perverse palate."

"Nonsense. Ripeness is all."

"That fruit is bruised and rotting."

"Poignant, Walter, my boy, poignant. Poignancy is a delicacy to which I am gradually becoming addicted. Slow and quiet, sharpened with an edge of grief. I recommend older women highly."

"Unhealthy, that's what it is. Take my advice, do yourself and her a favor. Stay away from her."

"Unfortunately, I haven't any other choice. They leave tomorrow."

"Good!" Walter took the stairs two at a time.

XXIII

LELA DIALED the Woodwards' number. There was no answer. She knew that the Woodwards were late risers; nevertheless, she was concerned. It had not been right to foist the Lessings off as she had, and it was not like Gail not to get back to her. She was tempted to drive over and make sure that all was well; however, Anne wanted to get a sketch at least, before the sun became unbearable. She decided to wait an hour or two; she would try again then and if there was still no answer she would run over and dig Neil and Gail out.

She found Anne in the living room asleep, unconscious for all to look at, showing her age and not pulling her weight for the moment. She had humor and strength; people thought she was beautiful and said she was gifted; but, sleeping, she looked old. Lela was moved by her vulnerability.

"Come now, it is time to go," she said softly.

Anne groped awake.

"Will this do?" Lela indicated the short terry cloth shift she wore.

"Very charming."

"Am I to have my own proper head?" Lela teased.

"Don't you care for my masks?"

"It isn't that. It's just I'd rather not be reduced to one."

"But of course you really are one."

"Many, I suppose."

"I shall give your one body several heads. Will that please you?"

"No, no, no. Why don't you just make me beautiful? Appeal to my vanity—or would that compromise your artistic integrity?"

"Yes, somewhat," Anne replied candidly.

In the hall they met Beth coming from the kitchen bearing a picnic basket, and Matthew and Walter coming down the stairs. A general chorus of impatience brought Mrs. Macleod and Richard down to the hall, and they all walked out onto the veranda.

"Daniel's just going after the boat now!" Lela pointed to a rock below the house. Naked except for his undershorts, Daniel poised, dove into the sea, and swam toward the sloop.

"That's exactly the right rock," proclaimed Anne. "I want you to pose on it. This is where we part," she said to the others, propelling Lela with a hand on her shoulder.

Richard blew a kiss to his wife and joined the others heading down the drive.

"You had better let me give you a hand getting settled," Matthew insisted, taking the suitcase from Anne.

Looking back at Matthew sorrowfully, Beth allowed Richard to take the picnic basket and her arm.

While Lela descended to the rock cautiously, Matthew arranged Anne's portable easel and fingered the tubes and bottles in the suitcase. "It has always seemed to me to be far more physical than words—after all one gets one's hands dirty —and, as such, probably more satisfying."

Anne moved the easel, adjusting her view of Lela on the rock below, and finally replied, "It is, I think, more direct, but I may feel that because I cannot bear to write. Having to reply to an ordinary letter throws me into a slough of despond and causes paralysis of the thumb and forefinger. Ought I to tell you that I like your poems?"

"Only if you do. If you don't, a discreet silence is in order. Either way, you have the advantage of me, for I've not seen your pictures."

"There are none in the States. Oddly enough, I am preferred by the French. I expect a showing in New York sometime next year, however, and you must promise to go." She began opening tubes and arranging her palette. She did not think they had anything in common—poems and pictures, there it ended. She suspected him of being one of those young chaps who resent women who "play" with art, and, no doubt, he thought she played. Nevertheless, she reminded herself, he was trying to be nice.

"I like your poems about places but not the ones about women," she said.

"Most women agree with you. Most women seem to think that what I intend as erotic praise is really a form of misogyny. Surely you're not going to accuse me of that?"

"No, I shouldn't go that far," she replied, thinking to herself that he was pricked because her praise had not been full-throated enough. She placed a canvas on the easel.

"How do you begin?" he asked.

"With a color and this." She held up a flat-bladed knife, and applied Prussian blue directly to the white surface in thick bold strokes. "You travel a good deal, don't you," she remarked.

"As often as I can. Usually only in the summer."

"Yes. You write as you go. And in the winter you teach. Poets must teach, these days. As a rule, I neither travel nor teach, I paint. It is one of the advantages of being a woman

—one need not keep oneself or anyone else." She became absorbed in the movements of her hand and was silent.

"Look at Daniel!" Lela called up to them uncertainly, for she had been watching his white arms strike the ocean, thinking, as she always did, when he did anything slightly out of the safe and ordinary, that life would be impossible without him, that his absence was the one contingency she could not possibly survive.

Matthew waved to her, as if to appease her noise and prevent her further interruption. Standing behind Anne, he placed his forefingers on her temples and traced the outline of her face. She did not move away from him, but rather leaned back against him and laughed. "You can't be serious!"

"Oh quite serious," he said. "You are very lovely."

"How delightful. Nothing could please me more. Now, please do go away, child, and play with someone else." She did not move away from him, but waited for him to leave her. Finally he did, stepping back, laughing himself, "I'm a fool. Forgive a fool."

"There's nothing whatever to forgive, I've not been so flattered in years. Now, do go away."

Matthew waved farewell to Lela and turned down the drive. He caught sight of the others and ran toward them. Anne had reminded him of the woman in London. That ghost was now laid to rest, for he had made a delicious fool of himself with Anne. Yes, he had exorcised the London lady for good and all. He did not know if it was time, the world, or himself, but lately he had found that sex was his only communication. All the other muscles of contact seemed to have gone dead. Anne was right, he wrote as he went. He hadn't talked about his work for years. Travel, movement: walking, climbing, riding; they were essential. They (not people) released the monologue in him. Even now, as he ran along the beach toward the dock, he could feel it begin to spin out in his mind.

He had almost caught up with the others. He saw them standing there and realized that he hardly ever spoke to anyone. He had no idea at all what Walter was up to and only a vague notion of the theory Dan had been working on all summer. He knew Lela wrote—charming things—and he had tried to encourage her. That at least was on the credit side. But there, ahead, was Beth with the Oxonian. He had no idea in the world who or what she was. He pounded down the last few yards of sand between himself and the dock, accusing himself of living in a dream and admitting that he thoroughly enjoyed it.

Richard had managed to sustain what could pass for a conversation with Beth by sheer perseverance. He saw Matthew coming, and brought the encounter to what he hoped was a satisfactory conclusion, remarking pleasantly. "And so you have your music and your sons and don't mind the social burdens of academic life. I have heard from the Relds that the social rituals are not so severe in the States as they are at home."

"That may be true," Beth said, "though I'm not sure Lela is any expert on the social rituals."

Actually the "burdens" were damn severe, no matter what Lela said. The wife of the Dean never left her alone. What did the man mean, summing her up like that—music and sons, as though they were a pleasing but not particularly functional fresco on the architecture of life? Although, to be honest with herself, she had to admit that generally one did regard the substance of the life of someone else in just that way.

She had spent the last ten minutes with the Englishman, understanding only five words out of ten (the other five disappeared down his throat). She had muttered, nodded, stared at her feet, and performed all the other gestures which indicated assent and alleged comprehension. She was tired. She gratefully surrendered the responsibility to Matthew, as he pounded onto the dock, shaking the already weakened structure as he ran.

He put an arm about Beth's waist and said to Richard, "I've just been talking with your wife."

"Have you really? I thought you two were going to be sensible and ignore each other. Anne positively abhors conversation with anyone even remotely involved in the arts. I suspect you feel the same way," Richard replied. He was sure their meeting had been antagonistic and that Anne had had the best of the confrontation.

Matthew politely supported Richard's assumption. "Yes, you're quite right. I like to think of myself alone in the endeavor. The only one in the world even remotely concerned with something which matters. Anyone going about the same business is a blow to the ego."

"Yes, yes. Solitude is important." Richard spoke more to himself than to Matthew. "That is why I must get Anne back home among her lakes and mountains as soon as possible."

He too would be happy to return. Once Anne was safely deposited in Grasmere, he could have his occasional long weekend in London; he could involve himself with the fortunes of the newest generation up from university and needing encouragement. There, at least, he could be of some use. Year after year they came—the tall and beautiful young men, and, although he knew that they laughed at him and pitied him, still they came to him, and still he loved them.

Richard, Matthew, and Beth joined Walter and Jean Mac-

leod at the end of the dock. Beth shaded her eyes and looked
out to sea.

"No sign of a sail yet!"

Daniel was just boarding the boat. He hoisted himself over
the side and onto the deck, started the bilge pump, and found
a pair of trousers in the deckhouse. The *Philemon* was fitted
out neatly with bunks, stove, and a head; she was self-suf-
ficient, for Daniel had promised himself that they would take
a long trip on her someday—cut her adrift and let her take
her own way.

Moving smoothly, automatically, he unfurled the mainsail, loosened the mainsheet, and hoisted the sail.

He was happiest when his hands were busy and his mind
was free, but he spent most of his life with the principle in-
verted.

He pulled in the mainsheet, and released the mooring line.

The clock ticked on and on (he hoped one of them would
have a watch; he had left his behind)—on and on, and there
were so few moments like . . .

"Now!" he cried aloud.

Turning off the wind, the boat was under way; he had felt
her tug and then smooth herself out. Joyfully, he turned her
downwind.

The summer was over. He had finished his paper; all that
was needed was to plug in some numbers. He'd throw that
job to one of his graduate students as a computer exercise. It
did not amount to much, he knew. Extrapolations from a
minor method. He had enjoyed the mathematics of it, the
beauty of the game. He had handled it with elegance, but use-
fulness was another matter. He wasn't sure how functional it
would prove. What had been sheer pleasure in the doing must
now be given over, talked about, published, criticized, sur-

rendered to politics and gossip. He knew they talked about him—his colleagues—said he was getting older, wasting himself, said he was lazy, said he was rude, said he would stay where he was, said that was exactly what he deserved. Ironically, he had almost decided that he wanted exactly what they threatened: to stay where he was and weed the garden on weekends. Most men did their best work before they were forty. He hadn't much time left. On and on it ticked. More and more he felt he wanted simply to be left alone. He had his own world, a world of right relations.

He sailed past the dock and waved.

"Oh dear, he's going without us." Mrs. Macleod sounded somewhat relieved.

"No, he'll jibe soon and come around for us," Walter explained.

"Gaff-rigged," she remarked. "I haven't seen one in years."

"Don't let her beauty fool you; she's not fickle; she's a genial creature and as stable as a mountain," Matthew assured her.

The clock in the town chimed nine. Mrs. Macleod readjusted her watch.

Daniel jibed, sailed on the wind toward the dock, then headed directly into the wind. The *Philemon*—almost miraculously—came to rest alongside the dock.

"Nicely done!" Matthew saluted.

"It's a perfect southeaster. What a beautiful day."

XXIV

"LELA, DEAR, you really must stop fidgeting, or I shall have to give the whole thing up," Anne complained.

"Well frankly, I'm damned uncomfortable, and bored too. It's impossible to carry on a conversation with the waves banging around me like this. Can't you put me someplace else?"

"Oh, very well," sighed Anne, "come on up then."

Lela climbed up the rocks and Anne posed her again, turning her head to one side. "Look over there, in the direction of the sail."

Lela turned back and looked at Anne. "Are you all right?" she asked quietly.

"Quite. Look to yourself, young lady. I've survived almost a half-century of public and private wars and grown up to be a very hardy perennial. What a child you are, Lela."

"It's just that you look so tired."

"I am rather. I'm still not used to your weather and find it hard to sleep. Now please look—there." Anne turned Lela's face again.

Lela watched the sail. So far Daniel had hoisted only the main. She wished she had gone with him, for Anne perplexed her. Yesterday she had wanted talk and today she wanted to avoid it. Lela decided to scratch at the surface of the woman's reserve.

"What was it like during the war?" she asked.

"Why is it Americans are so morbidly curious about the war?"

"You yourself brought it up a minute ago."

"That was only a figure of speech. However, if you promise to sit still, I'll tell you a story about the war. Once upon a time . . ."

"Now, do be serious. Were you in London?"

"Partly there, partly in the country."

"Was it terrifying?"

"Yes, I suppose so . . . one forgets." Anne put down her brush and palette and looked off to sea. "The waiting was the worst of it. It was a relief when anything happened— raids, bombs. Invasion was what we most feared, of course. In the beginning it was dreadful. How will we carry on, everyone asked. But after a while it became routine, part of the pattern. If you wait long enough, everything does, even fear. It all seems a very long time ago. Twenty years and more. I was even younger than you are."

"It is strange," said Lela, "for us it is a generation and a continent away, and yet it's close. We've forever heard it talked about, seen it on film. I think we live with the feeling that sooner or later we'll have to pay the piper. Sometimes I wake up at night sure in my mind that this shelter is false; the walls will soon cave in. I suppose that is why we are, as you say, morbidly curious about the sound, the smell, the taste of it."

"Do you really dwell on it so?" Anne hoped to keep Lela on the subject, for there was something in her face that she wanted to capture.

"Perhaps not. You know the gospel: in the process of observing we always distort; in the process of talking about it, no doubt I exaggerate. Nothing's true for more than a minute at a time. I'm hopelessly inconsistent and I never know what I really feel or if I feel at all. Oh God, what a sticky conversation. Can't I move about a bit?"

"All right, but just briefly, please. I'm finally getting someplace."

Lela stood and stretched. Anne continued to paint. She had blocked in Lela's figure against the rocks, experimented with the colors of the sea, and then given up the background in order to concentrate upon a large likeness of Lela's face in the foreground, the contours of which bore a suspicious resemblance to a mask.

Lela prowled back and forth, tossed stones into the sea, and finally settled on a rim of rock, dangling her feet in the air.

"If you're comfortable there, you needn't move. Just turn your face slightly to your left. I want something between a full face and a profile."

Lela did as she was asked.

"Tell me more about the gospel according to Daniel," Anne urged, for she hoped to preserve Lela's mood and face for another five minutes.

"It isn't really Daniel's gospel."

"Yes, I know. The gospel according to Heisenberg and company. What do you think it all means?" Anne was elated, for it looked as though Lela's face might hold in its present guise long enough for her to get it onto the canvas.

"The only fact of life is that there are no facts," recited Lela.

"Is that a principle for living or a lesson learned by rote?" Anne asked dryly. She regretted her tone immediately, for Lela's face began to change.

Lela answered her question with equal irony:

"Half principle, half lesson . . . as time goes on, more of the former and less of the latter."

Anne attempted to resurrect the mood and face: "I don't quite understand your feeling about the war. Talk about it some more, won't you?"

All the warning signals and storm flags were up; Anne's sarcasm threatened the safety of small craft. Lela spoke, protecting herself with flippancy:

"All this . . ." she swept her hand across the immediate horizon, from the boat on the right to the house on the left, "does rather read like the proverbial last garden party of the year. Surely you have noticed."

"That's overly melodramatic, isn't it?" Anne gave up the painting for the unity and intensity of Lela's face was gone; it was as usual, ordinary and unbeautiful. The angles did not meet; the forms did not cohere. What had interested her from the beginning, from their first meeting, was gone.

"There's no point in talking to you, if you're not going to listen." Lela's face paused between curiosity and hostility like a kaleidoscope between designs.

"Don't be ridiculous. You are such a child. I just happen to be more interested in your face than your voice at the moment, and I find it difficult to attend equally to both." Anne removed the mask with the edge of her palette knife. "It hasn't worked out anyway."

The *Philemon* was before them on the horizon, decorous and stately, under one sail. Lela focused on the downward curve of the bowsprit with momentary despair; upon the instant she was feeling exactly what Anne refused to believe in: to rise in the morning was dangerous, to part for even a day, an unnecessary hazard. She knew Anne was right, however;

it was pretentious to generalize her own personal mania. (She was afraid of life because, as Anne said, she was a child.) It was, after all, necessary to draw a line between a solipsistic complaint and historical necessity. The occasional tightening in the back of her throat was not the malaise of a generation.

She impulsively apologized. "I'm sorry, Anne; you're right. I'm being childish. I've had such a feeling of loose and tattered ends this weekend, I talk a lot of nonsense."

Anne smiled and waved her over. "Come here. It's my fault. I'm not used to working with a model. I'm very rude and untalkative while I work, particularly when it doesn't go smoothly."

Lela joined her behind the easel and surveyed the canvas. There was a mass of color—the sea, a crude outline of the rocks and Lela's figure. Lela's face in the foreground was almost obliterated.

"What a stick you're making me," Lela complained. "And that—what is that supposed to be?" She pointed to the scraped area of the canvas; the mask outline was still faintly apparent.

"Oh, Anne, you *have* been reducing me to a mask!"

"Dear child, it isn't reduction at all; it's a form of transformation. It has nothing to do with you." Anne ran her hand along the line of Lela's chin. "That interests me; it is simple and impersonal."

"Yes, I know. I don't really mind how you do me. Shall I go back and sit down? I promise to be quiet."

"No, not now. Why don't you take me for a walk along the ocean? If I see something that interests me, I'll settle down to it again." Anne began to replace things in the suitcase.

"There is nothing I would like better than a walk. But I must call the Lessings first. They seem to have dropped off the edges of the earth."

Anne paused in the midst of cleaning a brush. "Why are you so worried about them? They looked like the most dreadful people. I should think you'd be relieved to be rid of them."

"I am in a way, but I feel responsible. I've always felt . . . oh, let's not get into it. I'll just call them. It will only take a minute."

"Lela, what's the matter with you?" Anne asked with exasperation.

"Nothing is the matter with me; you're the one who needs explaining. Yesterday you insisted that I tell you all I know about Rachel; today you want to cover the whole subject over with a layer of paint. Well, that's perfectly all right with me. I'd prefer not to scratch the scab. I'd just like to know where we're at, that's all, what exactly it is you want of me . . ." Suddenly and unaccountably she was close to tears and could not continue. She turned toward the house.

"Now Lela, wait . . ." cried Anne, grabbing her arm. "Sit down here. You're quite right, I haven't been very consistent. And, of course, arriving with Claud and Mark, particularly with Claud in the state he's in, is rather like spreading a communicable disease. No wonder you're upset."

Lela regained control. "Yesterday, when you asked about Rachel, the Novocain began to wear off. I began to think about her. I hadn't really . . . not in years . . ."

This must stop; I cannot breathe, thought Anne. Whorled shapes of shells on the floor of the sea, the Himalayas, a sword swallower—she could spend forever writing in a large notebook the things she had not seen, the things she had missed. Anne Bennett's Book of the Undone. And why? For reasons usual and universal: the brevity of life and the wasting of time, the weakness of the body and the complacency of the spirit, the cost of travel. Traveling backward in time faster than the speed of light, could I catch up? she wondered. Instead she must stand on a rock by the sea (her husband was sailing on the edge of that sea, she reminded herself). Instead she must try to explain herself to a stranger in a white tunic. Lord have mercy on us, she thought, smiling the smile she had learned by heart, the false face of intimacy.

"I am not so mysterious as I seem," she said. "It's simply that Richard came to the point of decision last night. We are going home directly. There's nothing more we can do for Claud. In fact, he's made it quite clear that he would like us to leave. He thinks we meddle. Perhaps we do. At any rate, what with that and having had no sleep, I decided to let sleeping ghosts lie. Cowardly of me."

"Not cowardly, but sensible. I agree. It's best forgotten. There is no earthly point in dwelling on it."

"Is the *Philemon* fast?" asked Anne, indicating the sail on the horizon.

"She usually does about six knots. Dan maintains she'll easily do eight. I can't imagine why he hasn't hoisted the jib."

"How far will they go?"

"Perhaps to the town and back, or further, if the weather holds. I'll go call the Woodwards and ask them about my prodigal guests."

"Give a shout for Mark while you're about it, please. I've no idea where he's got to."

Lela made her way over the rocks and back to the house, resolving to shake off all temperament and nonsense. She swung open the screen door and walked down the hall, crying, "Mark. Mark!" Her voice and the floorboards echoed. The house loomed around her, large, hollow, cool. There was a scuffling noise on the second floor. The hound plunged down the stairs and slid to a halt at her feet, wagging expectantly. "Not you, old boy," she murmured. Someone else was in the house. She was sure. She could feel it.

"Mark! Anyone?" There was no reply. She dialed the Woodwards' number. There too, there was no answer.

Upstairs in his room, Claud lay upon the bed, praying that Lela would leave without disturbing him.

XXV

SETH WOODWARD LAY FLAT on his back on the living room floor, inhaling a cigarette with deep pleasure. Slowly he raised one leg in the air and admired it, flexing the calf muscle. The phone was ringing.

Gail Lessing was stretched upon the couch face down; one hand brushed the floor. The ringing grew louder and louder and finally exploded in her head: she was awake. The walls of her skull were thin, fragile, and the pain inside was pushing to get out. "I am a bruise," she muttered, opening her eyes, and there on the floor with one leg in the air was the instrument responsible. Seth tossed his cigarette into a half-filled cocktail glass. It hissed out and floated on the surface. Raising his other leg, he lifted his buttocks onto his hands.

"Prevents piles," he explained, seeing that she was awake.

Gail was under some kind of thick covering. Sweat rolled down her neck and between her breasts. The air was bitter with smoke. The phone was ringing. The thirst in her mouth and throat was no doubt what men lost in the desert felt. Her senses were working, but not her memory.

"Jesus Christ, Seth, you deaf bastard, the phone is ringing!" Sonja shouted from the bedroom.

Seth pumped his legs in the air. "Well then, my pet, why don't you answer it?"

"To hell with it," Sonja decided. Her naked body was involved in a sheet. She unwound herself with difficulty.

"God what a stench!" she said.

There, crumpled in the corner, was the mattress pad and bottom sheet, spotted with lumps of Neil's vomit. He lay on his side, next to her on the bare mattress. He had placed one hand between his legs defensively and with the other he clutched the pillow.

Sonja looked at him penitentially. He was pathetic enough, and she had been at him like some kind of animal, not that it had done her any good.

She smoothed out the sheet and covered him. "No damn good at all," she whispered.

Taking a deep breath and holding it, she picked up the pile of sheet and pad and carried it, arms' length in front of her, into the bathroom, dumped it into the bathtub, and resolved to burn it all with the trash. In front of the full-length mirror, she paused.

"The face of a horse and the body of a she-goat," she told her reflection, slapping the loose flesh along her thighs. She had tried to stay as thin as she could, as thin as was humanly possible at the age of forty-three, but still, there were distended layers of flesh hanging about her thighs and hips, practically dragging on the floor.

"You are disgusting!" she announced to the mirror, closing her eyes. Grabbing her bathrobe from the hook on the door, she fumbled into it and did not open her eyes until she was covered. As she brushed her teeth, she tried to avoid the mirror above the bowl. Finally she faced it straight on.

"Mirror, mirror, on the wall, who's the ugliest hag of all? You, you old witch of a bitch!"

The remainder of yesterday's makeup caked the lines of

her face. Her lips were dry and cracked. She had spent too
much time in the sun, she decided, and it had made matters
worse, more coarse-grained than usual.

"Skin of a horse, face of a horse, hair of a horse."

She took the brush from the top of the toilet tank; its
bristles were stained with black. The color was coming out.
The last job had cost twenty-five bucks and that little
French pansy had promised her it would last. She brushed
her hair. It was coming out, all right; the roots were already
showing gray. She'd look like a zebra within a week. A bath
was what she needed, a long hot bath. It would fix her up as
good as new, or at least as good as slightly used, but a glance
at the contents of the bathtub quickly discouraged her.

She filled the washbowl with warm water, loosened her
robe, and began to sponge her body with a damp cloth. Suddenly a flash of heat rose and slapped down within her,
knocking her breathless. She sank to her knees and braced
herself against the edge of the tub. It had come again. A thick
stream of blood poured down the inside of her leg and
stained the floor. The worst of it was that she never knew
when it was coming—three months, two weeks, a year—and
for the first day she could not control it.

She had last had her period six or seven months ago. It had
come in the supermarket with half of Scarsdale standing in a
line in back of her. She had bent over to empty out the cart of
food and blood had poured out of her like the first gush of an
oil well. Remembering the look on the checker's face, Sonja
shuddered.

First she was hot and then she was cold and then the pain
started opening and closing its claws in her gut. There was
no damn point to it; she'd already had her brats, she'd done
that much for the world. Seth was probably right. He said

get it over with; have the whole business out. It was an easy operation these days. She'd just been reading about it. They didn't cut you to pieces anymore; you were up and out in next to no time.

She dragged herself up and fumbled in the linen closet, hoping there were some napkins.

It seemed to Sonja that she had come from that awkward hulk of a girl in the maroon uniform of St. Mary's (she could see herself clearly—she was only eleven—crying in the girls' toilet because she was bleeding and didn't know why); she had come through all the cycles of the body to this hard and hungry middle age and it made no sense at all.

Seeing that the bedroom door was open, Gail Lessing went in to find Neil. He was on the bed, dead asleep, and he looked pathetic, like a child. His clothes lay on the floor by the bed. The smell in the room was nauseating. He had been there all night, but all she could feel was that it was funny, extremely funny. Gail began to laugh.

Looking down at Neil, she thought of their son, Michael. When Michael came, they had not even been married a year, but it wasn't her fault, not even Neil, for all his unfairness, could blame her for Michael. She hadn't wanted to, not on that particular night: they were sleeping in a strange room and it was hot. Neil had insisted and would not let her take care of herself. Afterward he had been angry, had accused her—she never responded, he said; she didn't really like it, she was cold, she only pretended, she had tricked him into marrying her. Then he made some ugly crack about her father, the butcher.

Lela. Gail felt the old envy. Lela had no children; Lela was perfectly free to do what she liked. Lela hadn't even asked after Michael. People without children never realized

how one's whole life . . . She had wanted to talk to Lela,
but what was the point; Lela would never understand, could
not be expected to understand.

Michael. She hoped his heat rash hadn't got any worse.
Neil had hated the idea of leaving him with her parents. The
apartment smelled, he said. He had commanded her parents
to speak English to his son. They had agreed, humbly, ob
sequiously. Their son-in-law, the scientist. It made her flesh
crawl. She would call Mama today and find out about the
rash. Her head felt as though it were about to blow open
She couldn't remember what had happened; she decided not
to try.

Neil was sitting up in bed, rubbing his eyes, shaking hi
head. He looked at Gail coldly, cautiously.

"I think I'll call Mama this morning," she said.

"It's about time you gave Mike a thought," he growled.

In a second she had a thousand answers. He was sitting in
that woman's bed, after all. But of course he thought she had
put him there. She left the room without replying.

Neil sat in bed thinking of his son. It wasn't Michael'
fault. Sometimes he had to remind himself of the fact. De
spite the tedium of conjugal familiarity, sex in a motel room
had seemed, at the time, pleasant. However, it was not th
kind of event which should yield issue. Because of tha
chance event (ten seconds at most) in the middle of summe
(it must have been just about the hottest day of that year)
in a room about fifty feet from U.S. 1 (diesel trucks shoo
the bed), because of that unnecessary and idiotic moment
his degree had been delayed five years (they could not affor
both baby and tuition). He was just now getting started an
it wasn't really the way he wanted it. He was starting in in

dustry, but he wanted pure research. They only gave him a day a week for research and then he had to work with a team in order to get near the equipment he needed.

Headache or not (and it was a beauty), he was going to get out of the rabbit hole. He put his feet on the floor and tentatively raised himself, testing his equilibrium. He stood, and suddenly gravity wasn't working anymore; he was spinning off, off, off and away to the tune of a high-pitched scream in the most secret chamber of his brain.

Down he went, taking a bedside table with him.

"What was that?" cried Sonja from the kitchen.

Gail froze in the living room as Seth streaked past her.

"Well, well, well, buddy boy has had a little fall." Seth picked Neil up without strain and put him back on the bed. "Not all the king's horses or all the king's men can put egghead back together again."

Gail rushed to the bed. "Is he hurt?"

"Don't worry. He was too flaccid when he hit even to bruise. Let him sleep it off. You know, if he can't play with the big people, you shouldn't make him try."

Gail ignored Seth. In the living room she sank gratefully onto the avocado sofa and stared with concentration at Campbell's soup.

Seth joined his wife in the kitchen. Sonja dropped two tablets in a glass of water and watched them dissolve. "Never again!" she stated emphatically.

"My pet, that's what you say every weekend." He spooned coffee into the percolator. "Have fun?" he asked lewdly.

"Oh leave me alone, can't you. I want to stop. I want to stop all of this." She drained the glass and, bending over the sink with her arms hugging her stomach, she began to sob.

Seth stared at her in disbelief. "That can only mean on
thing. You've gone and got it again. Good Christ, I though
you were done with that for good."

"You shut up, just shut the hell up!" Her voice rose to hy
teria, then fell to a plea. "I'm sick. I know I'm sick, and yo
don't help me, you don't help me at all. Why don't you hel
me?" She slid to the floor and rested against the cupboar
below the sink.

"Stop it! You stop it this minute or, so help me, I'll soc
you one to straighten you out. Cramps and a hangover, that'
how sick you are!"

"Tommy," she moaned, "I want to see Tommy, I want t
see my boy."

"Oh God, if you could hear yourself." He put his hand
underneath her arms and dragged her to her feet. "Tommy'
a thousand miles away, as you damn well know, and you'r
going to stop this or I'm going to belt you. If there's on
thing I can't stand, it's a sloppy female."

"He's always a thousand miles away. He hates us. Th
others are all right; but Tommy hates us. You know it's tru
Seth. The oldest, the first, and he hates us. It's unna
ural . . ." she gasped for breath.

"Either make breakfast or go back to bed." His voice wa
quiet with threat.

He knew she was right in a way. Tommy was different, u
natural, but it wasn't anything so positive as hatred . .
he could have understood hatred, he had hated his own pa
ents. Tom was indifferent, he ignored them, and that Set
did not understand. Tom took money when it was offere
but never asked for it if it wasn't. The giving and receivin
and the not giving and not receiving were equally insignifican

to him. The severing of connection between father and son, the . . . estrangement . . . was something that ought to cut deep. But did he, in truth, feel it deeply, Seth asked himself; did it hurt him, or did he just pay it a kind of lip service on the surface of his mind? Perhaps he was just as indifferent as Tom, but more given to making conventional noises to the contrary. What did it really matter; what did anything or anyone really matter?

The humanitarian, he sneered, for Thomas Woodward was a thousand miles away teaching hillbillies how to write. Last year it was the niggers in Mississippi (the boy had practically got his skull split in two—thirty-two stitches); this year it was the illiterate in Tennessee. Cause-hopping, Seth called it. The boy was gutless; it was all a sop for his own weakness. He couldn't face the world the way it was.

The coffee began to boil. Seth turned down the flame. Sonja was finally under control.

"Go inside and sit down," he said. "I'll make some toast."

Sonja blew her nose, splashed water on her face, and joined Gail in the living room.

"I'll just bet that was Lela on the phone, wondering what has happened to you," she said, testing her voice and finding it less hoarse than she expected. "It's just as well we didn't answer it; you might have found her questions difficult to answer first thing in the morning," she added, dryly.

"I think I must have been hysterical." Gail rubbed her palm across her forehead.

"Poor old Seth," laughed Sonja, "he really has had more than his share." She slid open the glass door, stepped out, and laughed into the morning sun, thinking how pathetic Seth was with his twitches, his abortive attempts at what he supposed to be sin. He hadn't the excuse of compulsion or obsession; he was simply infantile. They were poor creatures, poor creatures all.

And there she was, a girl again, in front of the ancient Sister, whose face said so plainly: poor creatures, poor creatures all . . . and the bells were ringing . . . one, two, three . . . so clearly she heard them.

They were the bells from the town clock. What an ass she was. The girl was sitting there staring at her. Sonja turned back into the house.

From the road Mark could see the angled roof and the stone steps leading down to the house of Woodward.

"Eight, nine, ten," he counted aloud, sitting down on a large stone at the edge of the road. He drew a handkerchief and a watch from his pocket. His father's watch was accurate, he noted; he had borrowed it an hour ago and told his father that he was going to take a walk. His father was glad to be rid of him he knew, for he was tired and wanted to sleep.

If he had a pedometer he could tell how far he walked; as it was, he could only tell how long. He had seen a pedometer once in a store. It had numbers up to twenty, which was a very long way to walk. He peered down the steps at the house of Woodward. It was the strangest house he had ever seen. It seemed to be stuck right into the rocks, but that was impossible. He decided not to explore the house, but rather to go on down the road. He hoped he could walk all the way to the town. The road stretched before him as far as he could see. When he looked out across the ocean, he could see Daniel's boat. It had been moving with him ever since he left the house. It was probably cooler on the boat. Mark scrubbed his face with his handkerchief, stood, and dusted off the seat of his pants.

From the front bedroom window of the house across the road, Mark was a small figure, frail but resolute, trudging down the road. Ida Hobbes wished she had been in her front yard and called the lad to her. He was probably staying with the new people down the road. She had seen strange cars turn down their road yesterday. Decent young people, they seemed. Very polite; not loud, not like those others. Ida looked at the angled roof across the road and curled her thin lips. They had been at it again last night. Up to all hours with music loud enough to be heard across the Atlantic. Things were changing.

She sighed and smoothed the skirt of her faded cotton dress. She would soon have to discard it, for it was beyond mending; but how she loved the print: a gentleman in top hat and a lady in a bonnet by a fence, etched in blue. It made her feel delicate, ladylike, even though she knew she was a shapeless, serviceable sort of woman really. Poised at the window, she looked out over the ocean. The young people were out for a sail. She wished them well, for since they had moved into the old place, she had felt they belonged to her in a way. She supposed they would leave at the end of the summer, board up the house and move inland; nearly everyone did. Winter would come in the usual way, with no one to see and nothing to look at but the weathered gray boards nailed to the windows of most of the houses along the road. Regretfully, Ida Hobbes watched the bowsprit of the *Philemon* inch across the horizon.

XXVI

DANIEL MANNED THE HELM. The others sat on cushions on either side of him. Mrs. Macleod was uncomfortable. Richard slept; his chin rested on his chest, his head nodded with the motion of the boat. Clad in bathing trunks, Walter was stretched on top of the deckhouse.

"Then you are not interested in truth," Beth concluded triumphantly. She had taken advantage of Daniel's captive position to start an argument with him.

"Only insofar as it suits my purposes," he confessed, wincing, for he found her adolescence embarrassing.

Mrs. Macleod grunted and shifted her weight. Here she was with scarcely the room necessary to draw a proper breath, sitting on a cushion which was much too small, listening to a lot of nonsense about truth. She interrupted them with annoyance: "It is a foolish matter of semantics!"

"You don't mind if I persist in my foolish notion that there is something to truth—a meaning to the word, I mean," Beth went on.

Daniel shrugged his shoulders. "Why should I?"

Denied an argument, Beth felt helpless, ridiculous, angry. Daniel did not think her sufficiently intelligent to talk about anything more serious than nursery rhymes. He had made that clear all summer. With a deep intake of breath she began again: "I don't wish to affront the dignity of your beliefs . . ."

"Oh, cut it, Beth!" Matthew commanded. He could not bear her occasional pomposity, a way of phrasing she had—as though she were addressing the combined faculties of Harvard, Princeton, and Yale. She hadn't the mind to go with the voice.

"Time for the jib and stays'l!" called Walter, easing himself off the roof. "All right, Dan?"

"Yes."

Matthew jumped to his feet and took the wheel from Daniel.

Richard was roused from sleep. "What now?" he asked.

"Walter and I are going to hoist some more sail and make some speed," Daniel explained.

Mrs. Macleod smiled indulgently at Richard. "Had a nap, have you? Very sensible." Her smile said clearly, we are of an age, you and I, we have that in common.

I suppose we do, Richard thought, although he found it difficult to relate himself to the age of an elderly lady with white hair and an absentminded hum (for Mrs. Macleod did hum, and quite without knowing it, a gentle intermittent coo, like that of the mourning dove). He was only fifty-three; she looked five years older, at least.

Anne was only forty. The thirteen years between them had seemed an immense difference when they were first married, but now he hardly ever thought of it. People had warned them that they were making a grave mistake, that they would mind it more as they grew older. It had been quite the other way around; they minded it less. There on the forward deck were the young bodies of Walter and Daniel, bending and stretching. They shouted nautical phrases to one another.

"They are nearly half my age," Richard muttered to Mrs. Macleod, who leaned sideways to catch his meaning. "Half my age," he repeated, lighting his pipe.

"You certainly don't look it," she said. "It's all in the mind, as they say."

"Yes, it's true, all in the mind. I always think of myself as twenty-five with all the world before me. What a fool . . ." Richard chuckled. He inhaled deeply. "All in the mind."

Mrs. Macleod asked herself if the thing they were saying, this automatic response, this cliché (used simply for the purpose of easing the contact of strangers, a preventive ointment of platitude to avoid the abrasions of conversation) were really true. In *her* mind were snow and a bird of prey, and she did not know what it meant.

"Hand over hand and sway," called Walter, hoisting a sail.

"There they go. They're drawing. Beautiful," murmured Matthew.

"Oh dear!" Mrs. Macleod clutched at Richard as the sloop sped forward.

"Easy on," laughed Richard.

Matthew watched her with concern. "Everything all right?"

She settled herself on the cushion again. "Some of your movable ballast moved. Keep your mind on your work, please; my seeming floatability is deceptive. I am a very poor swimmer and would most certainly panic if we capsized."

"Ay, ay!" Matthew saluted her.

"Full and by!" Walter and Daniel jumped back into the cockpit, and again Mrs. Macleod lurched off her cushion and had to resettle herself.

"And now, Daniel, my friend," Richard began, when they

were all seated, "I want you to tell me something about anti-matter."

"I should think you've had enough of all that after last night. He had me going for more than two hours," Daniel explained for the benefit of the others.

"I'm quite serious. I won't be put off. I've got a captive expert and I intend to make full use of him."

"Anti-matter," Matthew repeated, "it strikes a bell. Come on, Dan, give."

"What do you want to know about it?"

"Begin at the beginning. Does it really exist?" asked Richard. "Or is it just something you people have invented to make the universe come out even, equal in all cases, and without exception, to the absolute value of zero—all simple and tidy."

"As I've been trying to convince you, 'we people' do not invent," Daniel protested.

"Does it exist?" Richard repeated.

"Of course it exists."

"I'm still not sure what it is you're talking about," Matthew complained.

"Richard's the man of words. Let him explain. I'm curious to see how much you dabblers pick up. Discourse . . ."

"All right, I'll try. We'll title it 'Misapprehensions of an Amateur' and depend upon Daniel for corrections and addenda."

"Over my head already," said Walter, returning to the roof of the deckhouse.

Richard cleared his throat significantly . . . "Presumably there is something called a positron, a particle with the mass of an electron but possessing a positive charge. It's very short-lived, and when an electron and positron collide, conjugate, combine, meet—whatever you people call it—matter disappears and energy results. How am I doing, Professor Reld?"

"Very well. I might go so far as to say that I am impressed. The man of letters in the modern world is surely an amazing beast. Where did you pick all that up?"

"Do you know, I'm not really sure . . . an article on quasars, I think."

"Quasi-stellar, isn't that it?" Mrs. Macleod asked.

Daniel smiled. The old lady was a constant surprise. She went all over the world alone and knew something about quasars. He wondered why she traveled and where she got the money. Her husband had been a minister, he seemed to recall. Dead a long time. No doubt she believed that quasars were a manifestation of the deity.

"But what are they?" Beth was asking.

"Energy. Light. Traveling away from us at a tremendous rate, perhaps. At the edge of the universe we measure." Daniel watched the ambling of a low cloud above the mast. It was cumulus, but it might mean rain. They had better not go too far, halfway around the cape at most, then back.

"How long ago, Daniel?" Mrs. Macleod asked. "I once knew but now I've forgotten."

"I'm sorry, I've not been following . . ."

"The age of the universe. It's slipped my mind."

"I don't remember either. Ten or fifteen billion years, I would guess."

Matthew watched Beth. She was thinking about the new baby, he was sure of it. He was sure of very little else about her; for all their living and sleeping together, she was a stranger. The habit she had of holding herself off until he came

—why did she do it? He gave her pleasure he knew, but still, she held herself off until he was done. She liked to see him helpless, beyond control—that was his guess—she found it exciting to be conscious when he was not.

Mrs. Macleod sighed and hummed. The warm sun grew cold. The lazy, harmless clouds darkened. The bare bones of trees groped the air uneasily. The windowpane no longer separated her. The hawk circled. The winter wind pushed down into her lungs. She could not breathe.

With a finger to his lips, Daniel cautioned the others. Mrs. Macleod was asleep.

XXVII

"I'm afraid it's a case of hawks and doves," Lela explained to Anne. "The Lessings are victims born; at least, I've always felt that about Gail . . ."

"She is much plumper than the average dove, Lela."

"True . . . well, the Woodwards are the Woodwards. One can't help suspecting them of cannibalism or worse atrocities."

"Really? How fascinating. I should like to meet them."

"No. They are not an appropriate spectacle for tourists from abroad."

"Ah, I see, they are the essence of America, the real and true grass roots."

"Certainly not! What a thing to say."

They reached the path which led to the bridge and the beach. The dog ran impatiently ahead. Lela took Anne's paint case and grabbed hold of her wrist, moving ahead along the path. Anne winced as branches of bushes whipped and scratched her bare legs and arms. She achieved the bridge and stopped to investigate the long red welts streaking her skin.

Lela circled her wrist with her thumb and forefinger. "How thin you are."

"I weigh nine and a half stone which is more than you."

"But you're taller. Come, let's go down to the water and rub salt into your wounds."

Anne followed her dutifully across the beach and accepted a sea-dampened handkerchief. She dabbed at her scratched legs.

"I am sorry, Anne. We should have taken the long way."

"Nonsense. At home I scale mountains and traverse forests."

"I don't believe you."

"But I do, really I do. There is no reason in the world to treat me like a Victorian gentlewoman who swoons."

They walked along the beach, ankle-deep in the sea. In the heat of the sun with the sea brushing her legs and all other things suspended, Anne decided that she was really quite fond of Lela; they got on together. She did not indulge herself for long. Silence allowed the illusion of contact. Directly they began to speak—and they would, for one always felt it necessary to speak—they would be once again a young woman and a middle-aged woman, who had been formally introduced by a chance event and were making the best of it along the edge of the Atlantic Ocean. The least she could do was try to amuse Lela, for the poor child would have fifteen or twenty more years of the horror of human contact to live through than she herself.

Anne reached back into her catalogue of human character and came up with Laurence Denholm, the pathos of whom had proved useful on many similar occasions. Americans seemed particularly amused by him.

"You're quite right about there being such creatures as victims born," she said. "In some people it is a congenital defect. One of Richard's ancient friends, a school fellow from Oxford, dear Larry Denholm, lost all his hair before he was twenty and is always the shortest person in the room. But those are the very least of his difficulties. For poor, dear

Larry, the paradoxical conflict between human free will and divine predestination is a daily reality. For example, if he comes to stay in one's spare bedroom, there is always a tack on the floor. Sweep and scrub as one may, a tack will remain, and it is preordained that Larry's unshod chubby foot will step upon the tack. There is Larry, holding his chubby foot in his chubby hands. What does he do next? What the ingenuity and will of any ordinary person would indicate: he seeks the tack. However, there ends any similarity between Larry and an ordinary person. In the very process of retrieving the tack, Larry places his foot, as predestined as any foot in the army of unalterable law, once again directly upon the tack with predictable but immutable pain."

"Alas, poor Larry," Lela laughed.

"Ah yes. Just think of it— of all the numberless possibilities of life, poor Larry has experienced only two: being bullied and being pitied. An infinity of tacks in spare rooms, that is all he knows and all he will know. As you may guess, his temperament is consequently warped."

They walked out upon an arm of rocks which reached into the sea.

"You still haven't told me anything about the Lessings," Anne accused. "Your magic was magnificent. One minute they were there and the next, they were gone. Did you think we would eat them?"

"No, it wasn't that. The house was already crowded and Beth hates them; she positively hates them." Lela picked up a pebble and scratched a pattern on the rock. "Gail comes from a very poor family. She's always had a hard time of it, particularly in college. I don't know too much about Neil. He's some kind of engineer, I believe, and doing research on the side. He's just finished school. They have a little boy. You know, I forgot about the child; I never asked her about him. I can't even remember his name."

"The boy—Neil, you say his name is—interested me. He looked driven, about to be violent. His face intrigued me because I saw another one like it only yesterday, at the hotel. Here let me show you." Anne took a piece of chalk from her paint case and sketched on the rock surface. Soon the bellboy, crudely drawn but unmistakable, frowned back at them.

"Yes, he does bear a resemblance to Neil," Lela agreed.

"Perhaps both were deprived of the nipple at too early an age," Anne suggested.

"Or altogether. American women rarely breast feed. Beth does, of course, perpetually. It's an old-world custom."

"A sound one nonetheless, I've been told. Whatever the reason, your Neil Lessing is not happy and neither is this fellow." Anne continued to improve the sketch.

"Their marriage has been wrong from the beginning and the baby was born right off. I suppose Neil feels a captive."

Having completed a realistic likeness, Anne simplified the lines of the face, transforming it into a mask. "I'm thinking of doing a mural of masks with this fellow a part of it. Perhaps I should present them all as though they were projected from rocks . . . like your mountain . . . what is it's name?"

"Rushmore. Presidents, not masks."

"Ah, but a president is a politician, and surely a politician is more mask than anything else."

"Agreed, but you do everyone as a mask."

"Everyone but you. You won't sit, stand, or lie still long enough."

"As I told you before, I insist upon being a multiple mask. You haven't explored my many 'facets,' as they say."

"Complex, are you?" Anne asked, matching Lela's irony.

"Oh very."

"If you'll go down there," Anne pointed to where the rocks eased into the sea, "and just sit for a moment or two, I'll do a quick sketch of a complex you. I can work it up in oils later. In fact, I promise it to you as a Christmas gift. Would you like that?"

"Very much." Lela arranged herself as Anne had asked.

Anne turned over the page of her sketchbook and poised her pencil.

"Now, you must give me something to work with, you must tell me something about your complex self. Your love affairs, for example," Anne suggested.

"Nothing recent enough to intrigue you, I'm afraid," Lela replied, laughing.

"No complex sins? No excursions into the perverse, for example?"

"What makes you ask that?"

"Sodomy, for example . . ." Anne persisted, for her instinct told her that she had, quite by accident, quite without intention, struck the truth. "Sodomy is a fairly complex sin."

She examined Lela's face as she turned up to her. Her sea calm was gone; for a moment fear invaded. However, she recovered quickly and replied matter-of-factly:

"Yes, once, a very long time ago, but there was nothing complex about it. It was, as you put it, simply an excursion."

"Rachel . . . of course!" cried Anne. "No wonder you're in such a muddle about her."

"I am not in a muddle about anything!" Lela insisted.

"But you were frightened a moment ago; I could see it."

"Disconcerted, not frightened. After all, Anne, one does have certain compunctions about having broken a taboo of the tribe, particularly when the fact is being trumpeted abroad for the entire Atlantic coast to hear."

"My dear, I do not trumpet. Since the subject is not painful, you must tell me more about it. One is naturally curious."

"You, Anne, are unnaturally curious and really quite beyond belief."

"All right, all right, no further questions. I am going to get to work. Could you contrive to look as if you were about to swim?"

Lela stiffened and looked out to sea.

Anne worked rapidly. She had the expression. She knew what she wanted to do. The rest was easy. Blocking in the body was simple and the background forms were automatic and irrelevant. She would eventually change them anyway.

She had frightened Lela (despite her protestations to the contrary). Lela seemed such a sensible person. Surely she knew such things often happened, that it was a childhood experience best forgotten. Schoolgirls fell in love with the games mistress: it was a platitude of adolescence. Why all the fuss? Why should she suddenly look frightened?

Anne accused Rachel and shook an imaginary fist at the mahogany box containing Rachel's ashes. It sat smugly on the floor of the front closet in Claud's apartment for everyone to trip over. "Get rid of it!" she had once growled at him, for she was sure the cleaning lady gossiped about it, said he kept his dead wife on the floor of a closet. "But where?" he had asked helplessly. He was right. What could one do with it? Not scatter the contents to the four winds in the middle of Times Square and then advertise: "Empty urn for sale, hardly used." It was a problem without a solution.

She hoped Rachel had got what she deserved: damnation to hell, and not the circle of sodomy, nothing so glamorous as that—the circle of mischief (if there was one) was where she belonged.

The face was good. Yes, she had got it exactly, and the way the arm stiffened. That was a bit of all right. The rest would come later.

She looked off at the horizon. Richard's particular edge of the sea was no longer visible, for the house and its bed of rock eclipsed the progress of the boat. And what if they capsized, she wondered. Richard did not swim well.

Driving to the sea, she had not been able to remember the last lines of the final stanza of the poem from which Richard had quoted. Now suddenly she had it—whole and intact.

> We sat as silent as a stone,
> We knew though she'd not said a word,
> That even the best of love must die,
> And had been savagely undone
> Were it not that Love upon the cry
> Of a most ridiculous little bird
> Tore from the clouds his marvellous moon.

What a lot of Irish nonsense that was, she thought. He ought to have published a deathbed retraction.

Love was the invention of a malevolent deity for the torture of a substandard species, as any simpleton knew. On the most beautiful day in the world (although a cloud here and there did threaten), with all the things in the universe to do, one found oneself worrying about a husband sailing on the edge of the sea.

The dog appeared from nowhere, chasing a gull. He swam a short way out to sea after it and then came to Lela, rubbing his body against her, licking the salt from her legs. She scratched his ears absentmindedly, thinking that there was no getting around the fact that they wasted their lives. She furnished a house, read, and scribbled to amuse herself. Rachel had learned to play the dulcimer (or some equally esoteric instrument for which great music had never been written), given birth to Mark, and made clay pots somewhere in Morningside Heights. She had sent them a pot for Christmas one year, a comic pot with a red and white zebra. The sweet geranium she had planted in it still bore leaves, and when the leaves withered, she saved them for the scent. From now on she would put the dried leaves in the rose jar Claud had given her.

The dog nuzzled her hand. "Good boy, funny boy," she crooned, "it's all right."

"I've done with you, if you want to move," Anne called.

"Have you really?" Lela asked sarcastically.

The dog arrived at Anne's side, alternately panting and lapping.

"Lela, do call him off," she pleaded.

Shooing the dog, Lela looked down at the sketch.

"Seen a ghost, have you?" she whispered ironically to her face on the page.

"Steady on," Anne said.

"It's all right," Lela replied; "in fact, it's very good. Come, I'll show you Gull Island; leave your paraphernalia here, we can pick it up on the way back."

XXVIII

With the house to himself Claud had fallen asleep. He awoke on the last stroke of the chimes and looked at the alarm clock. It was eleven o'clock. He had been sleeping for an hour only, but it had been one of those hot deep summer sleeps which left one heavy-headed and confused. His damp shirt clung to his body and even the bedspread under him was wet. The thin curtains at the open window billowed and sank; the breeze reached him, a cool finger of air on his face.

He had not taken his shoes off and there were black heel marks on the white spread. Guilt. A lesson learned young. The process of civilization. Gentlemen did not put their shoes upon the furniture. His mother produced civilized gentlemen by virtue of their fear of that most potent punishment, her displeasure.

He had lived his boyhood in a dormered room under the eaves. High up it was, and always as hot as any American summer. All the heat and dust of the house collected there, a palpable and friendly presence. He had dreamed away his childhood lying on an old brass bed staring at the ceiling.

Although he had not smoked for years, he suddenly felt hunger for a cigarette. It was the result of thinking of home. He could remember his first cigarette clearly: he was eight or nine years old, Mark's age, lying on the bed, exhaling in the direction of an open window; he sucked the smoke in and blew it out the way he had seen his father do. There was a giddy, voluptuous moment and then . . . fear, for he did not know how he could clear the air before his mother came home. He solved the problem by purposely spilling a bottle of Richard's shaving cologne (awful stuff—dandy juice he used to call it to taunt Richard). His mother never guessed about the cigarette. Instead there was a row with Richard. "Dirty, destructive little bastard," Richard called him and flung his goldfish bowl out the window. The fish had died instantly; he remembered dashing down the stairs after it and the pain in his lungs. ("Goldie" he had called the fish, with a singular lack of imagination, and Richard had mocked him for the stupidity of the name.) One of the fragments of glass had flattened the postman's tire, and his room had stunk of Richard for weeks.

God, how he had hated him in those days—Richard, the young man down from Oxford on holiday, getting all the attention at dinner, talking a language he didn't understand, and never a word for him, the grubby little boy across the table who kept a fish and left a ring in the bathtub.

Richard still used the awful stuff and it still made him smell like a damned pansy. Yesterday when they had turned up the windows of the car because of the rain, he had thought he might faint from it. It lasted the whole day long; it was always there, hanging about Richard like a lethal repellent guaranteed to kill large, man-eating insects in the African veldt. No wonder Anne was an insomniac; the smell was enough to keep the dead awake.

Claud went in search of a cigarette, found an unopened pack in the drawer of a table in the hall, and returned to the bed. He watched the lit match char a path toward his finger and inhaled deeply. The ecstatic giddiness was the same, but it no longer mattered if the room filled with smoke and there was a mark on the spread, or if he burned the house down and himself with it. A long ash dropped on the spread.

Claud smiled, contemplating a life without the odor of Richard's shaving cologne. They would go home soon, he was sure of it; Richard would stand no more of him. And just in time, for he was turning into a regular old woman with a filthy mind, wondering what did—or rather did not—go on between them. Richard never took her properly, of that he was sure. His curiosity was a sop for his own failure, he had to admit, for he had not taken his own wife . . . Rachel, the polite stranger . . . there had been instead . . . liaisons . . . for want of a better word. Did Richard play that game? No, Richard was his mother's true success, a perfect gentleman.

A second ash dropped upon the spread, and burned a widening circle through spread and sheet. Yes, he had to agree, a destructive bastard.

Cupping his hand under the cigarette, he walked to the bathroom and flicked it in the toilet. He washed his face and regarded it in the mirror. Thin eyebrows and weakness with women. Genetics. A mother in common.

There was another reason why he'd be glad to be rid of them. For all her neuroses, Anne was a damned attractive woman for her age. "For her age"—that was a laugh. She could not be more than a year or two older than he was. Because of Richard, he always thought of her as much older. It worked the other way too; he knew she regarded him as Richard's little bad boy brother. The sooner she was out of his life the better, for recently, on several occasions when he had been made to endure lengthy expressions of Richard's pomposity, he had envisioned himself taking a sweet and intimate revenge—not that there was any reason to suppose that Anne would prefer the younger to the elder.

Claud wondered what had become of Mark. "Going for a walk," the boy had said.

XXIX

Mark hung his chin over the slat wood fence which guarded the swimming pool in front of the Tropicana Motel from the rest of the ordinary world. The water in the pool was green, and the man and woman lying on mats directly below him were red. Mark listened to them with clinical curiosity.

"Feel that sun, Ethel! Now what did I tell you? You never believe anything I say. Just as good as Florida, only cooler. Not so crowded either—and five dollars a day cheaper let alone the plane fare. Ninety-eight—the paper says it's ninety-eight in Florida."

"Cheaper—that's all it is. Nothing to do at night and the ocean's too cold to swim in."

"But how about that lobster? That was the living end. You said so yourself. 'Dave,' you said, 'that's the best lobster I ever ate.' You said it; you can't deny it."

"I wouldn't have said it if I'd known it was going to keep me up half the night with a bellyache. You and your bargains. Some vacation. They roll up the sidewalks at six. It's all right for you; all you want to do is lie on your back. But what about me? I don't get out of the house from one end of the year to the other. At least in Florida I can have a little fun. Every year we go to Florida and all of a sudden this year you decide to get cute. All of a sudden you have to get cheap—and me looking forward to it for months. Why don't you consider me for a change? It's my vacation too, you know!"

"Consider you? Are you out of your ever lovin' mind? Every year for eight years we go to Florida the hottest month of the summer because that's the way sweet little Ethel wants it. Well, this year we're going to consider me; we're going to do it my way. Is that clear? So you can just shut up that mouth of yours and keep it shut, because I'm sick to hell of listening to your lip!"

The lady cried. Her shoulders shook and her flesh rippled.

"Aw Ethel, come on."

"Shouting at me like that and everybody staring . . ." She sniffed and blew her nose.

"Tonight we'll go out, I promise. We'll take in a movie and have a couple of drinks later. Let's see what's playing." The man held a newspaper above him. "Tony Randall. You've always liked Tony Randall." He passed the paper to her.

"We've already seen it, Dave. Don't you remember? Last winter. November it was. We went with the Jewells and the car wouldn't run because you'd forgotten to put in anti-freeze. Don't you remember? It's as old as the hills."

"All right then. We'll go dancing. There must be someplace to dance around here. I'll ask the guy at the desk. We'll ask that nice young couple to come along . . ."

"What would they want with a couple of old fogies like us . . . they didn't even want to sit with us at breakfast. Couldn't you see that? Oh no, not you. You had to yell at them in front of the whole dining room."

"O.K. Since there's no pleasing you, let's just forget it!"

Mark could tell that the man was losing his temper again. That was how one said it, although it was very odd to think of it as something one had and then lost. Temper was like anger; one didn't lose it, one got it . . . sometimes very quickly. At least, that was the way with his father.

"You know, Dave, if you don't like the heat, we could always take a winter vacation. Ask the boss. You could stand up for yourself for once. Why should we always have the last choice of vacation? Good old Dave lets them walk all over him. Florida in the winter, wouldn't that be grand?"

"We can't afford it! I'm warning you for the last time, Ethel, shut up!"

The lady began to talk again. She was making it worse. Mark wished she would stop.

The man propped himself up on his elbows to answer her.

"Hello," whispered Mark. He had been caught; the man had seen him.

"Hey, what do you think you're staring at, kid? This is private property. Go on, get!"

Mark climbed down from the fence, thinking it was just as well. It was not really exploring.

He found his way back to the road which led to the town, stopped to scratch a bite at the back of his knee—he clawed at it and it bled—and to consult the watch. The long hand was between the two and the three, but the time had nothing to do with the two or the three. It was really twelve minutes after eleven. Time was complicated.

The boat was still there—faraway, but still sailing along beside him.

XXX

M<small>RS</small>. M<small>ACLEOD</small> woke from her sleep with a start and hummed a signal of her conscious state. Cranach. They were speaking of Cranachs which Matthew had seen in London. Did Cranach please or not please Matthew? It was impossible to tell, waking in the middle as she had. Walter was speaking. Apparently he knew all about art. He was a surprising young man. She herself knew nothing about Cranach, except a disgusting little tale—not to be found in any of Vasari's Germanic equivalents—about his means of exciting the muse. But perhaps it was not about Cranach but about Bosch. One was German; one was Flemish (but which was which, she did not know), and one had to do with Philip of Spain. They were hopelessly confused in her mind. She withdrew her attention from what was being said.

She had not been a week in the States and already she wished to be gone. She had deserted the clean and expansive perfection of Scandinavia (visions of pavement, impeccably swept, rose before her) for the squalor of New York on a whim, because of dear Lottie—née Lotus Mackensie (the wife of Carter Harn, who had died while fishing on Lake Champlain), now a victim of cancer.

"She is dying and knows it," wrote a mutual friend. "What they call terminal—in a room for two. Her children are grown and having other children. They visit on Sundays between two and four."

She had been to school with Lottie years ago. (Jean's father thought the farm bad for a young lady and sent her to board at Miss Wilson's Academy, where she and Lottie had been taught the virtue of forbearance—tolerance in contemporary idiom—the antique grace of pouring tea, and that one did not take off one's gloves to shake hands.) Now, more than forty years later, she hardly ever wore gloves; now when she shook hands, it was almost always flesh to flesh.

Truth be told, Scandinavia had proved something of a disappointment. She was feeling rather bored, rather restless, rather lonely, when the letter about Lottie arrived. Surely death was an important, an intimate occasion, she had thought, and notions swam before her of doing good and of giving and receiving a deathbed embrace. (Her sentimentality lately was appalling—another symptom of age.) Quixotically, she booked the next flight. Before the fact, it had seemed a profound and dramatic thing to be doing, tinged with the romance of their forty years of parting.

The fact itself was obscene. The dying body was a mechanical despot which allowed neither the mind nor the spirit an inch.

It was a new hospital and looked more like a hotel. The reception room was thickly carpeted, dance music wafted down from the ceiling, and everyone was very polite.

"Mrs. Harn? Yes, of course. Lottie is one of our pets," the nurse informed her, and her chatty use of the nickname had seemed an affront. "Down the hall and to your left, the third door. Cheery old thing, she is."

The gift shop, called "The Pill Box," displayed stuffed animals and potted plants, neither of which seemed appropriate

for poor Lottie would be dead, they claimed, before the
next germination and it would be cruel to remind her, even
indirectly, of spring). The cafeteria advertised Beef Stroga-
noff. Pretty girls in stylish pink dresses romped down the halls
pushing carts of magazines and candy. Everyone was very gay.
It was reassuring to find that death had become such a pleas-
nt, such a friendly affair.

Lottie was thin. That was the immediate thing about her.
The flesh under her eyes drooped, folded itself gently against
he upper ridge of her cheekbones. Her arms were sticks, embarrassed by the full sleeves of her hospital gown. Jolly Lot-
ie had grown dry in body and humor.

"Jeannie!" Lottie hooted. "I'd know you anywhere. You
till walk like a goose."

With infinite care, a nurse cranked the bed to a forty-five-
degree angle, while Lottie clenched herself against the movement. That accomplished, she breathed with bliss—the air
hortled in her throat and was expelled with a hiss.

They talked for fifteen minutes, about old friends, about
he school (now gone, Lottie said, for a shopping center).
"The last two years have been bad for native tomatoes," Lot-
ie said, "and oh how I miss native tomatoes."

Several silent minutes were marked crudely by the loud
icking of a cheap clock.

"Two of them have gone already," Lottie whispered, indi-
ating the curtained screen parallel to her bed. She sneered
er pride in the fact that she had outlived two of the previous
ccupants of the adjoining bed. "This one's a coronary.
Nothing to it!" she snapped her fingers in the direction of the
resent occupant, to demonstrate the brevity and ease with
which the heart ceased to beat.

"Blue Cross pays all," Lottie announced with sly satisfac-

tion. "All but twenty percent for private nurses, and I hardl
ever need them!" Another triumph.

The clock ticked its sovereignty over the room.

"I've been knitting," Lottie said brightly but heavily, mak
ing it clear that her uninvited guest was not doing her share
"The hernia next door knits too. He says it helps him to pas
the time. Imagine, he dove into a swimming pool and cam
up with a hernia!"

Lottie awaited a reply. Jean thought frantically and finall
said, "Sailors on those long voyages used to knit beautift
things between whales." For a moment she had been prou
of herself, delighted with the inspiration—but then she rea
ized that long voyages were hardly a fit subject. The meta
phoric possibilities were disturbing.

She had been saved from further conversational contribu
tions by the entrance of a girl with a porcelain pan and tw
angels of mercy in white.

"I thought you were never coming!" Lottie greeted them.

Jean rose to leave. Lottie motioned her to stay.

"I can almost do it myself. Most days they only have t
help bending my legs up."

"Yes," she said as the two nurses flexed a leg each. "I kn
each day, tear it out at night, and begin again next mornin;
I can't seem to decide what to make."

There was silence. The girl, the nurses, Lottie, and she he
self waited.

"Oh, I want to, but I don't think I can. Not today," Lott
protested.

"Of course you can."

"Oh no, not now."

"You must bear down!"

"I can't. Truly, I can't. Please don't force me!"

One of the white figures advanced over Lottie's frail body. There was a scream and the sound of a monstrous evacuation. Jean Macleod shuddered involuntarily; she could remember the sounds too clearly. She had not behaved well; she had fled (as they said in Victorian novels), and sent flowers the following day. Such was her weakness as a human being. She had deserted Lottie and called Lela, wanting youth, health, and gaiety. She had accepted for the weekend.

However, Lela too was involved with death. Jean concluded that all was abortive, her feeble gestures of connection, her twitchings of sentiment. Poor Lela was in the middle of it. Since they last met, the child had turned a corner and found herself in the midst of a crowd pushing its way to some spectacle. She herself had felt that way at thirty. It was a sense of time. Suddenly at that age one discovered time: it passed and one could not catch hold of any of it. When one confronted sixty the time sense ebbed; she was entirely at a loss to tell the hour or the day.

At sixty what did one want? Solitude. Solitude mitigated by sensible people to dine with on Thursday. Comfortable lodgings. Warm rooms in the winter. Yes, that was all she wanted. She would go abroad again. All that remained was a visit to her cousins, elderly ladies living in a suburb. They would urge her to stay, for the economics and politics of living were simpler with three than two. However, a life constrained by the frayed familiarity of all things would be intolerable; she was not so constituted. She would go abroad again.

What had she at sixty? She composed an answer for Daniel for he had a penchant for direct, rude questions and he was staring at her curiously. She had a vast acquaintance—"in all the countries of the world," she liked to say, for it was nearly the truth. The world, if it were limited to them (the people she knew and corresponded with), would not be a world constricted at all. For they were diverse. She saw them now as something tangible: letters piled on a chiffonier in a pension in Paris or Berne. She fanned them out and their stamps formed an arch of color. A continuum of humankind, her mind phrased for the elucidation of Daniel, who had not and would not ask, for he was attending to the helm. They were her fellow voyagers, who journeyed, for example, from Halifax to Istanbul via Montevideo. She had taken such a voyage in 1952.

At the captain's table she presided, spooning soup which keeled dangerously leeward; they discussed the effect of the bad weather on the pet iguana, for he—that fragile, melancholy, delicately carved descendant of the world's first sun—suffered, hopelessly caged in a cabin below. His master, the zoologist from Uruguay, could not eat for the thought of him The zoologist now lectured at Cape Town (they had dropped him there sans the lizard, which had tragically died at sea) and he wrote semi-annually of his researches. He now kept a boa constrictor which was plagued with a perverted palate Its normal, necessary, healthy appetite for rat had been subsumed by a deadly and decadent desire for the marinated artichoke. She had sent three jars for Christmas, and was still unsure whether the zoologist had considered the gesture thoughtful or cruel.

Jean Macleod laughed quietly to herself, for the zoologist's absurdity was the delight of her life. She was tempted to fly immediately to Cape Town and kiss him on the top of his bald head.

But no, she would not go to Cape Town, or to Paris o Berne. She roused herself to the problem at hand: the dis

osal of her fat and bones in some corner of the world, for
his was the last weekend of summer and winter would soon
e at hand.

The solution was not three feet from her. Richard's chin
ested on his chest, while his body rocked with the languor-
us pace of the sea. The deep moans from his throat kept
ime to an unplayed waltz, three longs and two shorts. She
ould go to London.

London was cold, but it was a manageable cold. Rooms
ould be found with central heating, in South Kensington or
loomsbury, if she had her preference. She would have her
ooks and her letters and the gruff good manners of the
ritish on Thursday . . . an ideal winter.

She surrendered with pleasure to the ambience of the boat,
bscrving her fellow voyagers one by one.

"Welcome back!" Walter called to her. "I'd offer a penny,
ut I haven't one."

He did wonder what she'd been thinking about. Whatever
was, she had been hard at it for quite a long time. Now she
as back with them, looking dazed. What did the others
ink of her when they looked? An old woman struggling
ith God? Hardly. Her placidity was fathoms deep. On the
irface she seemed to be a pleasant old pussy suffering minor
iscomfort without complaint for the sake of the social occa-
on. There was more, he felt sure, but he would never know.
ailboats and old ladies were a sweet, sweet life but he
ouldn't stay, not beyond the day. Brother-keeping was not
is idea of a full rich life, but this brother they had chain-
hipped.

They had met at a rally in a ball park—they were both on
eir way out, a coincidence . . . they had defection in com-
on . . . behind them the chant of a black sea, tribal, res-

onant, but they both knew too much about the elaborate de
tails of its orchestration for the sound to persuade. When th
orchestra was finally tuned, the baton would call for a cre
scendo. The hymns and the chants were true and righ
enough (as close to the rhythm of life as the pulse of blood
and the voices were good and pure; but the performance be
gan in the wrong place and with the wrong people.

Behind it all there was always a room with a long table,
committee composed of a hierarchy of other committees, an
the jealousies and antagonisms of internecine war, as orgar
ization argued with organization, group with group; for th
black man had learned the evil tedium of politics from th
white man, and learned it perfectly.

They knew it all, as they stood listening to the crowd re
spond, and so they had defected to the nearest bar for
drink, for several drinks. They had drunk to all the organiza
tions, not by initials but by name. They had pledged then
selves to a private war, a brotherhood of two without commi
tees, memos, or bureaucracy, a pact of common sense an
dignity. They had parted quite drunk.

Walter rolled over and watched the gathering clouds. H
had kept the faith, or tried to . . . had lived a paradox fc
months. He had kept himself separate from the burning, th
looting, and the committee room, and he had cohabited wit
the consequent guilt, for the absolute need of separatio
was always countered and met by his absolute need to act i
some way.

He had no idea whether the quiet brother had tried t
make the South safe for the black man or simply taken a wal
at the wrong time and in the wrong place. Now he was livir
carrion both for the white cock and the black crow; now h
was the subject of the committee room and a useful obje

in the endless quest for propaganda. Did quiet brother want or not want to be made a martyr of, that was the question. Unfortunately, if he did not want—it was probably too late. Even in the early press releases it was easy to detect the skill of a public relations man.

Quiet brother had been described as "steady," "reserved," "responsible" in the newspapers. All the sacred cows of the white middle class had been chosen to capture its sympathy and sharpen its guilt. It was a safe bet that the New York office of at least one major "rights" group had already laid on extra help for Monday to handle a sudden increase in contributions and inquiries.

Walter sat up and stretched. The paradox was over and he was relieved. He would call Noah Jaspers tonight. Noah had a finger in every pie and would be sure to know where quiet brother was. He'd go see the man and find out what he wanted. He'd keep his eye on the vial which contained a distillation of pure fact: his friend had been beaten because he was black.

"Hey, Matt," he called, "what was it the man said about arterial roads?"

Matthew closed his eyes, put his head in his hands, thought for a moment, and then recited:

"*You cannot be away, then, no*
Not though you pack to leave within an hour,
Escaping humming down arterial roads:
The date was yours; the prey to fugues,
Irregular breathing and alternate ascendancies
After some haunted migratory years
To disintegrate on an instant in the explosion of mania
Or lapse for ever into a classic fatigue."

"That's right, Matt, my boy, that's what he said. I don't know about the fugues, but ascendancies, that is right enough, that speaks to our condition, we're certainly prey to them. Did I ever tell you about my visit to the house of Lin Yu Chin in the street of the Maidens of the Camellia . . . all names remain fictional to protect the innocent . . ."

"At least thirty times," Daniel interrupted.

"The same man in the same poem also said something about 'ruined boys,' " said Matthew, in a stage whisper of warning.

"Don't give it a thought, my son. I know a very good doctor in Harlem: cheap and discreet. Furthermore, he's a great disbeliever in Public Health—perhaps because of his profession. He has a distinct preference for private disease. You name it, he'll cure it. He was a friend of my father."

Walter turned abruptly to Mrs. Macleod. "Jean, did I ever tell you about my father?"

"Walter, that is really quite enough!" warned Beth.

"Sorry, my love." Walter blew her a kiss.

Mrs. Macleod hummed her vague confusion.

Richard had jerked himself awake. "Been in China, have you?" he asked.

"Hong Kong." Walter embarked upon an assessment of the city.

Mrs. Macleod leaned forward attentively. She too had been to Hong Kong.

To Matthew the subject seemed dull. He had not been to Hong Kong. No doubt he would eventually go to the Orient but not in the near future.

" 'They gave the prizes to the ruined boys.' " Laughing, he lingered with the line. He himself had been given a minor prize for his last volume; the announcement had been in the pile of mail waiting for him. It would please Beth immensely. She inevitably paid for his freedom and she had a right to some return. He would tell her as a gift, presented when the occasion was perfect.

There she sat, fulsome, classic, listening to the chimes from town. He would wait with her for the birth of his child, then claim it quickly and firmly, withdraw it from her overzealous maternity.

How pensive she looked. It had just struck noon and he knew she was concerned with the deep problem of lunch. She rose and disappeared into the deckhouse, waving Walter to follow.

Daniel watched Beth return, and with the dignity of self-importance, draw forward the wicker picnic basket, methodically cataloguing its contents. She thought she was the quartermaster of the universe and this was her glorious moment. No woman he had ever met irritated him quite so much as Beth—pretending to talk to him about truth when she never thought further than lunch. He would remember most from these three precious months of his life, this compulsion she had about lunch. At twelve they must sit down to lunch, and all the boundless possibilities of the day were delimited by the fact. He was not used to lunch. He did not like lunch. He and Lela hardly ever ate lunch; nevertheless, they had allowed themselves to be bullied for the sake of politeness. (It was the children of course; they demanded a schedule. Beth's children were always intensely hungry. Children ironed out the infinite globe of life into a flat map of order.)

It was only noon; they were all at peace. Still she insisted upon breaking it up with lunch. Damn her. Beth, great mother of the western world, treated everyone as a child.

"Ham and cheese," she announced, proffering a package.

"I know you prefer ham and cheese. I hope it's completely defrosted; I took them from the freezer this morning."

Daniel declined with a wave of his hand. Beth insisted. He gave in but not graciously. Walter handed him a paper cup of wine sympathetically.

It was almost over. There was solace in that. Next week the fall semester began. When Lela had children, perhaps they too would be reduced to the bad habit of lunch. He hoped Lela's talent for disorder would exempt them from the pattern.

Lunches notwithstanding, he would like to stay long enough to get in one more day's sailing. There was a faculty meeting on Tuesday. He and Matthew could drive up for it and back again the same day. That would give them, if the weather held, two or three more days.

Matt might very well have to be dragged to the faculty meeting, but he was willing to do the dragging personally. Matt had not been to one of the damn things in all his five years of teaching. Not that he blamed him. They were tedious beyond belief and totally pointless. Four times a year without fail, the will of the trustees descended in the archangelic forms of their revered President and the Secretary of the Faculty, who counted the faithful, marking their names in a book of judgment. Four times a year without fail, Matthew proved himself heathen and the Secretary of the Faculty addressed Daniel, out of all that full and faithful assembly, as though he alone were somehow culpable, as though he were the divinely appointed guardian, the keeper of the prodigal.

"Well, Herr Doctor Professor Reld," declaimed the Secretary clearing his Germanic throat, "I see that the Chairman of the Department of Crafts is again not among us."

Having had his joke at Matthew's expense, the Secretary

subsided for another three months into the rigors of academic bookkeeping. The joke was five years old, the result of the creation of a special department for Matthew devoted entirely to creative writing. No one else had cared one way or the other (except Matthew, of course, with a child on the way, living on his wife's money and hating it—Matthew had needed the added increment of a chairmanship), but the Secretary had objected vehemently: creative writing was an applied art, it was not an academic subject, and such a department demeaned the scholarly reputation of the university. His objections had been ignored, and in all these five years he had neither forgotten nor forgiven.

Four times a year in that mahogany room underneath the portraits of shrouded and hooded Past Presidents whose right arms leaned affectionately on the crest of the school, the Secretary of the Faculty fed the worm which gnawed him—to the singular embarrassment of an innocent and lowly associate professor, serving as surrogate for the real culprit.

He would not put up with it one meeting more, Daniel resolved. This time Matthew himself would be there to anoint the old fool with the oil of his charm or throw acid in his face, whichever he wished. He had been eating that woman's lunches all summer and it was the least her husband could do in payment.

"Faculty meeting on Tuesday," he announced to Matthew, chomping into his sandwich.

"Oh?" Matthew sensed trouble. Daniel's voice was unusually decisive. He was afraid he'd end up sitting through it on Tuesday, although he had vowed he'd never let himself be browbeaten into that nonsense.

XXXI

The bells of noon had struck and with them hunger. Mark crouched on a strand of sea-smoothed rocks, watching the stone throwers. There were two games. Three small boys, younger than he, played one. They picked up handfuls of stones, rushed to the edge of the strand, tossed them into the sky and, when a wave came, they rushed back from the edge, shouting, "Here it comes!" The other game was more complicated and it took him longer to discover the rules. Two older boys played it, standing up to their knees in the sea. It was necessary to throw a flat stone as soon as a wave struck and before the next one had built to a peak. It was necessary for the stone to skim the water once, skip through the air, and then hit a solitary rock which jutted out of the sea at some distance from the strand. He wondered if it was very difficult. When the older boys left, he would take off his shoes and socks, wade out, and try it.

Mark turned from the games and considered an old lady sitting on a rock near the road. She gripped a large paper bag between her legs and watched the passing cars anxiously. One sleeve of her loose black dress was torn; she fingered the tear every few moments, looking carefully around at the picnickers on the strand as she did so; then her eyes returned to the road. Patches of pink scalp glistened between wisps of white hair. Mark had not known that women could get bald. The motion of her head followed the cars as they passed until he thought he could no longer bear it. He squeezed his eyes shut and commanded the next car to stop with all his mind. He heard the noise of its motor come closer. He opened his eyes. The car stopped, the engine ran, the door swung open.

"Hey, Ma, c'mon for Chrissakes, I haven't got all day. How the hell could you miss the bus? You'll be the death of me, you know that, don't you!"

The old lady lurched off the rock and toward the car. The car moved before she had got all the way in and closed the door. Mark could see her arm struggling with the door as the car raced down the road. Alarmed, he stood to watch. The door shut as the car swung around a curve.

The stone throwers were leaving. Perhaps they were going home to lunch. He too was hungry; a pain in his stomach reminded him from time to time.

A man rose out of the sea and ran up the sand, shaking off water as he came nearer. He stood shivering a few feet away, looking down at a lady sleeping on a red rubber mattress. Then he grinned at Mark and pointed to the lady's bare back. Mark nodded. Straddling the lady's body, the man shook water on her. She cried out, turned over suddenly, and grabbed the man's ankle; he fell onto a mattress next to her and rubbed her arm with his wet hand. Mark shivered sympathetically and the lady smiled up at him.

"It's his fault," the man said to her, "he told me to go ahead and do it."

"What a strange thing for a strange little boy to do," said the lady, pretending to be angry.

The man stood again, looked at the sun, and stretched his

arms out wide. "Observe, my love, our private yardarm. Close your eyes. Tight now."

The woman shut her eyes.

"Is the sun not setting?"

"Oh yes, it most certainly is," she said.

"Let me know as soon as it's over the yardarm."

There was a long moment of silence.

"Darling, you have such a slow imagination." The man knelt down and kissed her eyelids.

"Now!" she cried, opening her eyes and kissing his neck.

"Hold the chalices!" He drew two glasses and a bottle from a basket, pulled out the cork with his teeth, and poured.

"To which god shall we commit our first libation? Venus, in honor of you? Apollo, in honor of me? Or Ganymede, the original cupbearer, in honor of our young friend?" He waved his glass at Mark.

"Apollo—but not in honor of you, my lord, in honor of the sun. I'm worried about the weather." She squinted at the sky. "That cloud looks threatening."

The man shaded his eyes and looked. "It's cumulus, not nimbus, my love, barely a chance at all of rain, so set your heart at ease, we shall have a whole afternoon of wine and sun."

"That sounds like a dangerously intoxicating combination," she said.

"Intoxicating, but not dangerous. Now, if it's danger you want . . ." The man leaned over the woman. She pushed him away.

"Remember, we have a visitor."

"So we do." He squinted up at Mark, then lay back down on his mattress, balancing his glass on his chest.

"Tell us all about yourself, young man. Entertain us with psalms and tales."

"What's a libation?" Mark asked.

The man held up his glass.

"That's just wine," Mark protested.

"A connoisseur at the tender age of . . . seven."

"Eight," Mark corrected.

"Short for your age. Don't let that bother you. There's much to be said for short fellows. What kind of wine, my lad?"

"Red wine," Mark answered promptly, smiling at the lady.

"My dear, we have before us not only a connoisseur but also an incipient rake." The man leaned forward again. "When he's old enough and wise enough to seduce luscious ladies on public beaches, I'll be . . ."

"Bald, paunchy, and distinctly sodden," she concluded for him.

"Exactly my point, love; *carpe diem* and the rosebuds too."

The man and woman kissed with their mouths open. One of the wineglasses spilled. The wine seeped toward Mark.

He stood looking down at them. He was not sure what was happening. The man's moving body pressed over the woman, his mouth ate at her mouth. Her fingers dug into the man's back. Mark turned away and trudged down to the edge of the strand.

The other boys were gone. The sea was like ice against his legs. He picked up a stone, hefted it in his hand, and felt the curve of it with his thumb. He threw: sideways and underhand, as he had seen the boys do. The stone arched and plunged; it did not skip. The stone had been too large and not flat enough. He waded back and chose more stones, stuffing them in his pockets. He threw them one by one, perfecting the swing of his arm. On and on he threw. The trips back and forth to the strand and the swing of his arm became rhythmic and automatic. As he threw he looked only at the rock, the target, and soon he no longer really saw it.

Before him was the garden of Euzilpha and Carduff, blue trees and a green sky. His mother sat laughing on top of the stone wall. Holding out her hand, she called him to the forest. They would explore together. A tree stood in the path. On its lowest branch there perched, large and menacing, the bird with four feet. One of the stones struck; the bird became a rock again.

XXXII

SETH WOODWARD SURFACED and peered through sea-bleared goggles at the sky. Low dark clouds were sailing in from the north. They were in for another storm—but not for an hour at least, he estimated. He was out far enough to see the *Philemon* in the distance. They would be in for a hard time of it, if they didn't turn back soon. An electrical storm —and this one promised to be a beauty—was no picnic on a sailboat.

Seth looked back at his house. It looked good from the ocean, his cave. He liked to think of people passing it on boats and asking who had built it and who lived there. Yes indeed it was quite a feat—a glass house built into rock. He had drawn up the plans himself and flown in an architect from Seattle to iron out the details. It had cost him one hell of a bundle—that little palace. He lifted his goggles to admire it once again, checked his scuba equipment, and prepared to dive.

Gail Lessing could see his tanks from the living room. She watched him dive and hoped he'd drown. "Time for a visitation to my finned friends," he had said, deserting his tear-stained wife and his drink-drowned guests. In the kitchen Sonja attempted lunch, weeping intermittently into a Bloody Mary for her long lost son.

Gail tried once more to rouse Neil. He had not moved in hours. Above him, the widow and the movie star, larger than life in cartoon color, still kept the vigil. Gail hissed directly into Neil's exposed ear: "Wake up. Now!" Still he did not move. It was hopeless. He would not wake. It was getting late. Buses did not run after five. She wanted to go home.

She would have to find Lela and get some help. Half expecting alarms to ring and a hidden portcullis to descend from the ceiling, Gail let herself out of the cave of Woodward.

"And so you've seen our coast, our sea, our islands, and our lights; we've nothing left to show," said Lela.

"Very beautiful they are too, particularly now—see!" Anne pointed to the gathering clouds. "The colors are amazing." She dropped down on the sand and stretched out with her head on the paint case. "Oh, how wonderfully tired I am. I've not walked that far since we came to this new world. You know, in all of New York there is hardly a square box of air to move in. At home I walk every day. How I've missed it these past months. How long has it been?"

"Since the end of April. Four months. Remember when I picked you up at the airport? We were in the midst of a hot spell. I tried to explain that it was very unusual for April, but you weren't having any of it. You knew all about American weather, you said, and had thoroughly prepared yourself for the worst." Lela sat down on the sand and put on her shoes. "Four months. I don't know how you've stood it . . . and I don't mean the climate."

"But I keep telling you, it hasn't been at all difficult, really it hasn't; not until this little excursion, that is. Suddenly everything seems to have come to a head, Claud's antagonism toward Richard, the confusion about Mark, my own impatience to be gone. We were all doing a splendid job of keeping civil until yesterday. We seem to have suffered a sea change in reverse." Anne sat up and looked out to sea. "Speaking of sea changes, the ocean has shifted from blue to green in just the time we've been walking."

"This whole weekend's a mistake," Lela muttered remorsefully. "I had some foolish notion that it would be . . ."

"Therapeutic. Like hot springs for the rheumatic," Anne contributed. "Perhaps it has been," she added, sardonically, "occasional stress is good for the nervous system. I feel as if I've been sleepwalking for months and just woke up."

"Oh dear," laughed Lela, "and here I've spent the summer languishing in what I thought was a soporific landscape."

"Then I count the assault of us Bennetts and Sarums a success. We've taught you an invaluable lesson. Keep your landscapes to yourself, young lady, and above all, keep them pure of people."

"Anne, you don't take me in for a minute. I don't believe your cynicism is even skin-deep."

"Nonsense. I mean what I say. People do intrude; you've lived long enough to learn that. Relationships between human animals are based upon the laws of expediency, the survival of the race: food-getting, shelter-building and baby-producing. All the rest, the whole vocabulary—family, friend, and their subdivisions, husband, son, lover, acquaintance—is fiction, storytelling, the invention of a bored and masochistic creature who can only keep himself amused with torture. It is an instinct like that of the salmon; despite logic and gravity, he must struggle up the falls to spawn. Now, you see, the sea air does have an undesirable effect; I am making another speech."

"So you are," Lela laughed. "I suppose what you say is true enough, but I am not entirely persuaded that the word 'instinct' accounts for love. After all, one does choose to become hopelessly involved with another person for more reasons than biology alone can offer . . ."

"Nonsense, Lela, you are talking utter nonsense. Love is habit, a learned response. Love is the oldest lie in the world; it's been going on for centuries. Love is the tallest tale of all told to keep the winter cold away. Weakness—for who can bear the thought of himself in the middle of no place alone . . . much better to invent conversations and caresses, painful absences and physical ecstasy. If for centuries the tale had gone another way, if for centuries the storytellers had told us that the sexual act was a painful necessity, it would be just that, and our senses would offer no evidence to the contrary. The same touch, the same response to touch which we now count the sweetest pleasure would be, if that first singer of fiction had given his tale a different ending, the sharpest pain. And so . . ."

"And so . . ." Lela repeated, laying the back of her hand against Anne's cheek, "touch is pleasant."

"Oh yes, very pleasant, but love, unfortunately, is not all touch or all pleasant. It is getting dark. There is going to be a storm. Somewhere out there, on that very frail craft of yours . . . In an hour or so we shall both be worrying about that. Not so pleasant. I'm already a little apprehensive."

"There's no need to be. Dan's a very good sailor and the *Philemon* is anything but frail. For all your speech-making, you live the lie."

"Of course. I'm just as gullible, as much a creature of habit, as weak as anyone else."

"Good." Lela stood and patted her on the shoulder. "I'm

going back to the house to call the Woodwards and make some coffee."

"I shall stay here for a moment and watch the colors."

Lela called the dog and raced him down the beach and over the bridge to the house.

"Lela! Oh thank God!" Gail called to her from the veranda. "I was afraid no one was here."

"Gail. I was just coming back to call you. I've been trying all morning. What have you people been doing with yourselves?"

"It was just awful, Lela, just awful. They are terrible, terrible people." Gail began to sob as Lela led her into the house, mingling sympathy, apology, and the reassurance that she would see that the Lessings got home as soon as possible.

The car Claud had rented was still in the drive. Lela suspected that he had been somewhere upstairs all morning, although he had not answered when she called earlier. If he were there, the problem of transporting the Lessings to a bus was solved.

"Neil's still in bed," Gail sobbed. "I can't get him to move."

"Did those gargoyles get him drunk?" Lela asked.

"Yes, yes, I suppose so; but that wasn't all . . . there was much more . . . I can't remember all of it. I think he . . . that horrible Seth . . . gave us something. I don't know what it was. I can't remember clearly."

"Perhaps it's just as well. Don't think about it now."

Lela kept her voice calm, in spite of her inner alarm. She had a clear memory of Seth, weeks ago, in front of their fireplace, arms spread in an emulation of latter-day prophethood, proclaiming that the Second Coming had Come in a new form of transubstantiation which produced both the horrors of hell and the glories of paradise with the mere ingestion of a minute chemical substance. They had dismissed it as more of Seth's bombast. Apparently they had been wrong. He not only believed, he proselytized.

She left Gail to phone her mother and went in search of Claud.

She found him on the bed in the guest room. Smoke and the smell of burnt cloth surrounded him.

"I didn't know you smoked."

"I haven't in years."

"You might at least take your shoes off."

"I've been thinking the very same thing for the last . . ."

The chimes from the town struck two.

". . . hour and a half."

"What have you been doing, setting fire to the bed?"

"Ah yes, just the slightest accident." He moved his leg to display the damage. "See, just a very small hole."

"Where's Mark? Neither Anne nor I have seen him since breakfast."

"Gone for a walk. Borrowed my watch and gone for a walk." Claud lit another cigarette.

"Gone for a walk where?" Lela demanded.

"Wherever he likes. That little chap is a good deal more independent than you women like to think."

"How long has he been gone?"

"Hours."

"Oh Claud, what if he gets lost?" Lela sat on the edge of the bed and pictured Mark, a small desolate figure, alone on a deserted beach as the sky darkened around him.

"He's got too much sense to get lost. You and Anne must really stop smothering him. I simply won't have it."

"We don't smother him. Naturally we worry about him,

since you refuse to take any responsibility at all. You're positively abnormal when it comes to Mark. It's as though you had nothing whatever to do with him."

"It's a wise father who knows his own son."

"That is a disgusting thing to say."

"Quite right." Claud sat up and patted Lela's arm. "All right, my dear, all right. I'll go look for my son like a dutiful father, if that will please you."

"There's something else I wish you'd do while you're about it."

"Anything, anything . . . said the grateful guest to the perfect hostess."

"This is serious, Claud. I really do need your help."

"All right . . . I am both serious and flattered."

"There were two people here yesterday at lunch . . ."

"Yes, of course, the unexpected arrivals you foisted off on the neighbors. She kindly attended the funeral of my dear departed wife, if I remember correctly."

"Yes, that's true. I had forgotten about that." Lela remembered Gail's gloating face at the back of the chapel and felt less guilty about having subjected her to what had been, without doubt, a harrowing experience.

"It would seem that the neighbors have been a little too neighborly."

"What have they been up to, mate-swapping?"

"Even worse, I fear. I suspect they got the Lessings drunk and then fed them some kind of drug."

"You're joking!" Claud began to laugh.

"I wish I were!"

"You're exaggerating, as usual," he accused.

"Very well, have it your way. Nevertheless, she's here now.

It seems she can't get her husband out of bed and she wants to go home. Could you possibly go over to the neighbors with her, get him—his name is Neil—up, and get them both on a bus?"

"Why I'd be delighted, dear Lela, simply delighted. In fact, I can't think of anything I'd like to do more on a cloudy afternoon by the sea. Muscle or tact—which would you prefer me to use to persuade the Mephistophelian neighbors to unhand their victims?"

"Either or both. Whatever it takes to get them out of there and away from here. Suddenly I'm hating the sight of them, the neighbors, and nearly everyone else as well."

"Tut, tut, so young, so misanthropic. Come on, love, let's get you out of your trouble. That's the least I can do, when you've been so good. You think I don't care, but I do." He put an arm about her waist and led her out of the room and down the stairs. "Lela, Lela, Lela, cheer up, you've only got fifty years to go."

They arrived at the foot of the stairs laughing. Gail was still on the phone.

"All right, Mama. If the doctor says there's nothing to worry about, then there's nothing to worry about. We'll be back tonight. Somehow we'll get back tonight. So just you sit tight."

"Mike's come down with a sore throat," she explained, as she hung up. "It's silly to worry, but at this time of year, you always wonder if it could be something serious." Gail smiled tentatively at Claud. He bowed politely.

"I've promised to make sure you get home as quickly as possible. Shall we go pick up your husband?" He walked to the front door and held it for her.

"Don't forget to look for Mark!" Lela called after them.

From the kitchen window she watched the car back down the drive, and then turned to read the note from Beth taped to the refrigerator door: "If we are not back by four, the roast please: 300 degrees."

XXXIII

THE IRON GATE was open. Mark spelled out the name which was engraved upon it: Mount Olivet Novitiate. He did not understand the name. There were no mountains around, of that he was sure. Of the building beyond the gate, he could see very little. He walked through the gate and down the road to explore it.

He confronted the house. There was a fountain in front and six chimneys above. The fountain played into the heavy mist which had rolled in so quickly from the sea. Birds bathed in it, shook their wings, and flew away. Along both sides of the house were real gardens. He had seen flower beds before, window boxes, and vegetable patches. However, these were made entirely of flowers and they stretched out from the house in both directions and seemed to go on for miles. All the colors he knew and some he had never seen before splashed the mist and rippled as the wind from the sea blew.

He followed a path along the side of the house; it plunged him deep into a garden. There were no tall careless flowers, but long neat rows of low green plants bearing an occasional small white blossom, and in the midst of them knelt a lady in black from her head to her feet. Although he moved very quietly toward her, when she looked up at him she was not surprised.

"Do you like strawberries?" she asked with a smile.

"Yes, very much. I hardly ever have them."

"Come here then."

Mark knelt down beside her and she handed him a white bowl.

"To pick them you must do this: pinch the stem close to the fruit."

She held up a large red berry. "This is a ripe one. Now, you feel it so that you will know what a ripe one is like."

He took it in his hands and pressed its fullness gently.

"Yes, that's right. Take only the reddest ones, and touch them there, along the globe, ever so carefully, ever so gently, and if they seem tender, they are ripe. Pick as many as you can, and I will fetch you cream and sugar."

She walked away from him and he began the task with all his attention. He knew that the lady cared deeply about the strawberries and thought they were very important. He was afraid she would be angry if he made a mistake. He smelled the fruit; it was sharp and sweet. He was hungry.

The lady in black returned with a pitcher and a spoon.

"You've done very well," she said, and taking him by the hand, she led him through the rows of plants, explaining, "First there is the white flower, and then the hard green seed, and finally, these ripe red berries which you may eat. Come over to the bench here." She led him into a clearing.

She mixed the berries he had picked with cream and handed him the bowl and spoon.

He could tell she enjoyed watching him eat. "Not too fast, not too fast," she cautioned.

"I am going to town," he announced proudly when he had finished. "Is it very far?"

"No, it's just around the next bend and down the hill. Are you running away from home, young man?"

"I'm going to meet my mother," he invented.

"Oh, I see," she replied skeptically. "But first you must come with me into the house; we'll find you an umbrella and something warmer to wear." She ran her hand over the chilled flesh of his arm. "It's getting colder; soon it will rain." Her hand tightened on his arm.

He pulled away quickly, calling "Thank you" as he ran down the path.

She followed him to the front of the house and watched him disappear down the drive. He was a beautiful child, and he ought not to be wandering about alone with a storm coming on. Perhaps the police ought to be called, but she must ask Reverend Mother's permission first, and Mother Catherine would say that they must not involve themselves in the affairs of the townspeople or the neighbors. It was regrettable, she would say, that their seclusion was constantly intruded upon during the summer. With twenty girls to look after, a summer colony was surely the least appropriate setting. (The novitiate had preceded by many years the motels and neon signs which so distressed the Reverend Mother. It had been built when there were miles of deserted coast.)

Of all the things in the world that she had seen, the child was perhaps the most beautiful, coming so swiftly upon her there in the garden like a dream or a vision.

She knelt quickly and prayed forgiveness.

XXXIV

Wrapped in a towel and carrying a glass, Seth Woodward answered the door.

"I say, Mr. Woodward, isn't it? Claud Sarum here. I've come to take these good people off your hands." Claud pushed Gail on through the door and shook Seth's hand.

"Britisher?"

"Not for years."

"The wife's in the kitchen. Under the weather, for some reason. Can I get you a drink, Sarum?"

"No thanks. I really can't spare the time; I've promised to get the Lessings to a bus. It seems their boy is ill."

Seth turned toward Gail. His disbelief was obvious. "Sorry to hear it. I would have been happy to drive you into town, if you had asked. But then you didn't ask, did you?"

"I didn't want to put you out any more than we already have," she mumbled. "I'll just go see if I can get Neil up."

Seth gestured Claud to a chair which allowed a clear view of the soup cartons. With determination Claud ignored them; he was damned if he'd compliment the bastard's vulgarity. However, Seth pressed the issue.

"Well now, what do you think of our little nook?"

"It's not my taste."

"Is that so? Taste is surely a funny thing." Seth paused and swilled his drink. "Take me, for example. I'm what you might call an Anglophobe. It's a matter of personal taste. Mind you that's just a generalization and I'm always willing to make an exception. Give the individual a chance to prove himself, I always say."

"Quite right," Claud quelled an enormous, visceral laugh. "Tolerance makes the world go round."

"The individual, that's the important thing. That's the trouble with you Britishers, you never give the individual a chance. First monarchy, now socialism. Your country's finished, you know that, don't you?"

"Ever been abroad?" asked Claud, changing the subject.

"Why the hell should I go abroad? Bad plumbing and a few broken-down palaces." Seth drained his glass and returned to the bar. Claud addressed the back of his neck silently: Good. You stay right here, American manchild, and romp in your three-thousand-mile playpen.

Gail appeared, suitcase in hand, with Neil lurching after her. "Well we're off!"

Claud relieved her of the suitcase and took Neil's arm to correct his unsteady gait.

"Thanks for everything," Neil snarled at Seth.

"So long, tigers!" Seth called after them.

With consideration for Neil's fragility, Claud wheeled the car gently around and headed toward town.

"Feeling nasty, Lessing?"

"Much better now. The air feels good." He turned to Gail in the back seat. "What's this about Mike?"

"He's come down with a sore throat. Mama had the doctor. He says there's nothing to worry about."

"I don't care what he says, I don't like the idea of Mike's being sick when we're not there!"

"Well neither do I!" Gail defended herself automatically. "You're not the only one who cares about him. I'm worried too."

"What a grotesque that man is and that hallucination he calls a home . . ." Claud hoped the change of subject might establish a truce between his passengers long enough for him to get them on a bus. After that they could draw and quarter each other and eat the remains for all he cared.

"They are obscene, disgusting people. Hallucination . . . you don't know the half of it," Neil muttered in cold anger and turned again to Gail. "I hope you're satisfied. Why can't you ever be content? Why must you always be at me about something? Pushing, pulling. I'm sick to death of it."

Claud kept silent. There was really nothing he could say. In the rear view mirror he could see Gail, curled and whimpering like a wounded thing. It was a bit thick. He watched the speedometer and tried to clear his mind of them. At least he had felt no signs of dizziness. Perhaps, after all, it was nothing, or something very simple: fatigue or wax in the ears. One and two tenths miles had passed. They were almost into the town.

Watching his cowed and quivering wife, with the prospect before him of their four-hour bus ride, Neil decided to relent. "All right, Gail, all right. Let's just forget it."

Gail did not respond, for there was no use trying to forget when the very tone of his voice was a reminder. He could go on like that for weeks—it had happened before—informing her with cold courtesy that she was despicable.

Neil reached back his hand for her to take. "It will be all right. Now stop. Please, Gail."

At the sound of her name she took his hand.

Claud observed their joined hands in the mirror. Scissors

and paste, scissors and paste, that was all marriage amounted to. Cut each other into shreds at noon; glue the fragments back together at midnight. He looked again at their clasped hands. That was the best of it; a moment when, in spite of wound and counterwound, they held on, they touched.

They reached the town and he found the Lessings a three o'clock bus. Having discharged his promise to Lela, he strolled at his leisure through the town and found himself near the wharf where they had stopped on the previous day to ask directions.

He had been brought back to the place by the figure of a man he had seen in a window overlooking the wharf. The man was still there, in the same position at the window. He looked out over the harbor while his hand mechanically drew a needle in and out of a vast fishing net. His implacable gaze veered neither to the left nor right, nor did he ever look down at his work. Claud wondered if he was blind or an invalid confined to a chair, and if he was blessing or cursing the sea.

On the previous day he had been struck by the feeling that the man reminded him of someone. Now he had it. Sidney Greenstreet, Sidney Greenstreet weaving fate and looking inscrutably out to sea.

He felt better than he had for months. The strange face in the window and the obscurity of the harbor and sea in the mist delighted him. Everything on the wharf stood out as if freshly painted against the gray wash of the oncoming storm: fractured, blanched posts, spirals of discarded rope, one gull on a post spreading his heavy wings.

It made no sense, he admonished himself, this feeling of elation coming upon him for no reason save the mirror image of a man and a woman clasping hands. The woman was dull and coarse; the man was weak and couldn't manage his wife or himself; and yet, they had clasped hands, and he had felt compassion and respect for them, and now . . . this extraordinary excitement.

The gull lifted his wings and flew, and there was the thing he had allowed himself to forget, there was Mark, legs apart, hands behind his back, observing the flight of a gull. A moment before the wharf had been deserted, but now, there was his son.

He had walked all the way himself. He was a manly little fellow, Claud decided, small for his age but well grown. His legs were strong. "Beautiful," women always said of him, but there was more to the boy than a pretty face. Claud watched him and was moved. He had been moved before by the boy, but this was quite different. Mark stood there, separate and complete, thinking . . . what was he thinking? Something about the way the gull flew or the look of the sea before a storm, perhaps. He would go on, separate and complete, thinking one thing or another for sixty or seventy more years. He would make love to women and bury his father.

"Come all this way, have you?"

Surprised, Mark spun around and faced his father.

"Tired?" Claud laid a hand on his shoulder.

"No. It isn't really very far."

"Like a lift back to the house?"

Mark nodded. "Did you come looking for me?"

"Oh no, not really. I knew you could manage by yourself, although Lela was a bit worried. Women, you know. I had something to do in town and then I saw you standing here."

Mark smiled gratefully and they walked through the town to the municipal parking lot.

Partly because he sensed some change in his father and partly because he was tired, Mark chattered comfortably on the

drive back about his walk and what he had seen. His father
seemed to be listening and so he decided to ask him about
the strange bird which had troubled him for so long.

"A bird with four feet," he explained, "and great wings."
He spread his arms out to demonstrate.

His father laughed. "Now wait a minute, I'll believe you
had strawberries from a nun, but not that you saw a
four-footed bird!"

"But I didn't see him, not really, not today. In a
book . . ."

Claud thought for a moment.

"A griffin. That must be what you are thinking of. It has
the body and legs of a lion and the head and wings of an
eagle. It's an imaginary animal and it stands for vigilance."

"What's vigilance?"

"Watchfulness, to keep an eye out for something. The
man in a lighthouse is a vigilant man and so is the man
who keeps watch on a ship. Understand?"

Mark nodded and dug into his pocket for the watch.

"Almost four o'clock," he announced and offered the
watch to his father.

"No, you'd better keep it. A boy your age needs a watch
of his own." There was no need to look at the boy's face,
Claud could feel his pleasure.

"Speaking of ships, look there!"

Mark looked where his father pointed. There was the boat
again, barely visible in the mist.

"She's heading for home and looking smart about it too.
I'll wager Dan's in a stew, what with a bad storm coming on
and a deckful of nervous passengers. Your Uncle Richard is
going to have more excitement than he bargained for." Claud
laughed.

XXXV

A JAGGED BOLT of lightning tore through the sky to the sea; an explosive crack of thunder followed. A short, involuntary cry of surprise and outrage came from Beth as she threw herself against Matthew.

Walter stood on the foredeck and quoted into the wind: 'We split, we split, we split!—Farewell, my wife and children!—Farewell, brother!—We split, we split, we split!' "

Standing at the helm, Daniel surveyed the faces in the cockpit. There were signs of strain, but no panic. Again lightning cleaved the sky. He estimated the seconds between the flash and the clap. There were five or ten seconds between sight and sound; it was not as close it looked, but it was plenty close enough. They were heading right into it. He looked up at the mast; it was the tallest thing for miles.

The waves of thunder rolled in and struck. Beth, huddling against Matthew's chest, screwed her eyes shut and clapped her hands over her ears. Jean Macleod winced at the first impact of sound and then composed herself and hummed. Richard threw back his head and turned his face into the wind as though thunder and lightning were his purest pleasure. Matthew too, despite the burden of Beth's shuddering form, showed signs of exhilaration.

Walter danced along the deck from the bow to the helm,

and, striking a prayerful, suing pose, he fell on his knees at Daniel's feet.

" 'Now I would give a thousand furlongs of sea for an acre of barren ground—long heath, brown furze, anything. The wills above be done, but I would fain die a dry death.' " At every third word he salted his Robeson bass with a Gielgud tremor and had them all laughing before he had finished the speech.

Another bolt struck and the thunder broke almost immedi ately. The only thing for it, Daniel decided, was to run. The least and the most he could do was get it over with as quickly as possible.

"Jean, why don't you and Beth go into the deckhouse," he suggested. "It looks like we may be in for some rain soon.'

"I, for one, prefer to *see* what is happening to me. I'll stay right here if you don't mind." Mrs. Macleod settled herself upon her cushion.

In the time it took Mrs. Macleod to decline, Beth reached the door of the shelter. "I prefer to huddle indoors with my eyes closed," she stated and disappeared.

"We can get more speed if I have the feel of her. Take the wheel, Matt, and let's see what I can do."

Daniel loosened the mainsheet and played it in and out. The *Philemon* careened on the wind and heeled over until a foot or more of the deck skimmed under the surface of the sea.

"Superb!" Richard exclaimed. He dug his heels against the opposite side of the cockpit and put an arm around Mrs Macleod to steady her. Commending her soul to the Lord, she leaned against him and gave herself up to the enjoyment of speed.

"I'll be damned," muttered Matthew, "I didn't know she had this much in her!"

During the run Richard could hardly contain his excitement and even Mrs. Macleod found herself wishing it would never end. Despite the periodic flashes of lightning which split the sky directly above them, the summer house was sighted too soon for all but Beth in the deckhouse.

She crouched on the floor of the musty room. She could not breathe for the smell of wet wood. Thunder surrounded her. The room was a coffin speeding toward doom. This is the shadow of death, she thought.

Daniel tacked and brought the *Philemon* smoothly to the side of the dock. The rain had just begun and Claud and Mark were waiting with umbrellas. The women disembarked cautiously, staggering as they felt solid ground beneath them. Matthew and Walter furled the forward sails and pushed Daniel off toward the mooring.

Out to sea, Daniel secured the mooring, furled the mainsail, and sat for a moment on the roof of the deckhouse to watch the storm. It had grown darker and the lightning struck more frequently. It was magnificent, the most splendid spectacle he had ever seen. He was tempted to stay there on the deck until the end of the performance, but he saw the lights of the house go on and he knew Lela would worry.

He fastened a tarpaulin over the deck, stripped off his clothes, dove, and swam for shore.

XXXVI

In the front hall, phone to his ear and caught between kitchen dishwashing and living room conversation, Walter raised his voice to a shout. The connection was bad and Noah Jaspers would not come to the point.

"Look, Noah, I didn't ask for a history of the world. Just tell me where he is, that's all I want to know; the papers don't say . . . Yes, I do know what they're afraid of; cut the song and dance, will you . . . No I don't want to make a bargain, but if that's the only way I can get the name of the hospital out of you, all right, a bargain it is . . . what do you want from me?"

Walter held the receiver away from his ear and mouthed profanities at it.

"Yes, damn it, if he wants a three-ring circus, of course I'll march. I'll ride an elephant, turn cartwheels, and carry a totem pole. I want to talk to him first, that's all, before you people try to turn him into the Christ of the century. Is it a deal?"

Walter rummaged in his pockets for pencil and paper. "All right, Noah, give it to me slow and clear." He printed the name and address in large letters. "Good. With a little luck I should be able to get there on Monday. How about you? . . . I'll fly from Boston; see you there."

"Fly where?" asked Lela, coming from the kitchen as Walter hung up and flinging her apron over the banister with distaste.

"Tell me, Lela, is the female's habit of coming in at the ends of conversations which do not concern her an inherited gift or an acquired skill?"

"Acquired, I assure you," she replied. "I practice three hours every week." Walter propelled her by the shoulders into the living room.

The curtains were drawn against the storm. Lela helped Daniel pass cordials and surveyed the room. Richard and Anne were on the couch by the fire with Claud and Mark cushioned in front of them. They were deep in conversation; deciding about Mark she guessed. Jean Macleod had the red chair on the other side of the fire and was trying not to listen to what was being said. Walter seated himself on a stool by her chair and immediately made her laugh. Matthew and Beth arranged pillows on the floor and parted the curtains to watch the storm. When the cordials were served, Daniel beckoned Lela to a corner where he had set up chess.

"But you always win," she complained, contemplating his usual opening: pawn to king's pawn four.

"Oh good," called Matthew, "the Relds are about to demonstrate once again the supremacy of the male intellect." Laughing, he turned back to his wife, kissing the random strands of her hair that escaped the combs and bands with which she daily and unsuccessfully fastened them. There were streaks of gray, still disguised by the prevailing gold, but soon to be distinguishable even from a distance. It was because she had had all those children, insisted upon them year after year. There was something both comic and dreadful about her lust for sons. If she had her way, Steads would inherit the earth by the sheer overabundance of their number. Nevertheless, this next would be a girl. He willed it.

"We're going to take very good care of you," he whispered, laying his head in her lap. "No more sails in storms."

"I shan't miss them in the least," she confessed. It was pleasant to be inside with Matthew so close to her, looking out at the streaks of lightning and the breakers flaying the rocks, but not three hours ago, in the deckhouse of the *Philemon*, she had been sick with terror. No one could ever know how frightened she had been. Death was neither a reaper nor a horseman, neither friend nor enemy; death was not even strange. It was stale air in a closed place. Matthew had realized that the run had frightened her, and Lela had looked at her strangely when they got back to the house, but neither of them would understand that it had been more than a few moments of physical fear. She herself did not understand. Was it a sign? she asked herself and checked the thought, for she would not allow herself the indulgence of superstition; it was unhealthy.

Looking up at her, Matthew wondered what she was thinking. Women. They lived from minute to minute, victims of will-of-the-wisps—*ignis fatuus* in a lighted room crowded with people. The barometer fell and they fell with it into their version of despair.

He soothed her as he would a child. "In less than a week, we'll settle in again; we'll have the children back; we'll be just Steads at home, in less than a week."

He too found the promise of the familiar routine reassuring. The bits and pieces of fact and idea, the colors and forms, floating away, away, from his memory and grasp, and all the lines spinning off into nowhere, had reversed direction. He had turned the wheel of the *Philemon* to round the prom-

ontory on which the house stood, and all colors, forms, and
fact had collided in the center of his mind to form a perfect
whole, a solid structure. It took his breath away to think of
it. It would be a long poem, an apologia of sorts. He owed
one—all gods and saints stood witness to the fact—living as he
did from sensation to sensation, woman to woman, country
to country, with never a thought for his wife or the world.
The poem would move backward and forward in time. He
would set an arbitrary date for its completion—the birth
of the child. He would, in fact, call it "Poem for My
Daughter." The project would please Beth immensely, she
would gladly see to it that he had peace and time. How she
had basked at dinner when he told them about the prize. He
had known the news would please her most coming like that
in public with everyone there wishing him well, all their
pride in him clear to her as, lifting his glass, Daniel had
toasted: "Our poet."

He turned on Beth's lap. There was Anne Bennett across
the room, leaning over to whisper something to the boy. She
was one handsome woman, only a fool or a eunuch could
deny her that. She too had saluted him—with her water glass
—at dinner, but there had been mockery in her eyes. She had
thought him vain—and he was undeniably vain—preening
his minor prize at dinner. That was one London lady he
would have to forgo. Across the fire from her sat Walter
amusing the old lady. Matthew again gave Beth his attention.

Walter had been telling Jean Macleod of his plans.

"And so, I go south," he concluded.

"Yes," she replied. "You think of it as an obligation, but
you must be careful. One hears so much, even abroad, about
violence these days."

"Jean, they beat him like some kind of animal in the road
—just for walking."

"Oh Walter, when you say *they* in that tone, you frighten
me. My dear, save some pity for us. I daresay, all of us, all of
us here in this room are guilty, at least of sins of omission
and sloth. We do nothing; others suffer . . ." Her voice trailed
off and she stared into the fire.

"You're a good woman, Jean, you have no need of my pity."

He said it quite seriously and for a moment she almost believed him. Was she a good woman? No, she had to admit; she
liked too much to be left alone.

"And what about you, beautiful friend, what will you do
when the weekend is over?" he asked, for she did seem beautiful, her calm white head resting back against the crimson
chair.

"First good, now beautiful—very gallant of you," she
laughed. "I shall go visit my cousins in Pennsylvania and
then to London for the winter. I've just decided today. But
never you fear, we shall keep in touch through Lela," she
added, reaching down to pat his shoulder. "I write to Lela
nearly every month."

Walter drew himself up and bowed his head. "In honor of
our imminent parting, madame, I shall tell you the story of
my life."

"Oh dear," she sighed, composing herself for a long legend.

"A short and ordinary story," he began.

"I don't believe it, not for a minute," she interrupted.

"Oh, but it is, and you're the first to hear it. Scrap iron. I
descend from scrap iron. It provides a small but adequate
income. My parents died early, which is a singular benefit for
a young man who prefers not to work."

"But why tell me this?" she protested.

"Don't tell me you prefer the fictional, slightly risqué
Walter?"

"No, that isn't what I mean. Why tell me anything at all? I
haven't asked, and I don't wish to know. I'm a selfish old
woman, don't waste the truth on me."

Walter picked himself up from the footstool without looking again at her. "I shall be gone in the morning. Good-bye,
Jean Macleod," he muttered affectionately as he moved off
toward the chess game. He patted Mark on the head as he
passed. A fragment of the family conversation reached him
before he moved on. They were disposing of the boy, or so it
seemed.

"School, of course," said Anne. "The question is where. I
propose we leave it to the man himself."

"Quite right," Richard agreed. "Now which is it to be,
Colton, England or here? If England, you can come to us on
holiday whenever you like. That would please your aunt and
me very much."

Mark looked away from them and at Mrs. Macleod so he
would not have to answer just yet. They were making it so
difficult. There was nothing in his head. He didn't know what
they expected him to say. It wasn't a fair question.

Claud watched his son's discomfort and put an arm over
his shoulder. It was absurd, asking a boy of eight to decide the
rest of his life. Visions of complete freedom, of a one-room
apartment, and all of it library, gave way to visions of Mark's
growing up, of having a man of his own blood to talk to.
"And that is something I have never had before," Claud
silently told his brother, "and furthermore," he continued his
imaginary discourse, "my son is a manly lad and I won't have
him turned into a facetious little pansy."

Aloud, Claud said gruffly: "If he wants school, he might as well stay in the States."

"Yes, I do want to stay here," Mark said, feeling his father's arm tighten gently around him. "I'd like that very much."

Claud could see that Anne and Richard were relieved. He had been foolish to assume that they meddled; they were merely trying to do what they thought was right. He ought never to have dragged them away from their lives, to have demanded so much. He had not been fair to them. He would hurt them no more, he was resolved upon that, no matter what Richard had or had not done.

"Well now, that's settled," he said, holding his son closer. "We're married for life. Perhaps we'd better fetch a Bible and have a vow, do things properly for the relations."

Anne laughed as she had not laughed for months. "Claud, do shut up," she gasped.

Claud joined her, laughing, with his arm tight around his son, as though he shared with Anne release from the suppression of a tedious and overlong ceremony.

"Now Mark," said Claud, bringing himself under control, "what time is it?"

With pride Mark pulled the watch from his pocket and proclaimed the time to the room in a loud voice: "Seven past nine!"

Claud removed his arm and stood Mark on his feet. "Seven past nine and I'm exhausted and so must you be. Go say your good nights and let us take ourselves off to bed."

Mark stood by Mrs. Macleod's chair. She opened her eyes. "How nice of you to come and see me."

"I've come to say good night," he declared. He hesitated a moment and then held out his hand. She shook it and leaned over to kiss him on the cheek.

"Good night, young man, sweet dreams."

Mark walked quickly away to Lela.

"You're losing," he said sympathetically, noticing how many chess pieces there were on the floor by Daniel.

"True," she said ruefully. "What do you suggest I do next?"

"What's that?" he asked, pointing to a piece on the board.

"A rook or a castle. It moves straight up or straight across. Yes, I think you may be right, he's the man to do it." She moved the piece to please him and gestured no to Daniel's indication that she could take the move over if she wished.

"I'm going to bed now," said Mark. He wanted to say much more, to tell her about his walk and what they had just now decided, but Daniel was there and the other man.

"Would you like a story?"

"No, good night." He hugged her quickly and ran to the door where his father waited.

"Anyway," said Lela, continuing the tale of the Woodwards and Lessings for the benefit of Daniel and Walter, "from what I could make of Gail's rather garbled account of the night, it was positively psychedelic. You don't suppose Seth put some kind of drug in their drinks, do you?"

"Lela, you are being beaten unmercifully!" Walter warned.

"Yes, I know, isn't it awful? When it comes to chess, I'm Justine and he's the Marquis."

"Check and mate!" Daniel flourished the L of his knight. "If you didn't talk so much, you wouldn't make so many careless mistakes," he added with annoyance. He would never understand why she couldn't keep her mind in one channel. Her thought branched endlessly in a thousand directions.

He saw that the logs had burned down. "Shall I build the fire up again?" he called.

"No," they all replied, agreeing upon an early night.

Everyone rose and moved toward the hall. Lela and Daniel turned off the lights and brought up the rear.

"I think I'll make something hot and bring it up to Jean. She's had a brutal day and it's such a cold night."

"Right," Daniel replied. "I'm going straight to bed. I feel as though I could sleep out the century. Good night." He kissed the top of her head. "You are just about the worst chess player in the world," he called back to her from the landing of the stairs.

Lela boiled water, selected beef rather than chicken bouillon, and arranged two cups on a tray. A few moments later she knocked at Jean Macleod's door.

"It's Lela."

"Come in, dear."

"After being attacked by strangers and tossed about on the ocean during a storm, I thought you might be in need of something hot to drink."

"How thoughtful of you." Mrs. Macleod accepted a cup. "However, I'm drinking under false pretenses." She sipped from the cup. "For I've enjoyed the strangers and the sail." She sipped again. It was beautifully hot, and she was in bed under blankets with the window opened to precisely the proper height, and on such a night dreams of unseasonable landscapes were surely impossible. All things conspired for a perfect sleep.

"Strangers and boats . . . I'm very fond of them both," she sighed, draining her cup and sinking back on the pillow.

Jean was almost asleep. Lela collected the cup and turned off the light.

"Good night, dear," she murmured.

In their bedroom Daniel was already asleep. From the way he breathed she could tell he was exhausted.

He had left the doors to the balcony ajar, for he adored the sea air even during the worst of storms. The storm seemed to have weakened. The rain had stopped, and only a random, mischievous stroke of lightning threatened the mast of the *Philemon*. The doors to the Bennetts' room were slightly open; from within came the regular sounds of sleep. She hoped Anne would have a peaceful night.

At the end of the balcony Walter was reading by flashlight. "Come into our room and use our floor. It's liable to rain again," she whispered.

"Certainly not. This sleeping bag, I'll have you know, is guaranteed against glaciers, monsoons, avalanches, and nuclear explosion. No piddle of a puddle is going to get the best of it!" He moved himself and the sleeping bag to one side to make room for her on the air mattress. "Here, you can have one of my layers, but only for a minute or two, because I am going to sleep long and deep this night." He pulled out a length of fabric and covered her.

"What are you reading?"

"A poem I've been trying to remember. Matt found it for me." He recited aloud:

> "*To disintegrate on an instant in the explosion of mania*
> *Or lapse forever into a classic fatigue.*"

"Not very pretty, is it?"

"No, not very pretty, but that was another generation."

"You think so?"

"I pretend to think so. Now, Walter, I won't be put off; what was that all about on the phone tonight?"

"Lela, my girl, I've decided to rejoin the parade and beat the big bass drum."

"Must you get involved in it all over again? It gets worse and worse; one can't tell the torturers from the victims, the keepers from the kept. It's madness."

"True, but as the man says, I cannot be away. It's a private matter actually and has very little to do with the general madness. It's a question of friendship."

"You knew the man who was beaten?"

"That's right."

"What fatuous cowards the rest of us are, with neither youth nor age nor even ignorance for excuse. We do nothing. Sleepwalkers in the fields of plenty."

"And why not? I too am partial to somnolence. It's sweet to come back to . . . old ladies and sailboats."

"You liked Jean."

"Yes, an extraordinary woman."

"I feel there is something else about her this weekend. I can't quite get hold of it or put a name on it."

"Lela, Lela, unfurrow your brow. You'll be aged before you're forty. When will you learn? People live. People die. It is entirely their own affair."

Lela shivered slightly.

"Come here now and let old Father Walter, first magician of the universe, tell you a nightmare to keep the cold away."

He wrapped the blanket more closely around her.

Part Three

January: Afternoon at the Deserted House

Lela woke late from her deepest sleep in weeks. Feeling herself fall, she awoke panting and baffled, like a fish flung onto a beach, and gripped the deserted pillow next to her. No, she had not really fallen. As she rubbed her eyes with the back of her hand, the far-scattered pieces of her world moved toward the center of her vision and locked into place: the snow fringed crowns of the pines outside the window, the electric coffeepot on the table at the foot of the bed, cup, sugarbowl and creamer which Daniel had given her for Christmas, and a pile of mail, their Christmas mail. He had managed to do all that without waking her. She sounded the silence of the house around her—yes, he was already gone— and then laid out two facts in the front of her mind: they had just got back from their Christmas visits (two weeks in other people's beds) which was why she was so tired; she was pregnant which was why she was so uncomfortable (four months gone, as people put it, as though it were some dreadful process of deterioration from which one could never expect to recover fully).

She got out of bed and looked out the window down toward the main street of the town. The town of Wiley still had its Christmas decorations strung from the lampposts. No doubt they would still be there in March. Beyond loomed the spire of the university chapel. The streets had been plowed and a sand truck groped its way up the hill.

Perched at the foot of the bed, she argued the virtue of the toothbrush as opposed to the pleasure of the coffeepot and decided in favor of the latter. Pouring herself a cup, she argued the morning newspaper as opposed to the Christmas mail and chose the former. She spread the front page on her lap:

War Losses Highest To Date

She dismissed the paper with a toss to the other side of the room and plucked the Christmas mail from the table, dividing the foreign from the domestic and subdividing the out of state from the local. The phone rang and the dog padded into the room, expressing his curiosity with a cocked head.

"Beth, of course," she explained to him.

"So you are finally back," Beth declared with amazement, as though the fact that the phone had been answered two houses away was an eighth wonder and the absence of that fact for the preceding two weeks, a deliberately conceived treachery.

"Of course we are back. I told you we'd be back on the third."

"Ah yes, but I still hoped, indeed, I must confess, I fully expected, you'd be back in time for our party."

"But Beth dear, I told you, it couldn't possibly be done; my people for Christmas and Daniel's for New Year's—we always do it that way, you know."

"I hope you had a pleasant eve."

"Oh dreadfully pleasant." Lela poured another cup of coffee. "We had eggnog at twelve, laced with cinnamon, and then we all sang 'Auld Lang Syne.' Houseful of Scots Presbyterians—perpetual mourning, even though the whole family has always lived to one hundred and fifty. One hundred and fifty, it is marked very distinctly on their genes."

"Oh Lela."

"Tell me how the party went." Lela drank the coffee in three quick gulps and lay back on the bed. Beth had been known to go on for hours. Daniel had once clocked her at two hours and fifteen minutes. It was absurd, for, as Daniel never failed to point out when she called, their upstairs bathroom window looked directly into the upstairs bathroom of Beth and Matthew (the roofs of the two intervening houses were low). On a clear day with the shades up they could all urinate together. There was no need to drag the Bell System into it.

"Drunk as a lord, drunk as a very drunk lord, in fact," Beth was saying, "she plumped down on the lap of the Provost without so much as a by-your-leave."

"Tut, tut, New Year's Eve will be New Year's Eve."

"You would think the wife of an instructor would have more sense. How are you feeling, Lela?" Beth's voice softened with solicitude.

"Terrible! So terrible that I think I'd better hang up and go into the bathroom."

"You shouldn't be having morning sickness this far advanced. Are you sure you're all right? You know it was the fourteenth or fifteenth week that I began to have my trouble. You must be careful. You must not . . ."

"Look Beth, I'm quite all right. I just have to go to the bathroom. I'll call you later." Lela hung up and chose an envelope from the foreign pile. She could bear anything, anything but another minute-by-minute, detail-by-detail account of Beth's recent miscarriage. After four full-born, wholly healthy babies,

one would think that she could take a miscarriage in stride;
but that was not the case. She had relived it for Lela's benefit
at least once a week since it happened. Actually the blow
had been to Matthew rather than Beth. For some reason he
had not been the same since it happened.

The letter she held was postmarked Liberia. The uphill
slope of the handwriting was unmistakable. It was from Walter. He had actually gone to Africa; he had been joking about
it for years. Inside was the typically ambiguous woodcut one
always received from agnostics in lieu of an "Adoration of
the Magi." It was quite a nice one, rather primitive and
brightly colored. "Les Quatre Ages de l'Homme." They were
all there too: papa, grandpapa, big brother, and baby. There
was a letter enclosed, penned with what appeared to be a dull
quill. Didn't they have fountain pens in Liberia? she wondered.
On second thought, she remembered hearing that it was quite
up-to-date. She had a vague impression of a sort of model
farm run by a man named Tubman.

Nov. 23

Dear Lela and Dan,

I'm writing this a full month in advance, since the post
from Liberia is reputedly slow. Let me now wish you
both the best for the new year. Thanks for the mail and
gifts while I was in jail. I meant to write saying I got
your package, but while lingering in prison, I contracted
a malignant disease—lassitude, and couldn't do a thing
for six weeks. They finally turned me out because of good
conduct, which is one of the symptoms of the disease.
All in all, I enjoyed it completely. I hadn't slept so well
in years. I must march for a cause again sometime and
disturb the peace—when I'm tired and my blood count
reads low.

About your homemade cookies, Lela, they were ter-

rible. I was constipated for a week. Please don't make
them again. Nothing else to say except that I am married.
The lady is yellow. I've finally indulged my long nur-
tured taste for things oriental. Send me a wedding present, something gaudy and American, for I almost miss
that big happy playpen.

All the best from me and my yellow spouse, who
knows all about you but loves you anyway—sight unseen.
                                                      W.

P.S. If you're ever in Liberia . . .

"Now how much of that can one really believe?" muttered Lela. All of it, except the wife, she decided. The postmark
was real enough, but it was impossible that Walter had married. She did not want him to marry, she had to admit. She
liked him to arrive, every so often, more or less helpless and
with no place to go. He had arrived with pneumonia the first
month they were married (Daniel had been apologetic, but
she had been delighted to nurse his old friend) and with
mumps two or three years later (he had been wretchedly sick,
but they saw him through it—saved his potency, he liked
to joke). No, she simply couldn't believe he'd married. She
was tempted to call Beth and find out what she'd heard from
Walter. It would be just like him to write them two stories
as different as night from day. But no. She would not call.
Instead she selected a letter from the domestic pile.

The envelope was dark green, and on the back of it, in
alternating lines of red and gold raised lettering, without
capitals or marks of punctuation, was the return address:

> mr & mrs seth woodward
> 2 willow drive
> crofton   new york

Covering the front of the enclosed card was an American flag with which certain liberties had been taken. Green stripes had been substituted for the usual white, and small gold Christmas trees, for the fifty stars.

Within was engraved a nounless greeting: "have a happy and a merry." Beneath the engraving was a terse note from Sonja:

> We are missing one dozen soup plates loaned to you August 26. They cannot be replaced. Return them at your earliest convenience.
>
> S. Woodward

For a moment Lela was baffled, but then the August weekend came back to her. Yes, they had borrowed soup plates. No, they had not returned them. She had promised Beth to run them back to the Woodwards the very first chance she got, but she had forgotten. They were in the kitchen cupboard of the summer house, more than 100 miles away.

Sonja's so-called Christmas card sounded more like a summons to court on a charge of petty larceny. Beth would raise a tempest, if she ever found out. She would have to drive to the summer house as soon as possible and pick the damn things up.

Lela grimaced at the flag and threw it aside. Paging through the pile of foreign letters, she took solace in Jean Macleod's script. London. Lela envied her that. They hadn't been over in three years, but Daniel had promised, as soon as the baby was old enough . . . the summer following this next . . .

Nov. 30

Lela, my dear,

    This year I'm obeying the injunctions of the post office and getting my Christmas overseas mail off a full three weeks in advance. I'm comfortably established for the winter in a dear little heated flat in South Kensington, and I'm actually looking forward to the first snow, which as yet we have not had. How could we survive without a change of season? I wonder that people in the tropics or arctics manage at all.

Anne Bennett and I happily collided in Selfridges a week ago (both doing our Christmas shopping early). Coincidence on top of coincidence, she was just having them send you a box of potpourri for your rose jar. (My own gift won't be so charming by half—but I know how Daniel adores marmalade.) Apparently her husband has had the most awful time. (I remember him fondly from our sail last summer.) A stroke, she said. His legs are paralyzed. She must do everything for him. She seemed in the best of spirits, nevertheless. Apparently her painting goes on splendidly. Some of her pictures are being shown in a gallery on Bond Street and I must go see them. She's done one of you, she says. But, of course, you must know that. It's been sent to New York with some others. There's to be an exhibit there late in January. We went off to tea together and spoke of you, missing you dreadfully.

Now Lela, you are not to worry. I simply won't have it. My concierge, a Mrs. Stacey, delightfully articulate, as even the least educated of the English are, takes very good care of me. She is most attentive to my comings in and goings out and regards me as family, a long lost relative rather deficient in her senses and in need of a strong and steady arm. She indulges all my whimsies. So you see, I am not only taking care, I am being taken care of. Your airmail alarms are quite unnecessary—superstitious premonitions. Really Lela, I thought you had more sense.

The older I get, the more I ramble on. I send my best love and thoughts to you both.

Jean

Yes, it was true, she had written Jean a silly letter. She had been worried by a dream about Jean. When she was ten she had dreamed her great-grandmother's death, and when she woke, the old lady was dead. One expected someone so ancient to die, her mother had explained; it was natural to have a bad dream about it and only a coincidence that the death had occurred simultaneously.

Nevertheless, the dream about Jean, coming twenty years later, frightened her and she had written in a panic—several letters: exhortations to Jean to take care of herself.

She had made herself ridiculous, and here was Jean writing as always, quite well. Of course, that was six weeks ago. Lela quelled the thought and returned to the content of the letter. Anne's picture of her. No, she hadn't known about it. Anne had promised the picture as a Christmas present, but she had heard nothing about it since summer, although both she and Daniel had been in touch with the Bennetts several times since Richard's attack.

Being sent to New York, Jean said. Herself on exhibition. It was a horrible idea. Particularly since she hadn't an idea which self or version of self was to be displayed. Perhaps it was not herself at all, but something Anne had conjured up: a mask.

Lela turned with relief to the domestic pile. There was Mark's round hand on an envelope. The stationery had obviously been chosen by the department of manners, for Mark had been sent to one of those expensive schools where behavior and taste comprised the major part of the curriculum and were considered matters of profound importance. At least, that was the vision she had of the place. Mark had been sent there—somewhere in the depths (or was it the heights) of New Hampshire against all their better judgment and advice. Mark himself added insult to injury by thoroughly enjoying the place:

> Dear Aunt Lela,
>   Dad says since Aunt Anne is so far away, I can call you aunt if I wish. Thank you for the dictionary. I did want one. I know everybody always says that about Christmas presents. But it's true. I did want one to look up words in. I like it here very much and have two boys in this room with me who are nice. Tomorrow Dad is coming and we're going to Vermont for the holiday, so I'm getting my letters over with now. Why don't you come here to see me? Please?
>   Love Mark (xxxxxxxx) Those are kisses.

"How charming!" Lela sneered. They were turning him into every other boy who says Dad not Father and kisses at random any Theresa, Doris, or Harriet.

"Not you, my friend, not you," she declared, patting her belly.

Again Lela addressed herself to the overseas mail. She hoped Daniel would remember to stop at the post office and pick up the packages waiting for them. Anne had sent potpourri. The Satsuma jar sat on their living room mantel, sadly in need of refreshment. She searched the pile for Anne's card or letter and found it at the bottom.

The letter was dated three weeks later than Jean's and had been sent airmail.

> 20 December
>
> Dear Lela,
>   I can't tell you how pleased we were to hear your good news. Richard and I do regret never having had a child of our own, and, of course, now with Richard's illness, it is perhaps more than ever on our minds.

You must tell Daniel that Richard has so enjoyed his letters; it is very kind of him to remain faithful; many of Richard's young friends in London have not proved so.

Your question about the damage done is not at all tactless—how silly of you to think it might be and how silly of me not to have been more explicit when I last wrote. Originally the right arm and hand and both legs were stricken. The hand is beginning to come back and we have hope that the arm will also improve with therapy. There is little hope that the legs will ever be right. Richard is an angel, very patient with my clumsiness. And I become more deft at caring for him as time goes on. No, oddly enough, I don't find nursing wearying at all. I much prefer doing things myself to having a stranger in the house. Needless to say, we are closer now than we have ever been before, and I don't feel at all the sacrificing wife. I have time and quiet for my painting and I feel I am finally coming into my own with it. By the way, I have enclosed a photograph (black and white and rather blurred, I fear) of your picture. You perhaps remember I promised it to you for Christmas. It will be in New York at the end of next month, so you can see it in the pigment if you have a mind.

It was perceptive of you not to press Claud for details about Richard. He has been more upset by it all than any of us would have believed possible four months ago. It was all I could do to prevent his flying immediately over. (I felt and still feel that a sudden visit from Claud might alarm Richard unduly.) Claud writes almost daily and whatever breach there was between them no longer exists. At least that much good has come out of the terrible time Richard has had. The convolutions of family relations are impossible to parse; I don't fully understand the change in Claud, but I am grateful for it. Richard has always worried so about his brother. Mark writes the most appallingly ordinary letters about games and masters. I hardly recognize him, I'm sure.

Last month I got up to London for two days and met, of all people, your Mrs. Macleod. I whisked her off to tea. We managed to avoid the subject of God for an hour and got on together very well indeed. She seemed buoyantly at ease in the sea of London, which, I must confess, I am not. Perhaps I shall see her again; she is staying the winter. I would much prefer to see you. Why not come visit my hills and lakes? The two of you would do Richard a world of good.

Look after yourself and write again soon.

Anne

Lela withdrew the photograph face down from the envelope and revealed it to herself cautiously. There she was, looking scared by the sea. Anne had been as good as her word. She bore her own face and not a mask and the expression on it was the same as in the preliminary sketch Anne had made on the beach. Anne had placed her on a ledge of rock, just descending to the ocean below; her legs and arms, bare in the white tunic, were more muscular and more tense than the fact. The look in her eyes was terror. Yes, she was capable of that. The remarkable thing was that Anne had seen it and got it so clear. The thought of this self of hers on public exhibition was unnerving.

She spread the remaining letters so that their postmarks were visible and selected one. The script was tight and barely legible and the address—Gilbertville, Pennsylvania—was strange. She tore open the envelope.

December 31

Dear Mrs. Reld,

It is a very unpleasant duty to make your acquaintance in this way, for Cousin Jean has spoken of you often and with deep affection. It is odd to call her cousin, for we thought of her as a sister, although we could never prevail upon her to stay with us for very long. I might as well tell you right off, Jean died a week ago Sunday; it was all very sudden and a dreadful shock. She caught cold and contracted pneumonia; it was viral and nothing could be done—although her landlady has assured me she had the best possible medical attention.

Lela put down the letter. She could not go on with it just yet. She could see it all too clearly. Jean alone in a room abroad with a temperature of 104, helpless, with only a stupid woman who brought broth instead of penicillin. The best medical attention! No doubt, but entirely too late. People need not die of pneumonia in the second half of the twentieth century.

She was not being fair, she knew. It was virus pneumonia and penicillin would have done no good. Penicillin was for infections not viruses—so Daniel said, and surely he knew what he was talking about. But still, they had let her die.

She had written Jean about the baby, but it was unlikely she had been able to read the letter. She had not known this wonderful thing was happening. But how selfish to wonder about that straight off. Had she had pain, did she know it was happening, had she been lonely . . .

To cease to breathe, to cease to live, never to come back— so she had defined death for Mark—a simple and truthful definition. The mortuary and the labor room were part of the same comedy. She would not allow herself to be shaken by this. She would read the rest of the letter and then call Daniel.

I fear at the very end dear Jean was not herself—delirium, you know, is quite common in pneumonia. She left a long letter which she had dictated to her landlady. It said she wished to be cremated without a service. However, we have decided to have the body sent here, and we will see to it that she is properly buried in family ground. In that last letter she also made known her desire that you be given her books and letters. We will, of course, respect that wish, and when her effects arrive, we will forward those things to you immediately. It was Jean's habit to keep all her letters, and, as I'm sure you know, she knew people all over the world.

"I don't want the damn letters!" Lela shouted into the silence of the house. She could see them too clearly: packed in a trunk, sere, smelling of mildew, long angular strokes like skeletons across the pages.

With a disgusted sweep of her hand, she scattered her own letters onto the floor. She had to get out of the house. She needed the cut and brace of the winter morning, the sting of the snow.

The magnificent tail of the dead raccoon stretched out onto the road. Lela turned the wheel sharply; the car swerved, skidded, and corrected its path. Ice had bent the trees to the breaking point and sometimes beyond. Branches littered the road.

It had been a difficult trip from the beginning but the final stretch was the most hazardous. The wind blowing in from the sea drifted wall after wall of snow across the road. She drove down the center of the road with the high beams on, sounding the horn every few feet. Dead white swirled everywhere. She was afraid she would miss the drive to the summer house and perhaps drive off a white rock into the white sea. Her gloved hand wiped the mist from the inside of the windshield.

Instinct informed her that the drive was directly ahead. She slowed the car (praying that no one was behind her),

sounded the horn long and urgently, and turned into the next
gap in the trees. The drive was impassable.

Parking the car, she trudged cumbersomely through the deep
snow. The front lock resisted the key. She struck match after
match and held them to the aperture; finally the key turned
and the door swung open.

Imprinting the floors with her wet boots, Lela toured the
house. The dog's ball and a dirty sock lingered in a corner of
the upstairs hall. In their bedroom the mattress had been
folded in half for some reason. She sank wearily onto its bulk
and contemplated the bed springs. They had taken the captain's chest and other furniture back home with them. Only
the bed remained—and a damned uncomfortable one it had
been.

The chill penetrated her overcoat in spite of its alpaca
lining. It seemed even colder in the house than out of doors.
Her legs felt numb. It would not do to sit too long. Move,
she commanded herself, and obeyed.

In the closet of the small guest room last occupied by Mrs.
Macleod she found an old army blanket and draped it around
her. One of the shutters had blown off and the window was
cracked. Snow drifted into the room.

She found adhesive tape in the medicine cabinet, a shirt
cardboard in a waste basket, and covered the crack. It was a
temporary measure at best.

"You have come for the soup plates," she reminded herself, surveying the room from the doorway.

In the kitchen "Jonah" was much the worse for a winter's
wear. The glue had not held against the cold and damp. The
edges curled away from the cupboard doors. She pried them
open and took down the plates. She thanked heaven that
they were all whole. She began wrapping them in old news-

papers, pausing to read now a headline, now a paragraph from the last week in August and the first week in September.

At the front door of the house, Ida Hobbes, warden of winter and self-appointed guardian of deserted summer homes on Gull Point Road, knocked the snow from her boots and pushed fearlessly into the hall. Hearing the rattle of dishes in the kitchen, she brazened toward and confronted the blanket-draped figure of Lela.

"Well!" she announced.

Lela let fall a soup plate onto the table. "Good God," she cried, "you scared me half to death!" She turned away angrily and examined the plate. It was not broken.

"Sorry. I saw the car. Thought I'd better investigate. Prowlers, you know. Can't be too careful."

"They can prowl all they like, there's nothing whatever to steal," Lela replied coldly, and then relented. "How are you, Mrs. Hobbes?"

"Can't complain. Bad winter. Not so bad where you are, I'm sure. We always get the worst of it, what with the wind off the sea. I see you've got a shutter off."

"Yes, we'll have to get it fixed as soon as possible."

"Good idea. Something like that can ruin a house: water all over the floors."

"Actually we're not sure we'll renew the lease. Too many problems."

"Oh, what a pity; we'll miss you young people."

"Kind of you. I'm sorry I can't offer you something hot to drink; the water and power are off."

"Don't give it a thought. Why don't you come down to my place and let me give you a cup of coffee? I'll just give you a hand with the wrapping and then you come on down," Ida suggested with gruff affection.

"Oh that's very nice of you, but this is the last of it." Lela held up the final soup plate. "I've got a long drive. I had better be on my way soon."

"Well there's not much new here—except Mrs. Vanidore, you'll remember Mrs. Vanidore; she used to clean for you, didn't she?"

Lela nodded.

"Gone. Terrible thing. Her husband got drunk one night and hit her with the electric iron. Terrible thing. She died of complications. Quite a scandal in these parts. But I never did hold with foreigners."

Lela simply stared. She did not altogether believe it. It was impossible to take in.

Pleased with the effect, Ida Hobbes stared back, examining Lela's face with curiosity.

"Expecting, aren't you," she stated emphatically.

"How ever did you guess?"

"Shadows under the eyes. Dead giveaway. I can tell a mile off. Never been wrong yet. Good news, eh?"

"Yes, it is rather." Lela smiled.

"Boy or girl—which would you like?"

"A girl, I think."

"Named it already, I'm sure." Mrs. Hobbes winked slyly.

"Yes, I suppose I have," said Lela, more to herself than to Mrs. Hobbes. "If it's a girl we'll call her Jean after a friend of mine who's died."

"What a pity, but you don't want to think about that. Not at a time like this," Mrs. Hobbes sagely advised.

Mrs. Hobbes insisted upon carrying six of the soup plates to the car, and Lela escorted her to the door, giving her the replies she expected. Yes, she had heard more snow was ex pected by nightfall. Yes, she would be sure to be on the road before dark. Yes, it did get dark so early these days.

She stood on the veranda in her blanket, watching Mrs. Hobbes stride down the drive, and then returned to the house.

Most of the furniture in the living room was gone (the Steads had taken it for their basement playroom). By the fireplace the red chair sagged disconsolately, keeping a lonely vigil. She smiled at its decrepitude, sank gratefully into it, pulling the blanket around her, and looked out the window.

There was nothing to be seen. The snow obscured all boundaries. The land was not divided from the sea, nor the sea from the sky.

In the distance, the clock chimes struck, but it was impossible to hear how many times.